The
Siren,
the Song,
and
the Spy

The Siren, the Song, and the Spy

MAGGIE TOKUDA-HALL

CANDLEWICK PRESS

Copyright © 2023 by Maggie Tokuda-Hall
Map and wave illustration copyright © 2020 by Rita Csizmadia

First edition 2023

Library of Congress Catalog Card Number 2022923583
ISBN 978-1-5362-1805-3

23 24 25 26 27 28 APS 10 9 8 7 6 5 4 3 2 1

Printed in Humen, Dongguan, China

This book was typeset in Warnock Pro.

Candlewick Press
99 Dover Street
Somerville, Massachusetts 02144

www.candlewick.com

This is still for Clare,
and the adult you've become.

PART ONE

The Siren

Genevieve

Genevieve was not dead.

Thanks to the Emperor, she was alive. She was aware of her body, which lay on the sand, aware of the sun that cracked her skin. But she could not open her eyes.

Time had gone in all directions, and Genevieve did not know where in its vast landscape she had fallen. Sometimes she was at her mother's dinner table. Then she was back aboard the *Dove*. She had heard the *whumph* of a submerged explosion breaking the surface of the sea. The Lady Ayer called to her and bade she braid her hair. A boy her age held out his hand, his name lost in the blare of cannons and pistols firing.

The wind carried a name: Thistle.

She had not heard it aloud in years. She tried to move her chapped lips around the sound, but all that arose was a hiss. She coughed, her throat dry and aching.

She was alive.

Her survival was not the only impossible thing that had happened. The Imperials had lost. The Emperor's ships capsized and crushed. The Pirate Supreme had escaped the Emperor once again. The Lady Ayer was dead.

The Lady Ayer was dead.

Genevieve had watched it happen, had seen her lady fall. It was the slowest and fastest thing she had ever witnessed: the sudden and terrible explosion of blood at her lady's neck, the inexorable crumple of her body. The great Lady Ayer. The Emperor's greatest spy. She watched it happen again and again, but she could never stop it from happening. Her mentor's blood hung in the air, a fine mist.

Genevieve pushed her fingers into the wet sand. She made a fist. She could hear the Lady's voice in her mind, willing her to move. To open her eyes. She blinked against the blazing sun.

Sit up, said the Lady.

Genevieve obeyed her orders, just as she always had. It did not matter if she was dead or alive, real or only in her mind; the Lady Ayer would always be her master, her mentor. Her voice was a comfort and a compass, and Genevieve dearly needed both. Her body screamed in dissent as she sat up, but Genevieve did not listen to it, not even as the world spun around her.

You need water. All the seawater you swallowed is making you sick. You need fresh water or else you'll die.

At this, Genevieve let out a mirthless laugh. There was no fresh water here. There was only the stinging seawater and the burning red sand. The laugh turned into another round of racking coughs.

Where is your pistol? Genevieve felt down her leg. Still in its holster about her ankle. *Where is your dagger?* She felt her thigh and found the handle of her dagger.

The effort of sitting up, of moving, of coughing had been too much. She lay back down.

Get up, said the Lady's voice, but Genevieve could not. Tears did not fall, but she was crying all the same, ashamed of her disobedience. Lady Ayer had taught her better than that.

She saw Rake's face, the face of her countryman, the face of her captor, saw it alight with triumph after he pulled the trigger on the gun that would kill her lady. She could feel her hate like something corporeal, something literally in her belly, heavy and pointed and hot.

Distantly, she could hear laughter, high-pitched and echoing over the dunes. It was Rake, she knew, the Pirate Supreme's man. Rake laughing at the demise of the Emperor's men. Rake laughing at her pain.

"Hey," said a voice. He did not speak the Common Tongue, but Genevieve understood him even if she could not recall which language he spoke. "Hello?"

That accursed laughing, the giggling was closer now, so close she could feel hot gusts of breath against her burning skin. All around her was the stench of blood, of meat gone to rot. She flinched away from the reek of that breath, tried to blink open her eyes once more.

Your pistol.

She was in danger. The Lady had taught her to defend herself, and her voice was insistent now, urging her to grab her weapon. Genevieve was no damsel in distress. She had been molded by the Lady Ayer; she was her right hand.

She could see the man only as a shadow that loomed enormous over her, backlit by the cruel sun, which added to her confusion.

There was a man there, but his voice was absent, and the

Lady's voice was there, but she was absent. The world had become nothing but a flurry of noises and shapes and pain, and Genevieve could hardly parse it.

The figure nudged her with his foot, not hard but enough to bring what little remained of her last meal—eaten when? days ago maybe—in Genevieve's belly up and burning through her throat. She retched, and she was distantly aware of his sounds of consternation and disgust. It was, if uncomfortable, also a perfect cover. She curled into herself on one side and let her hand drift to her ankle.

She saw the animal before she saw the man, its great square head too close to her own, sniffing at her with interest. It let out a high giggle, chittering and chilling. She startled away from it, and the animal startled away from her, but not far enough. It bared its teeth at her, and she knew at once where the stench of blood had come from.

Hyena. The familiars of Wariuta warriors, the keepers of the Red Shore.

Genevieve remembered. She had seen etchings and paintings of the hyenas: vicious, horrible animals with blood dripping from their maws, their gnashing teeth that could take off a man's leg. When the warriors came of age, they found their familiar, and from then on, the two would be inseparable, and deadly. The warriors of the Red Shore had killed many Imperial men, even if their means were crude. But they did not have pistols. Genevieve's pistol was there, on her ankle. She let her fingers wrap around it.

It's him or you.

If this man was a warrior, then he would kill her.

"Are you OK?" he asked. He was easily twice as big as she was. If it came to hand-to-hand, she would lose unless she was extraordinarily lucky or he was extraordinarily stupid. She could not take that chance.

Shoot.

With what little strength she had, she turned on the man and pointed her pistol at him. He held his hands up. Genevieve squeezed the trigger.

• CHAPTER 1 •
Thistle

For nearly as long as she could remember, it had been Thistle and Dai. Dai and Thistle.

Dai Phan had been Thistle Vo's best friend since their first day of school. Dai had tried to push Thistle into the mud for the crime of being a girl, and, refusing to go down without a fight, Thistle had wrestled him so they both landed in a puddle, leaving them drenched and already in trouble by the time they arrived for class. Sensing that they had met their equals, the two became fast friends after that.

And now, all these years later, they were nearly grown, and often the adults around Gia Dinh wondered when they'd be wed. They were only thirteen, but marriages could be agreed upon around that age, and their close friendship did give rise to the question not *if* their parents would have a conversation about terms but *what* those terms would be. This was the way of things in Quark.

Thistle didn't find the idea of marriage all that appealing, but if she had to be married to anyone, she'd rather it be Dai. That would be fun, at least. And anyway, her mother had made it abundantly clear that she would not let her daughter marry poorly. Dai was a good match and Thistle would be grateful one day for the fine work her mother had done by her when she had a big expensive house full of healthy children and probably even a servant to do some of the cleaning like Dai's mother had.

Thistle did not like this idea, but she knew better than to argue when her mother took that tone, so she tried to push the reluctance deep into her belly, where she stored all her inconvenient thoughts and desires. She liked Dai. There was that. Not like *that*, but a *complete* lack of romantic desire didn't seem to matter when making life choices in Gia Dinh.

Though currently Dai was hard at work being as annoying a husband-to-be as husbands seemed universally to be. He'd promised a big surprise for her that morning and had yet to arrive. It was midday already.

Thistle watched from the kitchen window as the Imperial soldiers marched by. They did this each day at noon, the changing of the guard at the Consulate, and whenever she could, Thistle would wait by the window when the time came. She liked the orderly way their legs moved in unison, the way the golden lion epaulets on their uniforms glinted in the sun.

A new guest would arrive at their house that night. Thistle's mother was off at the market to purchase better-quality ingredients—fresh fish from the rivers, water spinach, and amaranth—than they would ever eat themselves. The stone guesthouse they called home was larger than many other native Quark homes; most of the largest estates had been taken over by Imperial ownership after Quark was colonized. But all the best rooms were reserved for paying guests. Thistle had busted her back this morning getting all the rooms clean as fast as she could so that she'd be ready for Dai's surprise, and now she regretted it. Of course he was late. He was always late.

Finally there was a knock at the door. Thistle ran to it, and there was Dai. But he looked . . . different. His hair, which was always a mess, was neatly combed to one side. And his clothes, which were usually stained with mud or food from the restaurant or Thistle didn't want to know what, were clean. Suspiciously clean.

"What's your deal?" Thistle asked. "You look like a ding-dong."

Dai ran a hand through his hair, mussing it a little. He looked fractionally more like himself. "Whatever. My mom made me do it." He heaved a heavy sigh, then held out one hand to Thistle. Like she was a girl. Like she was a girl he was asking to marry him. "Thistle Vo." His voice dripped with dreary obligation. "Our parents have begun the sacred discussion of terms, and it is upon me, your future husband and keeper, to tell you how glad I am that you will be my . . ." He trailed off. The rest of the script was nauseating, both of them knew that, knew that it was best unsaid. "Anyway, you get it."

Thistle curtsied as she was supposed to, but as soon as she looked up, both she and Dai broke into body-racking laughter. Relief.

"Was this the big surprise? Because I'm not really surprised." Her mother had been in talks casually with Dai's parents for ages and wasn't particularly coy about it. She thought getting married was the best thing Thistle could do with her life. Thistle wanted to disagree, but she also couldn't think of any realistic alternatives.

Anyway, it would have been a lousy surprise.

Dai grinned. "No. It's just why I'm late—Mom made me, like . . ." He motioned to his hair in a dismissive way. "But. I found something," he said. "By the river."

9

"What?"

Dai didn't answer. He looked over both his shoulders as though someone might be trying to listen in, as though anyone in all the city of Gia Dinh would possibly care what these two thirteen-year-olds were up to, let alone saying. Thistle rolled her eyes. Dai may have been her best friend, but he was certainly prone to theatrics.

"Come on," he said.

He took her hand.

A jolt ran through Thistle. They had never held hands before. In her shock, she did not pull away but rather let herself be led down the cobblestone streets out of town, downhill—past the rice paddies and the farms—to the river. His hand was hot, and he did not let go until they'd arrived. Where his hand had been, a sheen of sweat remained, cold with the sudden exposure to air. The sky had opened into a drizzle, and Thistle could feel her hair flattening against her neck.

"I was down here digging, you know?" Dai's parents owned a small restaurant favored by Imperial officers. The only discernible help Dai ever was to the enterprise was digging up wild root vegetables. Thistle nodded. He led her to a pile of recently overturned dirt. "And. Well. Look."

He started digging with his hands, and Thistle hustled to help him, her curiosity piqued. It was loose and damp, and soon they'd unearthed a plain crate. It was the kind in which goatskins were imported from the Floating Islands. Stacks of them were found all over Gia Dinh. It was hardly newsworthy.

Thistle glared at Dai. "It's a box," she said coolly.

"Open it."

Thistle could see that the crate had been locked—a broken bolt hung from it. She assumed Dai was responsible. Dubiously, she lifted the lid.

Inside, pistols gleamed among boxes of bullets.

Thistle slammed the crate shut, her heart racing.

Guns were not permitted in Quark. They hadn't been since the Colonization. Only Imperial soldiers could carry pistols, and Imperial soldiers did not keep secret weapons caches stowed by rivers—they kept them in the many official military outposts all over the country.

Whoever owned these guns owned them illegally.

"Whose are these?"

He could barely keep the grin from his face. "I think the Resistance is coming back," Dai whispered.

But Thistle did not smile.

• CHAPTER 2 •

Koa

Koa should have been at the oasis, standing guard. But he couldn't bear to see Kaia squander the current peace. And so he had followed her. Or tried to.

The thing was, Kaia was a better scout than he was. Not just because she was smaller but because she was quicker, too, and silent. She and her familiar, Chima, moved in concert so easily. Not at all like Koa and his hyena, Tupac. The Wariuta said that familiars reflected the souls of their warriors, and maybe that was true. Koa and Tupac were both a little soft around the corners—all goofy and light and nervous giggles. There was nothing severe about either of them, no edge. They both made for poor warriors, a reality Koa had long since made peace with.

Kaia, on the other hand, was born to handle an ax. And Chima, at her side, was born to skulk and stalk and strike. And so his sister and her familiar had easily lost Koa and Tupac within the first hour of his attempt to track them.

Kaia had said she was hunting for weakness to leverage against the Colonizers—not exactly a tall order in her mind, but a dangerous one. And Koa suspected that was only a partial truth.

Still, he had gone where he assumed Kaia had gone: to the shore.

The Wariuta had lost dominion over the shore to the Colonizers. Many long and drawn-out months of battles had led to that, and though no Wariuta liked the arrangement, it was still a relief not to mourn, daily, the warriors and fishermen who'd been killed. And so the Wariuta were not supposed to be on the shore, Kaia especially. As the daughter of and heir to Ica—Koa and Kaia's mother and the leader of the Wariuta warriors—Kaia was too recognizable, too important. If she was spotted by a Colonizer, the tenuous peace that had settled would be destroyed. She knew that! And still she could not help herself ranging down to the shore.

Kaia hated the Colonizers and wanted them gone; that was genuine. No one wanted to fight them as ardently as Kaia did. But Koa knew his sister well, could see the dark corners of doubt behind her bravado. As long as they were at war, Ica would lead. And if Ica led? Kaia would not have to. Despite all her competence and her talent, Kaia was scared by nothing more than the weight of the leadership they all knew she'd carry—of that, Koa was sure. Neither sibling spoke this truth aloud, and neither needed to.

But Koa did not find Kaia on the shore.

Instead, he'd found a foreigner. She'd washed up on the beach like a piece of driftwood, her black hair seeping into the red sand, her pink skin so burnt it looked as if it had been flayed. She was like a gift from the sea. And a gift from the sea, Ica always said, was not to be trusted. Her arms stretched out as if in supplication to a god he did not know, her face turned to the sun.

She lay in the sand, letting the tide roll over her feet and her legs. Around her, jagged pieces of wood stuck out of the ground, remnants of whatever boat she'd been on. All thoughts of finding Kaia evaporated, and Koa rushed to the girl. She would die from exposure if she wasn't dead already. She needed water. She needed shelter. She needed care, and she needed it as soon as possible.

At his side, Tupac giggled in the way all familiars did when they were excited or nervous. They had only just been paired and were both in their youth. Tupac could sense Koa's worry, and Koa reached down and rubbed him behind the ears, feeling the prickle of his coarse fur beneath his fingernails. Tupac's coat had come in with more black spots than those of his siblings, but Koa could still see the likeness. Maybe someday he'd grow into something better than he was. Maybe Koa would, too.

"Come on," Koa said to Tupac. "She needs help."

Stilled by Koa's purpose, Tupac quieted, and the two made their way down the winding, rocky cliffs that abutted the shore.

As he got closer, Koa could see a few things about the girl: For one, she was about the same age as he was, maybe a year or two younger. She was dressed as a Colonizer, but she did not have the complexion of those from Nipran. Her yukata was in tatters, but even so, Koa could tell it had once been expensive.

Most important, he could see that she was still alive. Her chest rose and fell out of cadence with the waves. He ran to her.

He needed to be careful, he knew. Koa wasn't just tall but fat, too. Like his father before him, Koa was one of the largest of the Wariuta. He was easily twice the weight of this girl, and he did not know her. She'd be scared of him. He needed to counter that, needed to be gentle. He'd learned long ago that his big voice could scare those who didn't know him. And so it was in his nicest, most friendly voice that Koa greeted the girl.

She did not stir.

Was she asleep? He nudged her with his foot as delicately as he possibly could. Her body rocked to one side violently, as though he'd punted her, and she vomited onto the sand.

Cool, Koa thought. *Great job.*

What would Ica do? His mother had an uncanny sense for how to best handle people, to meet them where they were so she could navigate their needs and the needs of the Wariuta with equal respect. He needed to get this girl to Yunka, where she could be tended to by healers. But it was a long walk to Yunka, and as strong as Koa was, he didn't think he could carry her the whole way. He would if he had to, though. He had enough water on him to make it through the night, and he knew well how to put together makeshift temporary shelters from the cold and the wind. He just needed to get through to this girl!

Lost in his pondering and planning, Koa had not noticed Tupac as he snuffled up to the girl. She let out a yelp of terror and tried her best to scuttle away from him. Thinking she'd just started a fun new game, Tupac smiled his toothy grin and tried to get closer.

This, Koa knew, did nothing to help the girl feel more at ease, and so he called Tupac back. Tupac listened and, with resentful eyes, returned to Koa's side.

"It's OK. He's just curious. He wants to be your friend." Koa tried to comfort the girl, but he could tell his efforts were insufficient. "Are you OK?"

The words were barely out of his mouth before Koa was staring down the barrel of a pistol. Instinctively, Koa took a step back and put his hands up, and in that moment, the girl squeezed the trigger.

Nothing happened.

She squeezed it again and again and then let out a cry of despair. The powder, Koa realized. The gunpowder in the pistol had gotten too wet to ignite. He kept his hands up but took a step closer to the girl.

"I'm not here to hurt you," he said. "But you gotta stop—"

Whatever dignity or reconciliation he had hoped to garner did not come to pass.

He should have heard them coming. Chima's laugh was higher, sharper than Tupac's. But his mind had been on the girl and the pistol, not on the sounds that heralded his sister's approach. Chima charged the girl, snarling and baring her long yellow teeth.

The girl's scream was terrible and piercing even over the roar of the sea.

CHAPTER 3

Kaia

K aia was only a little surprised when her brother threw his body in Chima's way, forcing the familiar to slam her forepaws into the sand so she wouldn't collide with him.

Koa was a trained warrior, as was Kaia. They had not learned to fight for nothing, especially with Colonizers all around them. But he seemed determined to ignore his training, even if it meant shunting the responsibility of keeping him alive onto Kaia's shoulders. Which, of course, she would do, whether it meant sullying her conscience or not. Sometimes loving her brother felt like a curse.

She had watched from her spot in the cliffs as her brother meandered up to the Colonizer, trusting. Despite everything they had done! She would have stopped him then if she'd not been so sure the girl was a corpse. Or maybe it was her anger; he *had* followed her. As if she needed his supervision. But as soon as the girl vomited, Kaia had started moving toward them.

It did not matter how close to death a Colonizer was, they could still spring forth with deadly intent. And Kaia had been right. Koa was just lucky that her pistol was either out of bullets or broken. Kaia had her ax at the ready. She had sharpened it only that morning.

"Kaia!" Koa shouted. "Stop!"

It was no secret among the Wariuta that despite his size, his lineage, and the painstaking training Ica had seen to herself, Koa was a terrible warrior. He had all the wrong instincts. Sometimes the injustice of it rankled Kaia, and she resented her brother for things that were not his fault. He had not decided to be born big and strong. Nor had he decided that her left arm should end below her elbow. But here they were. And somehow she was still the better warrior of the two. She would hate him if she didn't love him so much.

Chima circled the girl, her laugh rising above them, mingling with the violent crash of the sea on the shore. And, giving Chima a wide and reverential berth, Tupac circled, too, his smaller form like a shadow of Chima's. Once the girl was dead, Chima would get first pass at what was left of her. And even if both animals ate well in Yunka, there was no substitute for fresh meat.

It did not take long for Kaia to reach the girl, who crouched, huddled and pathetic, on the sand. Up close, she was so small, so weak—her eyes full of tears, her lips cracked. If Kaia was not mistaken, the girl had pissed herself. It would be a mercy to kill her. Kaia lifted her ax.

But before she could bring it down, Koa caught her by the wrist. Kaia turned on him, her eyes wide with fury. He knew better than to interfere with her. But his jaw was set, his grip firm.

"Don't," he said quietly.

Kaia made to pull her arm from his grip, but Koa would not let go. In all their lives, he had never once stood up to Kaia. If she weren't so angry at him, she would have been proud. Had she not been telling him do to exactly this for years? In his eyes, finally, she could see the fire that forged warriors. Annoyance flickered in Kaia's chest. Why was this the moment he chose to ignite?

"Fine," she spat. She let her arm fall to her side. "But we tie her up. She can't be trusted."

"Fine," he replied.

His voice was tart, and he didn't have to say that this was all Kaia's fault for Kaia to know that was exactly what he thought. And anyway, it wasn't her fault that this was now complicated; they could have executed her and been done with it, and there'd be no reason to lie about where they'd been, where they'd found the girl. So, really, his mercy was the problem.

Kaia stood still as Koa undid the leather straps that criss-crossed her back.

Kaia pointed her ax at the girl. "You're lucky," she said. And even though they did not speak the same language, Kaia could see that the girl understood. She did not try to run again and instead kept a wary eye on the familiars. Chima did a good job looking intimidating, snapping now and again in the girl's direction. Tupac, on the other hand, lolled behind her and stopped, briefly, to lick himself.

"What are we going to tell Mom?" Koa asked.

What he meant was *Are you going to tell her you explicitly disobeyed her command? Again?* Kaia frowned.

"This wouldn't have happened if you hadn't followed me," she muttered.

She yanked the girl to her feet, and Koa, with an apologetic look on his face, bound the girl's wrists.

And, no, she wasn't going to tell Ica the exact truth.

The truth was, Kaia had a lot more at stake than Koa did. If Koa got in trouble, well, who cared? Everyone knew him, everyone loved him. Everyone knew he was a poor excuse for a warrior, knew that Koa's father, Chimu, would have been ashamed to see who his son had turned out to be. And everyone also knew that Ica loved Koa more, even if she had named Kaia her heir. In fact, everyone loved Koa more. Even Kaia. He was lovable. Just. Also really annoying.

"If you promise not to kill her—*or* advocate for her execution—I'll take the fall," Koa said.

His eyes were still on the girl, and Kaia wanted to shake the shit out of him, to yell at him. Colonizers were not friends! But Koa thought everyone was a pal just waiting to happen. If she hadn't known her brother so well, she might have thought he was nurturing a crush. But Koa wasn't like that. His immunity to desire was his greatest strength. That or, perhaps, his negotiation skills.

The girl was getting better than she deserved. For Koa's negotiation on her behalf. That Kaia could not afford to lose face in front of the other warriors again. The last dressing-down Ica had given her had echoed through the ranks for months, it felt like—no one listening to her because she had not listened to her mother. Kaia sighed.

"Here." Kaia thrust her waterskin at the girl. "I'm not hauling your corpse back to Yunka."

The girl drank greedily. Koa watched, smiling. Of course he hadn't thought to bring water with him. Koa was no tactician. But even through her irritation, Kaia was glad he was glad. His happiness was like that. Contagious.

The Colonizer presence had disrupted the relative peace not only of the Wariuta but of their family, too. Ica was forever occupied and defensive. When she did speak to her daughter, she was prone to lectures and admonishment. Kaia could not remember the last time her mother had simply listened. And the normal placid playfulness that rested between Koa and Kaia was constantly strained; Koa, true to Koa's form, thought a live-and-let-live arrangement was perfectly viable.

Kaia did not agree.

She looked at the Colonizer girl. She would need healers' attention for her skin, which was ruined. It'd take at least a few days of constant salve application. Pathetic. How was it possible that a people so ill-equipped for the world had managed to conquer it?

She stood before her and waited until the girl's eyes met hers. It did not take long. The girl had a steel spine, at least. She looked into Kaia's eyes without blinking, and Kaia could see fire there.

"If you try anything," Kaia said, "I will kill you without hesitation." Behind her, Chima giggled high and loud, and the girl swallowed but did not break eye contact. "Do you understand me?"

And though the girl did not respond, Kaia knew she had understood.

Kaia, none too gently, pushed the girl forward with the tip of her ax.

• CHAPTER 4 •

Florian

Florian let his fingers entwine with Evelyn's hair. He tried to let his mind rest. Above them, the moon's silver light filtered through the constant motion of the Sea. If he focused his eyes, if he really tried, he could see the cold pricks of starlight. But why would he?

Curled in his arms, Evelyn traced shapes Florian did not recognize on his chest. He had not known life could be like this: safe, calm. Quiet, not as in silence, or as in stealth, but as in quiescent. As in peace. As in contentedness.

They lay nestled in a soft bank of sand at the base of a great kelp forest. It was a spot Evelyn had quickly come to favor, since so many otters fed there. Together, they watched the otters as they dove and hunted and played, their little faces alight with mischief and mirth. They made Evelyn laugh, which made Florian laugh, and so they returned often.

"Do you remember day?" Florian asked. "The sun, that heat."

"I do," Evelyn replied. She pulled herself up, and Florian immediately regretted asking, for they were no longer touching. But he did not pull her down to his side. Evelyn smiled at him, and he smiled back. How could he explain to her that she was like the sun now? The thing that burned bright and beautiful and necessary and warm in his life? She leaned down, gave him a kiss on his forehead. "But I do not miss it."

"Nor I." An incomplete answer.

What was the sun in Florian's life, except a reminder that another day had passed him by? So many days he had awakened in Crandon to the cold white light of another day breaking, and he knew he would need to find food, shelter, a coin if he could. Sunrise had been just the opening shot of daily battle. And though he mostly felt so far away from those days, still there were moments when his mind would return, as if the tide of his thoughts could not help but bear back ceaselessly. Happiness, he was learning, did not guarantee forgetting.

"How long have we been here?" Evelyn mused.

Florian followed her gaze upward, where the shadow of a great ship had, for a moment, eclipsed the moonlight.

"I don't know," Florian said. Time no longer passed in days but in great swaths—the time they spent with the humpback whales. The era of manta rays that passed overhead like great birds.

"Do you ever wonder what happened?"

Evelyn did not need to clarify. Days or months or minutes ago, Florian had become a child of the Sea, left his brother and Rake behind to fight a war that was still raging. Above them, the Emperor's men still hunted the Pirate Supreme. On the Floating Islands, a witch remained with all of Flora's secrets. On the Red Shore, enslaved people waited for freedom that would likely never come. In Crandon, there was always cruelty, always heartbreak. All the Known World still squirmed beneath the Nipran Empire's fist.

Distance, Flora was learning, did not guarantee forgiveness.

What was Alfie doing now? she wondered. Was he safe without Flora there to watch over him? Would Rake keep his word and protect him? She trusted Rake with her own life, but she was less sure she trusted him with Alfie's. They had never shared the same bond. And besides, they were up against more than anything Rake could take on alone. The Empire of Nipran had crushed thousands of men just like them in a single breath and never stopped once to wonder at what it had done. The thought caught in her throat, and she felt sick.

Was her life truly so separate from all that now?

Flora pushed her worries down as best she could. Time may have passed, but not so much that she could not recall how to feed herself with her own fear. *Let it nourish me,* she thought. *Let it pass through me.*

"No," Flora lied. "I don't."

Evelyn watched her with a curious face. Then, with one finger, she touched the crease between Flora's eyebrows that formed when she was worried.

"Liar," she whispered.

• CHAPTER 5 •

Koa

Ahead of them, Chima and Tupac led the way back to Yunka. Chima in the lead, of course. She was bigger and dominant over Tupac, who seemed to want both to be as close as possible to her and to stay clear of her powerful jaws.

The girl fell again, her feet unsure in the sinking sand of the dunes. Koa tried to offer his hand to help her up, but she ignored him, and Kaia scoffed at him, and so Koa chuckled, because what else could he do? He'd take the blame for Kaia's disobedience, and everyone in town would think, *Oh, that Koa, he's a lovable idiot,* and no one would know that he, too, had the Wariuta's best interests in mind. And both the girls were treating him like he was either diseased or stupid even as he saved them both, in his way. If he didn't laugh, he'd scream.

He knew that with the Colonizers, the men were in charge. It was mostly men who came to Puno. And while Koa, like all the Wariuta, regarded all Colonizers with equal parts pity, fury, and disgust, he did wonder sometimes what it would be like to be listened to. To be taken seriously. Like his father had been. It was not that Wariuta men never led, but it wasn't a given the way it was with the Colonizers. He had no urge to lead. But it would be nice, he thought, to be listened to.

But the thought was gone as quickly as it had arrived, and Koa went back to wondering what would become of the pink girl he'd found. And just how much trouble he'd be in. And if she'd receive the healing she obviously needed. And where she'd sleep.

He'd offer her space in his hut, except he was pretty sure that—given the opportunity—the girl would stab him in his sleep. Which, he thought, was fair enough. As far as she knew, she was just a prisoner.

As far as Koa knew, too, he supposed.

He smelled Yunka before he saw it, smelled the smoke of cook fires, the warm scent of roasted meat rising in the wind. The girl was likely hungry, and he was glad the wait for food would be short. Though she should receive attention from the healers first.

"You'll eat soon enough." Kaia gave him a withering look, her face smug.

Koa tried his best to ignore the sting of hurt her words brought, but he failed. He wasn't even hungry; he was just worried for the girl. Kaia knew that. She was angry with him—for what? taking her blame? being right?—and lashing out, as was her way. She wanted him to be as sour as she felt. The only thing Koa could really do was refuse to take the bait, so he smiled at his sister until she—reluctantly—smiled back.

"Sorry," she said at last.

When Koa smiled again, it was for real.

He turned and walked backward so he could try to make friendly eye contact with the girl. "Do you smell that?" he asked her. "The night meal'll be ready when we arrive in Yunka. Do you eat cows where you're from?"

He didn't expect answers, and he was given none. Still, he wanted the girl to hear his voice, as soothing and as affable as he could make it. He smiled his big smile, the smile that made Kaia laugh, but the girl didn't smile back. That was OK. He wouldn't want to smile, either, if he were her.

"I really don't think we need to keep her tied up," Koa said to Kaia. "She hasn't tried to run for hours."

Which was true. After the one time, the girl had not tried to bolt again. Koa would not have tried twice, either. Chima had chased her down, and the girl had shrieked in terror at the sight of her jaws. Koa may not have screamed if faced with Chima, but he certainly understood being fearful of the creature. Chima was young, but her forelegs were already burly with taut muscles. He looked to Kaia hopefully.

But Kaia just gave him a poisonous glare and yanked the girl forward for good measure. She staggered but couldn't quite brace herself properly before hitting the ground. When she stood again, half of her face was coated in the red sand of his home. She spat a mouthful of it out and coughed, a horrible, dry, hacking cough. She needed more water. Koa winced apologetically at her and offered her the waterskin. He tried to look small as he handed it to her. He thought small thoughts. But she flinched away from it and didn't accept it. She looked to the ground.

Which was too bad. First, she was dehydrated, and badly. But also, Yunka was beautiful as it rose over the dunes. The fires flickered orange in the dwindling light of day. The huts leaned together like the people who lived within leaned on one another, each dwelling as individual and unique as the person who owned it. It was lovely the way nothing was exactly the same, the way each hut was built to its own dimensions, took its own shape. And there, in the distance, the bathing pools shone with the bleeding rays of the sunset. Koa wished the girl would look up, see where she was headed, see what he saw. How could any place so beautiful be frightening?

Nearing the town, both Chima and Tupac sprinted ahead of the group until they were just black dots in the darkening landscape. Perhaps with the animals gone, the girl would be less afraid. If only for the remainder of their walk.

"See?" he asked her. "Yunka. You'll like it."

The girl did not meet his eyes or respond. But she did look into the distance at Yunka. He wondered what she was thinking, wondered if she thought it was beautiful, as he did. He hoped so.

Wariuta cities were as varied as the people who lived there. In Puno, he knew, the houses were built of stone. In Nema, on the far lakes, the houses were built into trees, and fishermen hung their lines from their balconies at night. But Yunka was special. He would have chosen it as his home even if he had not been born there.

"The best city in the world," Koa said. He meant it.

"How would you know?" Kaia snapped.

Koa watched her back as she made her way to the city he loved and she resented, his lips pressed into a thin line of irritation.

Someday, he hoped, she would appreciate what they already had.

He reached out a hand to help the girl, but she gave him a quick, hateful glance that made it clear she did not need or desire assistance and made her way on her own.

CHAPTER 6

Kaia

Ica already sat in her place before the bonfire that raged in the center of Yunka. At her side, her hyena, Puka, groomed herself with long, steady strokes of her thick pink tongue. Kaia had hoped that maybe she would catch her mother without the whole town watching, but no such luck. She braced herself at the trouble her brother would surely be in and stepped forward into her mother's view, dragging the girl in her wake.

Not long ago, Wariuta were split into townships, each with their own leadership and rules. But when the Colonizers came, the necessity for unity had arisen. No one was confident that anyone could lead the once-disparate groups, but Ica had won leadership through her cunning and also her strength—she was undoubtedly Yunka's finest warrior, but she was known to be merciful, too. So nearly all the former foes had raised their fists for her, and Ica had led all the Wariuta ever since.

They had lost Puno, though. Ica blamed herself—she thought the years of violent conflict between Yunka and Puno had soured their relationship past the point of any potential reconciliation.

Violent conflict that, in her youth, Ica had often led, often insti-gated. But Kaia knew better. The greed of the Colonizers was a contagion, as infectious and terrible as the sores and fevers that often came with them. The Wariuta of Puno were no different from all the others who had been colonized before them. But she'd die before she let Yunka go the same way.

Ica's silver eye glinted in the firelight. Long before Kaia had been born, Ica had lost that eye in battle. A scar from where her opponent's battle ax had nearly ended her life cut a straight line from her hairline to her chin. But she was still sharp-eyed, even in her older age. And so it did not take long for her to spot her daughter, and the prisoner she had with her.

Following Ica's gaze, Puka regarded the prisoner with a curl of her lip, letting out one whoop into the night. Like her master, Puka had lost one eye in battle and, like her master, had a silver eye in its stead. The mirroring of their eyes, the Wariuta said, spoke of the divine relationship the two shared—as the finest fighter and the most ferocious familiar that lived.

Ica stood and motioned to the girl.

"Who is this you've brought us?" she asked. At the sound of her voice, the rest of the Wariuta hushed, their eyes all pointed at Kaia and Koa. Without looking, Kaia could feel Koa shrink under their collective gaze. He hated to be looked at. Not Kaia. She stood with her chin up, meeting her mother's eye. Someday she would lead these people. She needed them to know that she would do so with courage, just as her mother had.

"A prisoner, Mother. Found on the shore." Kaia yanked the leather straps, forcing the girl to step forward. She could see the suspicion creep across her mother's face as she beheld the girl's pink skin.

"She needs the healers," Koa chimed in. "She was shipwrecked and nearly dead when I found her."

"Shipwrecked?" Ica's voice was like the pass of metal over a whetstone. She took a step toward her children and their prisoner, and even in the darkness, her might was obvious. She wore the same leather tunic of all the people in her town. Yet on Ica, it looked like armor. Pride swelled in Kaia's chest, forcing the curl of a smile to her lips. For all their differences, she knew that the best of her came from her mother.

"Tell me, my son. What were you doing on the shore?"

Koa did not answer. Ica looked to Kaia, who said nothing. Kaia could feel her mother's eye as if it were boring through her.

"My mistake is not this girl's fault," Koa said at last. His voice was stronger now, and Kaia fought the urge to encourage him in any way. He needed to stand up on his own if he would ever garner respect and not just affection. "We know nothing of her, and yet we treat her as a prisoner?" He looked around at the gathered Wariuta, meeting the eyes of his people.

Ica nodded. "You make a kind point, son. But this is no Wariuta girl you have brought to us. She hasn't earned our trust."

"I will," the girl said. Her voice quavered, but her words were clear. Kaia whirled on her. She could speak their language? Why hadn't she said anything? What trickery was this? "If you will hear my story."

Ica looked to Kaia, who tried with her eyes to tell her mother that she had no idea the girl could speak the Sky Tongue.

"Go on, then." Ica leaned forward, and Puka did, too.

The girl eyed the animal with visible fear. She took a deep breath.

"My name is Genevieve," she said haltingly. "I am on a ship that

did battle with the Pirate Supreme. We lose. My lady killed. I"—
her voice cracked—"am not. I am in the sea, and now I am here.
I am not bad. I want to survive."

Ica nodded. "How is it that you speak our tongue, girl?"

Many merchants and pirates spoke the Sky Tongue, but that
was from multiple visits. It was clear from the girl's evident fear of
the familiars that this was her first time among the Wariuta.

Genevieve bowed her head. "My lady says education is speaking many of languages," she said. "She tells me great things of
Wariuta. You raise cattle from dust. Your alchemists have no equal
in the Known World."

"Ah." Ica's face hardened.

The girl had said the wrong thing. Kaia smiled to herself.

Colonizers had long wanted to know the secrets the Wariuta
alchemists kept. They made salves that cured wounds, oils that
burned for days without depleting. And, probably of the most
interest to the Colonizers, a brutal explosive called kau. But the
Wariuta had no intention of sharing their secrets with those who
showed so little regard for life.

Koa sensed the change in his mother's disposition as well. "Are
you here," he asked the girl carefully, "to colonize?"

Genevieve mulled the question over carefully in her mind. "I
am sorry," she said. "I do not know that word."

At this there was a murmuring among the gathered Wariuta.
Koa looked triumphant.

Kaia had had enough. "Her ignorance isn't evidence against
malice. When has a Colonizer's ignorance ever limited his
destruction?"

The murmuring grew louder. Kaia did not let herself meet
Koa's eyes, even though she could feel the heat of his gaze on the
side of her face like flames. He was too soft for this conversation,

too weak. His kindness—regardless of the situation—was like an open door to pain, and Kaia meant to close it. It was possible to be Koa, to be so sweet, and not also be easy prey. He needed to learn this. Kaia had to protect him and her people. The deal they had made was aside from all that.

"You say your lady was doing battle against the Pirate Supreme," Ica pressed. "Tell us why."

A flicker passed over the girl's expression. Kaia could see it for what it was. Guile.

"To end the slave trade."

But that wasn't the whole truth, and Kaia knew it. The girl knew that Kaia knew it. She could see her eyes dart to Kaia and then back to Ica.

"See?" Koa asked a little desperately. "Let's show her that we are better than the Colonizers. Let's give her safe quarter. Perhaps she can be of some use. You speak Colonizer, too, yeah?"

Genevieve cocked her head a little, confused. "I speak the Common Tongue. And the tongues of Tustwe, Iwei, and the Floating Islands."

Kaia felt her heart fall into her belly. If there was anything the Wariuta genuinely needed from an outsider, it was someone who could speak the many languages that arrived on their shore. Though several of the merchants surely spoke the Colonizers' language, none wished to stand between them and the Wariuta. And in this regard, the pirates were doubly useless.

Koa had won, and she knew it. Koa knew it. All the gathered Wariuta knew it.

Ica turned on her son then, her face hard. "I wish I could trust you to guard this girl," she said. "But your heart is too soft, and until we know if we can trust her, you will see to her care and comfort only."

Kaia knew what was coming before it did. She closed her eyes as if she could guard against it, but it still came.

"And you, my daughter," Ica said, "will be responsible for her security."

"Of course, Mother." She shot Genevieve a look of pure venom. "I'll keep a very close watch on her."

But when she met Genevieve's eyes, she did not see fear anymore. The girl was smug in her victory.

That was fine.

Kaia could change that.

The Sea

At night, she comes alive. Everywhere the hum of life, the buzz of activity.

The Sea hears it all, but she listens to her mermaids.

The Sea knows her children all, and she sighs for her newest pair, her happiest. They are so small. How can she tell her children that love may not be enough?

In a kelp forest, a bioluminescent speck floats through Florian's outstretched fingers, and his eyes follow it as it illuminates the deep lines in the palm of his hand. Those lines look like great chasms in the world of that little glowing speck.

How can she tell her children of scale; how they are like the speck in the palm of her great hand? How she is like that speck in the great canvas of time?

Close to a harbor for merchant vessels off the coast of Crandon, a small, slippery seal darts directly into a fisherman's careless net. This is happening and concerns her, and yet it is also happening and will continue to happen without her interference. How can she tell her children of priorities or impossible choices?

On the Red Shore, the child from Quark has made it to land, and perhaps to safety. The Sea cannot know, not now that the child's so far from what she can see. How could she explain to her Pirate Supreme that she saved this child but not so many of their men? Just one of countless choices she makes in an instant, every instant of every day of every era, unending. There is no rest for the Sea, no respite, just a world that keeps violently ending and perpetually continuing.

She has begged her daughters to keep to the deeps, to find the trenches and the canyons. How can she tell them that their sisters, her daughters—her daughters whom she swears always to protect—are being murdered not one by one but en masse now? How can she explain such wanton destruction?

If she once had the words for this, she has lost them along with her murdered children. She knows, in some distant part of her mind, that the Empire of Nipran is responsible, but she cannot always hold this fact in her memory. Her grip on this truth slips, fades, is transformed into all humans. With their avarice and their greed and their unending propensity for violence.

She awaits the Pirate Supreme's call, but she cannot hear them.

And she fears they have forgotten her.

CHAPTER 7

Thistle

The walk back from the river was an odd one. Clearly hurt that Thistle did not share his enthusiasm for the totally illegal guns, Dai had been cold and testy the whole walk back. Annoyed that he had made her a criminal by proxy—knowing there were guns was a crime against the Imperials in and of itself, and snitching would make her a criminal against Quark just the same—Thistle did not have the energy or inclination to soothe him. Instead, they'd stalked back in heavy silence.

A bad omen for their eventual marriage.

When she returned to the house, her mother was a whirlwind of activity. Their guest would be there shortly, so Thistle was rushed off to wash her face and comb her hair and change her clothes and otherwise make herself look respectable and presentable, which she did without argument. She needed a moment alone.

Still marveling at what a strange day it had been, Thistle stood by the door and waited for the guest as her mother had bidden her do. Her name was Lady Minami, apparently, and Thistle was to be on her absolute finest behavior. They'd never had a *lady* stay with them before. If this went well, Mrs. Vo said breathlessly, perhaps there would be more.

Unspoken: *So don't mess this up.*

For the second time that day, there was a highly anticipated knock on the door, which Thistle answered with a deep, Imperial bow.

"Welcome to our humble domicile, Lady Minami. We hope you find it and our hospitality to your liking." She looked up and felt the breath catch in her throat.

The Lady Minami was tall and imposing, unlike any person she'd ever seen in Quark. Her hair was knotted in a complicated pattern on top of her head, her back straight, her eyes sparkling yet impassive. She wore a corseted kimono in the Imperial style, of course, but hers had thin gold thread woven into its pattern of flowers so that it glinted in the early-evening light. She smiled.

"You must be Thistle Vo." She made a quick motion with her hand, and two young Imperial soldiers bustled into the house. Each carried several bags. Thistle motioned to them where their rooms were, and they sped off, needing little help from her.

"Yes, milady."

"My lady," the Lady Minami corrected, but in a gentle tone. "I hear you are to be wed."

Thistle looked at her feet, embarrassed on a multitude of fronts.

"Lady Minami!" Mrs. Vo bustled into the room and bowed low, her back curved incorrectly. Thistle could tell from the way the Lady Minami's eyes tracked her mother that she had noticed this and didn't approve. She surely did not approve of her thin black hair tied in a low tail at her neck, either, or the shabbiness of her dress. Or Thistle's dress, for that matter. How had Thistle never noticed how . . . poor they were?

"Please," her mother said. "Come. I have dinner all set for you."

The Lady Minami gave a small tilt to her head, the bow of a superior to an inferior, and followed Mrs. Vo into what now was, in Thistle's opinion, a completely inadequate dining room.

Her mother had set the table with their best porcelain bowls, with the actual silver. It was not often she turned the key to the cupboard that stored all their finest dishes. A bottle of rice wine sat to the side of a sparse bouquet of her mother's favorite purple flowers.

"My goodness," said Lady Minami. It was not that the woman was beautiful but that each detail that comprised her whole was expertly chosen to communicate her wealth and class. Thistle catalogued her every sartorial choice and stored them away for future reference. "Quite the spread."

Thistle, who had never even imagined a lady of such . . . ladyness, was at a loss for words. All thoughts of Dai and the guns faded as she stared, open-mouthed, at the goddess who had just materialized in her home. The Lady regarded her with a warm but amused smile, her black eyes twinkling.

"Such lovely flowers," the Lady added. Finally, Thistle recognized that she had been prompted to speak—several times now— and, not wanting to seem dense, she shook herself back into the world of the living. And the cognizant.

"They're thistles!" Thistle blurted. Her voice was altogether too loud. "For me. Or my mother, really. They're her favorite flowers. Because my name. That's why she named me that. But be careful and don't touch them. They've got spines. Not terrible ones, but they're very. Poky." She was rambling, and she knew it, but at least she'd mastered the volume of her voice now. She wanted to close her eyes against the shame of acting such a fool in front of such an illustrious guest, but the woman emitted a tinkling laugh. It was a friendly sound, high and light.

"They're almost as lovely as you are," she said.

Thistle loved the way she spoke, each word precise. She grinned at the compliment.

"Mm. You are too kind to us, Lady Minami," Mrs. Vo said quietly. There was an ice in her voice that Thistle did not recognize, nor did she like it. Was she trying to mess this up?

"Is there a specific seat I should take?" the Lady asked after some time.

"Oh! Right!" Thistle led the Lady to the nicest spot, the one with the only nonlumpy pillow. "Here, my lady." Thistle took care to enunciate both *my* and *lady*.

The Lady nodded her approval and gracefully swept into her seat, the silk of her kimono soundless with her movement. She sat, as Imperials did, with her knees discreetly tucked under her. Thistle made a mental note to sit this way from now on.

Mrs. Vo poured the Lady Minami some rice wine. "What business do you have in Gia Dinh?" she asked.

"Just some shopping," Lady Minami said. She flashed a small smile. "Quark does have all the best soaps in the Known World, after all."

Mrs. Vo gave a polite smile, but Thistle could see the flicker of suspicion across her mother's face. She hoped it was subtle enough that the Lady did not see it, too. Dinner passed without any egregious faux pas, and just after it, the Lady Minami excused herself to bed.

As they washed the many dishes from the evening, Thistle noticed her mother's brow furrowed in worry.

"What's wrong?" Thistle took a clean plate from her mother and started to dry it.

"Nothing—just. Nothing." She sighed, looking behind her as though someone might be in the doorway. There was no one there. She leaned in close to Thistle so that their foreheads nearly touched. "Watch your mouth around this one."

"Lady Minami?" Thistle tilted her head, a little surprised. Hadn't everything gone well?

"She's not . . . hmm." They could both hear the Lady moving about upstairs in her room. Mrs. Vo took a deep breath, then continued in a hurried whisper: "I don't believe she's told us the whole truth about her visit here. And it's been my experience that one should never trust an Imperial who's clearly keeping secrets."

Thistle nodded, but she didn't understand.

It had been a very long day of not understanding things.

CHAPTER 8

Koa

When Koa was a boy, his father had told him that one day a girl would come back to his hut with him and everything would change, and he'd become a man. Clearly, he had not imagined it'd go like this.

Genevieve had pushed herself to the very wall of the hut, her eyes darting between Koa and Kaia with undisguised hatred. Kaia was taking the downtime to sharpen her ax, which was unnecessarily menacing and annoying. First of all, she'd sharpened it, like, the day before. And also it made it harder for Koa to braid her hair because she was constantly shifting around. Her braids were loose because of it, and Koa figured that was what she deserved.

"She speaks our language," Kaia said. "Think she can fight like us, too?"

Koa rolled his eyes. Everything with Kaia was a fight. It was the worst side effect of her training, like the only tool she understood how to use was her ax.

"She's our guest," Koa said. His voice was quiet but, he hoped, also firm. He was not interested in Kaia starting another fight in general, and he was extra not interested in her starting a fight in his hut. "There's no reason to be rude."

"Do you remember the first Colonizers that came?" Kaia asked. Of course he didn't. They had come before either of them had been born. But he had heard the stories. All the warriors of Pilau, massacred. Over a quibble about fishing boats. "They were guests of the Wariuta once, too."

"That was years ago." He did not like the waver in his own voice, the weakness of it. He hated the way Kaia could bring that out in him, and he hated that Genevieve could hear it. He felt his cheeks prick hot and stupid, and he hastily completed Kaia's braid.

"Do you think they have fundamentally changed in the years since?" Kaia asked. "Or do you think this girl is the same as all the other grasping, ugly little foreigners who come to our land to get sunburnt and rich?"

"Please do not talk like I am not hearing," Genevieve said, her voice quiet.

"I bet she can't," Kaia said, as if to no one but clearly to Genevieve. "Fight, that is. I hear all those Colonizer women just lounge about all day, waiting in their big cold homes for the men to come home and lie with them."

"Kaia," Koa hissed.

Why did she always need to start shit? What good would it do her? Do anyone? She was supposed to be a leader, not a stupid kid itching for a fight. She was supposed to be better. She was better than he was in so many ways. How come she was so small in this one regard? Was she really that scared?

"My lady," Genevieve bit out, "is a great warrior."

"Was," Kaia corrected. She wore a snake's smile.

"Kaia!" Koa stood. He didn't know what to do, but he had the

43

sense that he needed to stop whatever was about to happen from happening.

"What?" Kaia said. "Our tongue can be difficult to master. I'm just helping the girl with her grammar so she doesn't look like a complete fool in front of the others." She gave Genevieve a deeply condescending smile. "It'll be our little secret."

"I do not know this word," Genevieve said slowly.

"What, *fool*? It means—"

"Someone new to our land and our language and our customs who is still learning, that's all!" Koa interjected. He gave one of Kaia's braids a gentle tug, a nonverbal *Please, for the love of all things good and nice in our world, shut up*. Kaia shrugged in a completely transparent *Whatever you say* gesture that only a real fool would have missed.

"I do not think this is true," said Genevieve. Her expression was unreadable. "I think she calls me stupid."

"Not just you, to be clear," Kaia said. "Your entire empire. From your dead lady to your emperor, wherever he sits ordering his minions to our nation just to ruin our lives." She paused, examined her nails. "But I guess especially you."

Koa might have missed it if he had not been watching Genevieve so closely, so concerned for her hurt feelings; and though he saw it, he was utterly powerless to stop it.

In a lightning-fast, practiced motion, Genevieve pulled a dagger from her thigh and flung it at Kaia. It landed in the packed-dirt floor of his hut with a reverberating thud that stole the breath from Koa's chest. Next to Kaia but not *in* Kaia. For a moment, both Kaia and Koa simply blinked at the dagger. Then Kaia pulled it from the ground with what, Koa could see, was more effort than she had anticipated. A very thin trickle of blood dripped down Kaia's thigh where the blade had just barely grazed her.

44

"Only 'fool' leaves an enemy armed," Genevieve said coolly. "This is something my lady teaches me long ago. Perhaps a lesson you will not forget?"

"You," Kaia roared. She was on her feet, her hand raised and ready to strike, but Koa was ready, too.

"Whoa!" Koa crooned as if he were trying to calm an ornery bull. He was glad in moments like this for how big he was. He could physically block the women from each other by merit of size. "Hey, now. Let's all just take it easy, huh?" He tried to ignore the sweat that rolled down his face and back. "Have some chicha drink?" His mind raced, desperately trying to find purchase on something pleasant, something nice they could do that didn't require any weapons. "I'll rebraid your hair! You were moving around so much that I did a crap job and we both know it."

Kaia lowered her hand. She was still furious, but Koa knew there was some part of her that was aware she should not kill Genevieve, however much she'd like to. It'd cause hell with their mother, and though he knew well Kaia was not afraid of him, she did still fear Ica. She regarded her brother coolly.

There was a horrible beat of silence during which Koa had a seemingly infinite amount of time to picture the many courses of action Kaia might take next that would end in blood and death and suffering. He could only hope that Kaia's fear of Ica's authority would hold strong against her desire to fight the Colonizers.

"Give me the dagger, Kaia," Koa said. He was proud of the steadiness in his voice. How firm he was despite the wiggling doubt in his belly.

Kaia glared at Genevieve.

Genevieve glared at Kaia.

"Please."

"I could kill you with your own weapon," Kaia yelled at

Genevieve. "Only a fool would throw her weapon into her enemy's hand for pride's sake. But I suppose only the gun was worth anything to your kind, and yours is rusting on the shore."

"You will not kill me," Genevieve replied. "You need me."

Kaia spat on the ground, then tucked the dagger into her belt and, much to Koa's relief, sat back down.

"I want four braids this time," she said to Koa. "And make them tight."

CHAPTER 9

Kaia

Ica walked steadily.

Kaia stumbled.

She was glad to see her mother's back, to know that Ica did not witness how gracelessly her daughter followed her lead, even if she knew their forebears saw. That could not be helped. The forebears saw all, and most clearly in the Canyon.

The narrow path into the Canyon of the Moon was treacherous even in the day. The cliffs were steep and falls fatal. But for those who sought wisdom, the trip had to be made at night. Throughout Kaia's childhood, Ica went alone, but as Kaia had gotten older, Ica brought her more and more. The invitations always filled Kaia with equal parts pride and dread. The path was not the only thing terrifying about the Canyon of the Moon.

Kaia knew why they went. They were losing the war.

They had lost the mountain city of Puno when Kaia was a child. More recently the shore. And now they had a Colonizer in their midst, and while Koa may have been hopeful for what Genevieve could offer, Kaia knew better. The girl was a snake. Kaia still had her dagger in her belt. She would die before she gave it back. She felt her hand reach for it involuntarily, checking to make sure it was still there. As if a dagger could protect her from what she might see tonight.

Elders visited the Canyon of the Moon to seek the wisdom of the forebears. It was where the veil that kept the dead and living apart was the thinnest, where those who came with pure hearts could seek answers in their times of need. The answers were not always encouraging, but they were always true. Kaia hoped that tonight they would help her mother see reason. To guide her away from her guilt, and to remind her of the powerful warrior she had always been. The one Kaia had always looked up to. The one who had taught her to live with courage.

Ica's familiar, Puka, led the way. Her enormous haunches relaxed even as she traversed the perilous terrain. Whereas Yunka was nestled into the red sand of the shore, the Canyon of the Moon was carved straight out of the moon-white rocks left by volcanoes long since sleeping. The Canyon of the Moon had been there ever since the first of the Wariuta had found this land. It was the most sacred space for her people.

Behind Kaia, Chima followed at a short distance. She could tell her familiar was as frightened as she was. The relationship between warriors and their familiars was an intensely intimate one; it was said that the familiar's personality was a portent of the warrior's destiny. And so far, that bore out for Kaia. Chima was small. She would never be as big as Puka or as strong. But she was fierce and stubborn. Kaia had seen flares of red-hot anger in her familiar, and it had been like watching herself. The animal was powerful, despite her size. Kaia was, too.

She waited a beat so Chima could catch up to her, and she rubbed behind the hyena's ear. Chima growled quietly, reassured.

"We're almost there," Kaia whispered.

A whoop from up ahead told her that Puka had reached the Canyon. Kaia swallowed her unease. She was aware of every breath she took, could hear the rush of blood in her ears.

Her mother waited for her at the entrance to the Canyon. She stood nearly a head higher than her daughter, and her hands were rough from years of handling a spear. Kaia would never be Ica. Ica was a legend. Kaia liked to tell herself that she had squared herself with this years ago, but the truth of it still made her stomach turn over. Someday, when the war was done, she would likely ascend and lead the Wariuta. If it had not been for the war, the vote may have been taken already. And everyone knew Kaia would be the presumptive winner, when the time came.

What would happen, she wondered, if she failed?

Ica squeezed Kaia's shoulder.

"When we walk into the Canyon of the Moon," Ica said, "we walk in with our minds clear."

Kaia made to keep going. But Ica did not move. She looked at Kaia as she so rarely did these days—as her daughter, not as her protégé. Kaia fought the urge to hug her, to let her mother's arms fall around her like a spell of protection, like she was still a child scared of the dark.

"You can do this."

Kaia nodded. She was only sixteen, but her childhood had ended long ago. War had seen to that. Whether she could or not, she *had* to do this.

She watched as her mother's figure cut a straight line down the rocks to the bed of the Canyon. It was as if the Canyon had been made for her, cut to her dimensions. It was the only place where a person as powerful as her mother made sense. As if her mother had been carved from the very same rock.

Kaia followed carefully, more mindful of her feet now.

In the center of the Canyon, equidistant from the great rocky cliffs that rose on either side, was the firepit. Who had dug it, no one knew. Who had lit the fire, none could say. But the fire there never extinguished, no matter the rains or the wind. It had been burning for as long as the Wariuta had been on this land; legend said the first Wariuta explorer who had disembarked her canoe and called this land her own had lit the flame. And there Ica sat, waiting for her daughter, Puka at her side. In the firelight, their twin silver eyes glinted.

Kaia took her place across the fire from her mother. As Ica prepared for the ceremony, Kaia watched as the moon moved into place overhead. When it was directly over the fire, it would be time.

Stars appeared as the sky darkened, each a cold pinprick in the heavens. Kaia knew, as all the Wariuta knew, that the stars were like the firepit—great fires that burned eternal. But while the firepit showed the future, the stars were so far away that by the time they appeared in the night sky, those who looked upon them with wisdom knew they looked upon the past.

A satisfied growl from Puka told them all it was time.

Ica passed Kaia the cup full of tea she had steeped in the firepit. It was a mixture of calafate root and dried mushroom stems. Kaia winced as the hot liquid burned her throat.

"Slowly," said Ica. She sipped her own tea methodically, silently, her chin tilted toward the sky.

The roots in the tea tasted of wood and sick and ants. As Ica and Kaia drank the tea, the shadows cast by the ancient fire sent strange shapes dancing across the cliffs. In them, Kaia knew, they would see their answers. If they looked hard enough. If their minds were clear and their hearts were pure, they would see. As ever, she prayed she would not disappoint her mother, her people. Herself.

Time dilated.

Kaia saw the night sky in fast motion, the night turning to day turning back to night, stars falling and blinking out as new ones shot across the sky, only to recede back into clouds that rushed with unfelt wind. There was a part of her that knew, rationally, that perhaps only a few minutes had passed, but the part of her that mattered, the part of her that saw through her eyes and smelled through her nose and felt through her fingertips, no longer lived time in a straight line. No matter how many times she did the ceremony, Kaia did not think she would ever grow accustomed to the strangeness of it.

When she looked down at Chima, her familiar's eyes were two bottomless black pools that contained all her anxieties: That she was unfit to lead. That she could never live up to her mother's legacy. That she would fail her people. That the Wariuta would lose everything that made them distinct in this world that trended toward sameness. That she was simply the one-handed girl who should never have been taught to fight as some in Yunka had always whispered she was. That no one respected her. That she would lose her mother and Koa to this war. That she would lose everything. She looked away before her fears engulfed her.

Kaia watched as a shadow on the eastern cliff formed the shape of a great city on a scale she could barely comprehend. Buildings, cold and sharp, loomed enormous over the people. She could barely stand to look at them, for the way they cut into the earth was so thoughtless, so savage. Beyond them, a great battle raged upon the sea, composed of all manner of ships: Long and narrow Wariuta canoes. Cold World galleons. The Colonizers' gunships. But. There. On the shore. A girl dressed in Imperial clothing skulked about the perimeters of the scene. Kaia watched her with suspicion.

It was Genevieve. It had to be.

All around her, destruction reigned. The buildings came crumbling down. But Kaia kept her eye on the girl as she slithered away from the unending darkness that swallowed the city until she met a great tall figure in an open field.

It had to be Ica. The figure had the bearing of a leader. The confidence of years of battle. Kaia watched with her breath held as the girl and the figure circled each other. Her eyes hurt from watching, unblinking, as their hand-to-hand combat began.

The girl won. Ica was dead.

In a howl of rage, Kaia flung the girl's dagger at the eastern cliff. In an instant, the images evaporated. By the time the dagger hit the ground, time had returned, the visions were over, and her mother was looking at her with something like fury or disappointment or disgust in her eye.

"She killed you," Kaia panted. "Genevieve, that little snake, she—"

"That is not what I saw," said Ica. She stepped over to where the dagger had fallen and picked it up. Her eye followed the blade, pausing on imperfections so minute Kaia had not seen them. Then she met Kaia's gaze once more. "You have sullied this place."

"I . . ." Kaia felt stupid. What she had thought throwing a dagger at a vision would accomplish was suddenly a mystery to her. She was a child. Out of her depth. Unfit. Everything she feared she might be.

"You must be better," Ica said. She wasn't cruel about it, her tone was even, but Kaia felt each word like a stab in her chest. It seemed these days she could do nothing but court her mother's rebuke. "For our people, you must be."

"I'm sorry." As if Ica had never been angry. Her fury had been legendary. The people of Puno carried many tales of it, and the people of Yunka were safe and fat and happy because of it. Her mother never seemed to remember.

"What good that may do us."

"What did you see?" Kaia asked finally. She did not know what else to say.

"I saw a coalition of many. I saw unity in purpose. And I saw the girl."

"Yes!" Kaia grinned. "Yes, I saw her, too!"

"We must work with her. Without her, the Colonizers can never be beaten."

"What? No. Mother, please, I saw her kill you, I saw—"

"She will not kill me," Ica said calmly.

"But I saw you die!"

"Death comes for us all, Kaia." Ica cupped her daughter's face in the palm of her hand. Her silver eye shone in the moonlight. "It will come for me, too. And when it does, you must be ready."

Kaia pulled away from her mother's touch. "No," she said.

Ica only smiled sadly. "Well. Whether you will be ready or not, it's coming. Until then, we will work with this Colonizer child. Not just for our own people but for all those who live under the Imperial violence and their greed all over this world. My life is nothing stacked against so many. A good leader understands this."

With dawning horror, Kaia realized her mother had seen what she had seen. She knew her own death was assured. And yet here she stood, looking like nothing unusual was happening. Why was her mother so resigned to martyring herself?

"But—"

"This is the path I choose. And until I am gone, you will walk it with me. Do you understand?"

"I understand that you have forgotten who you are," Kaia seethed. "You were a warrior once, the best of us. What happened to you?"

Ica pressed her lips into a thin line of disappointment. "I grew up, Kaia. Painstakingly, and often too late." She took a calming breath and met Kaia's eyes once more. "I made so many mistakes, so many terrible and cruel choices. But you . . . you need not make the same mistakes I did. You can be something better than me. If you'd just *listen*. Ferocity is not the only thing that makes a warrior great. Knowing this will make you a better leader."

Kaia shook her head. "Not a day went by when I was small when you wouldn't tell me to use my own judgment, not to be swayed by popular opinion. But now you lecture me about just doing as you say. Do you not see how infuriating that is?"

Ica smiled, and Kaia felt heat prickle at her cheeks. Was she amusing? She was not some precocious child; she was the next leader of the Wariuta.

"I wish you had not done such a good job learning to be yourself," Ica said finally. "Somehow you have turned into both the best and the worst of me."

The worst of me.

Unable to name the feelings roiling in her throat, Kaia simply turned away from her mother and stalked out of the Canyon of the Moon.

CHAPTER 10

Thistle

Thistle had heard the rumors. That her father had been part of the noble and defeated Resistance and that he had betrayed them. That it was the Resistance, not the Imperials, who had either killed him or run him out of Gia Dinh. She was barely a year old when he died or left, so Thistle didn't know what to think. She had never met him.

But she also had never known her mother to lie.

And though her mother now ran a guesthouse that catered almost exclusively to Imperials, she still held her dead husband's supposed heroism in her heart. Each year on the anniversary of his death, she would light a candle for him beneath the shrine of Death and whisper his name.

The shrine was hidden from guests, of course. Shrines to the many gods were forbidden after Colonization. And though Mrs. Vo was rarely prone to rebellion, she did have her one statuette, hidden in the stone basement along with the stores and the gold coin she had squirreled away in case of emergency.

Thistle sat before the shrine of Death. They said that those who lived in peril could feel him stalking, but Thistle had never felt anything like that. She looked upon the marble statue. He was small, maybe just the length of her forearm, but imposing regardless of size. Death could take many forms, but when captured in a statue, he tended to be a young man in soldier's garb, and this was what Mrs. Vo's Death wore. He held a spear close to his chest and glared down at Thistle from his plinth.

"He was always the most imposing of the many gods."

Thistle whirled and, to her abject horror, saw the Lady Minami standing behind her. But Lady Minami smiled warmly and beckoned Thistle to stay seated. Thistle was shocked when the Lady, in her immaculate silk kimono, knelt next to her on the cold, dusty stone floor.

"I always thought it was lovely, the way you people speak of death. Like he is an old friend." She placed a warm hand on Thistle's. "Who is this statue for?"

"My father," Thistle said. Her throat felt very dry.

"Ah. Mr. Vo. I wondered where he might be."

"He died when I was still a baby," Thistle said. "I never knew him."

"A pity, I'm sure."

And then, as if someone else controlled her mouth, Thistle felt words come tumbling that should never have been spoken. "Mother says he died in the Resistance." Why was she talking? Why would she tell an Imperial of all people that the illegal shrine in their basement was for a dead Resistance fighter? "But I've heard the Resistance killed him. Dai says that the Resistance killed a lot of people who were just suspected of betraying them, and that maybe that's why there's rumors that my Dad did, and that actually he might not have done anything wrong at all. He says

56

that was the way it had to be then, because there were so many betrayers. But I don't know. The Resistance lost."

"Dai as in Dai Phan, your future husband?"

Thistle turned to the Lady Minami then, her heart pounding with alarm at her potentially fatal mistake. "Please don't tell," she whispered. "That I was down here. That we have a shrine. That my father was in the Resistance. He's dead anyway. And I'll throw out the shrine, I promise; Mother will understand. We just. I don't mean any harm. I'm glad Imperials are here. Girls get to go to school now, I get to go to school now, and I know that's thanks to the Emperor. Please, I—"

"Shh." The Lady Minami squeezed Thistle's hand. "This will be our little secret."

"OK," Thistle said, but still the blood drummed loud in her ears.

The Lady pulled a long, slender pin topped with a pearlescent sakura flower from her hair and placed it—just as was tradition—before the statue of Death. An offering. "In his name, we ask for his blessing."

It took Thistle a few moments to realize what the Lady Minami had said. Not because she didn't recognize the words—they were the customary prayer for the many gods—but because she spoke them in the Old Tongue. In the language of Quark, long since outlawed. Thistle knew only snips and snatches of it herself, gleaned from listening to her mother's prayers.

"You speak our language?"

"Not as well as I'd like," the Lady admitted.

"But . . . how? It's illegal to speak it."

"Not in Crandon, it's not. And it's good for the mind to learn other languages. To be nimble."

"Oh." Thistle sat with this for a moment. How strange to think of Imperials learning the languages they forbade in the colonies.

"Perhaps I can earn your trust if I lend you a secret of my own?"

Thistle nodded her agreement, eager to know any secrets the Lady might hold.

"I don't think it's right to outlaw worshipping the many gods," Lady Minami whispered. "Or to outlaw speaking the Old Tongue."

Thistle smiled. "Really?" Her mother did not think so, either. It was nice to think of the Lady Minami and her mother agreeing on something. It gave her mother rather more credibility.

"Really. I believe the Empire of Nipran is strongest when we celebrate our diversity rather than eliding it. And I for one am proud to have Quark in our Empire."

"I'm proud to be in the Empire," Thistle said. She was startled to find that she wasn't lying, exactly. Not entirely. Her mother, just like all the adults in Gia Dinh, bit her tongue in public. But in private she gossiped and maligned her Imperial customers. They were a bossy, brutish lot, loud and demanding and often rude. Ignorant of their ways, though everyone in Quark knew how to bless the Emperor. An ugly people. Supposedly. But this was not what Thistle had seen.

She thought of the soldiers who tossed her candy, of them marching in their orderly formation.

Of the smooth roads the Imperials had built.

Of all the money they spent in businesses like her mother's and like Dai's family's restaurant.

Of the fine things—leather and apples and glass—that were now imported from all over the Empire.

Of the Lady Minami, who was interesting and smart and good.

Perhaps Thistle was not lying at all.

"You know, when I was a child, my nanny's name was Genevieve. She was from Iwei, strong woman, smart woman. She

58

knew the Emperor's words better than any official, could recite the royal line all the way back to the First Emperor. She had hands like a man's." The Lady chuckled, and so Thistle did, too. "And she instilled in me a profound respect for the immigrants who come to Crandon. We are all part of the Empire's might, thanks to the Emperor, but it takes real courage to come to the center of that power and find your own."

Thistle thought about this. She wondered if she had that kind of courage, if she could be strong and smart, too. If she could make it in Crandon.

"What happened to her?" Thistle asked.

The Lady Minami looked down at her hands and gave a rueful smile. "She passed, sadly. But not a day goes by that I don't think about her."

"I'm sorry for your loss."

"And I for yours."

They both looked in silence at the shrine for Thistle's father for what felt like a very long time.

"Thank you for sharing your shrine with me." Lady Minami stood. "It's beautiful." She gave Thistle a deep bow of respect, which Thistle did her best to re-create. "I think you and I will become very good friends. What do you think, Thistle Vo?"

・ CHAPTER 11 ・

Koa

Koa was pretty sick of Kaia's shit.

She had taken to looming over him and Genevieve, her presence like foul weather. Koa loved his sister, and even liked her most of the time. But she made it impossible to talk with Genevieve, to soothe her into comfort. How would they ever work together if she was constantly afraid for her life?

Koa tried that morning, unsuccessfully, to get Genevieve to bathe in the bath pits. It was Koa's favorite place in Yunka. Dug deeply out of the earth and packed with hardened clay, the pits were filled each day with steaming-hot water and emptied each night. No one talked in the bathing pits. It was a quiet place but not a lonely one.

However, Genevieve only regarded him with chilly horror when he pulled off his tunic, and it became very clear that she did not think being naked was normal. Which. OK. So that's why Colonizers always smelled so bad. Koa was willing to skip a single day if it meant getting Genevieve to be more comfortable, so he pulled his tunic back on and tried not to think about the warm, sour scent that came off his body.

Instead, he took her to the oasis.

There were many oases tucked away, too deep within the mountains for Colonizers to find. It was the secret to the Wariuta's success raising cattle—the oases were all uniformly rich with fresh water and with water lilies and seagrasses for the cows to graze upon. But one was different. It was full of seawater, and it was Koa's daily charge to keep the Wariuta away from it.

Genevieve stumbled as she followed Koa along the rocky pass, but she kept up. Before they got too close, Koa turned to her, already apologetic.

"So. You're going to hate this. But there's just no other way. I have to tie your hands."

Genevieve glared at him, her face red with exertion, exposure, and now anger. "You have to," she repeated, and even in her heavy accent, her disdain was clear.

"I have to," Koa said. "For your own protection. My job here is . . . weird? Please don't be mad." He placed his spear on the ground and bound her hands carefully, tight enough that she couldn't break free but as loose as he could manage. He did his best not to let their skin touch, kept his body as far away from hers as possible. A gesture of respect.

But Genevieve was still mad.

Koa didn't know what to say to her but figured once she saw, she'd understand. Or rather, once she heard. They walked in silence, Tupac padding alongside them, his big paws leaving craters in the sand.

When he could see the green of the oasis, Koa led Genevieve toward the lean-to he had constructed so he could have shade while he tended his post. The oasis itself was lovely. There were worse places to sit for the day. Three lanky palm trees on the water's edge leaned in the direction of the nightly winds. Distantly, he could already hear the singing that told him his charge was awake. Her voice was high and light as it drifted across the dunes. She must have sensed that Koa was not alone.

"I am going to touch you," he warned Genevieve. Though it pained him, Koa reached out and took her hand. "I'm sorry," he said, and he meant it. But she didn't tug or protest. She flinched when their skin touched but allowed him to lead her to the shade.

Why didn't she react to the song? Koa wondered as he tied her to one of the four wooden posts. It was as though she couldn't hear it.

"Hello, boy," called the siren. Her voice was soft like a baby's skin. "Have you brought me something good to eat?" She pulled herself to the edge of the green water of the oasis and rested her head on her arms on the red sand.

Koa looked at his charge. She was beautiful—she had smooth black skin and a mischievous mouth. Her eyes and hair were the same dark green of the water that was her home. But she had drunk the blood of enough Wariuta for Koa to know she was dangerous.

To all but him.

Her song was a lure. He was told it promised pleasure, but he couldn't hear that. All he heard was a melody, no more interesting or alluring than any sung under full moons or on naming days.

"You know my name, Lilith," he said. This was a game she played each day. She pretended not to know him, pretended he had not been her only company for the past five years. Each day, Koa sat by her lagoon. Some days she did not come to the surface at all. If Koa was honest, those were sad days. She may have been a murderer, but she was amusing—if occasionally rude—company.

62

"Oh, my," Lilith drawled. Her eyes dwelled hungrily on Genevieve, who stared back at the siren, agog. "Do you finally have a lover? I never thought I'd see the day."

Koa laughed his big laugh, felt the humor true and deep in his belly. "That's Genevieve," he replied. "And I'm pretty sure she hates me."

Lilith cocked her head. Her long green hair fell over one green eye. "Does she." It was not a question.

The siren regarded Genevieve with open curiosity. Koa could see that Genevieve's shock had already passed, and now she looked at Lilith with cold appraisal.

"I will not hate you so much if you do not tie me up." Genevieve glared at the siren. "What are you?" she asked.

"The better question is, What are you?" Lilith retorted. Her tail, long and elegant and covered in glittering green scales, thwacked against the surface of the water. She let her eyes wander over Genevieve, unblinking, and Koa lowered his spear so it was level with her head.

"No eating our guest," he said calmly.

"Wouldn't dream of it," said Lilith, who absolutely would.

"Lilith, this is Genevieve. Genevieve, this is Lilith," said Koa peaceably. "Lilith is a siren. Like a mermaid, but her song is dangerous. It's my job to protect people from her so she doesn't eat them, because she will and she has, and she'll eat you if you get too close to the water." Koa smiled at Genevieve. "That's why I had to tie you up."

Lilith pushed back from the shore and disappeared beneath the cool water of her oasis.

"But . . . you don't seem affected by her song," Koa said. He looked at Genevieve. She was calm, if annoyed. Usually those who heard Lilith's song were frenzied in their desire to reach her.

"It is nice," Genevieve said, but this was all.

Genevieve was like him.

Koa hated the word. *Unwanting.* It wasn't true, for one thing; he wanted all kinds of things. Good company. A nice place to sleep. For Kaia to be happy. Respect. But he understood it, too, probably better than the rest of the Wariuta did. For everyone else there was only one *want* that defined their lives. And Koa didn't want it. Or maybe it just didn't interest him. Sometimes he felt curious about it the way he might feel curious about a lizard. But, he figured, he was mostly curious why it mattered so much.

Whatever the reason, the fact that he didn't "want" meant Lilith's song had no effect on him. Koa was as safe by her side as he was in his hut. If he ever forgot the danger she posed, he needed only to remember Jia—a weaver by trade and a nuisance the rest of the time—who had assumed that since she did not typically favor females for lovers, she would be safe from the siren's song.

That was not so.

Koa found her, what was left of her, on the bank of the oasis. There was a word for what had happened to her, Ica said. *Exsanguination.* Her skin had gone ashy and terrible and vacant, all the warm color of her gone, gone, gone, her eyes still open, still wide with fear and realization, her mouth contorted in pain. Koa knew she was going to die before she died, had felt every drop of her blood leave her. Koa had retched, not when he first saw her but when he realized what and who she was. When he realized it was his own failure—to simply be at his post—that had allowed her to die.

Before him, Lilith had resurfaced and now rested her face on her thin arms, looking both harmless and lovely for her harmlessness. He tried to imagine her drinking blood but couldn't, even though he knew that was how she lived. On every seventh day, he brought her a calf to eat. But she always waited to eat it until he left.

Today was not the seventh day, however. That didn't matter. Lilith was still hungry. She was always hungry.

"Why not just kill her?" Genevieve asked.

The question startled Koa. She was a Cold Worlder, she didn't understand, but still. To be so callous.

"Because she is alive?" Koa replied. "Because it's not her fault she's like this."

Lilith openly glared at Genevieve. So she'd heard. Great.

"Because I am a gift from the Sea, girl," Lilith hissed. "Banished from my home for the crime of loving one of *you*." She licked her teeth, and Koa looked away. He hated when she was like this. Bitter. Cruel. "I sought the help of a witch, and my mother knew it. She always knows."

Genevieve smiled at Lilith, and Koa regretted her words before they were spoken. "That is your own fault. For trusting a witch."

To Koa's great relief, Lilith laughed. "What a little bitch you are," she said. Koa's relief dissipated immediately. "With your Quark face and your Crandon accent. You've trusted the wrong people, too, little miss. You'd be a fool to think otherwise."

She disappeared under the water again, and Koa looked to Genevieve.

"You're a part of the Empire?" So she was a Colonizer. He didn't realize how much hope he'd been holding out that she was not. There were so many immigrants from the Cold World who'd folded into Wariuta life with little problem. He had hoped she would be one. But the Empire's Colonizers were different.

It was the Colonizers' fault that the Wariuta had been relegated to only the largest of their cities. Outsiders had always been welcome, their best customs adopted—but there was one thing the Wariuta held fast to: the belief that life was sacred. It was the only demand they made of newcomers.

And Colonizers didn't respect that.

"Yes," she said tartly. "Proudly."

And they did not speak after that.

CHAPTER 12

Kaia

The Colonizers were a blight that predated Kaia's birth. They were a part of the world she had always known, a cancerous growth in her heart that was, unfortunately, as much a part of her as her stubbornness or her athleticism.

Kaia did not hate all outsiders, as Koa often accused her. She was half outsider herself. Her father had come from Tustwe and simply never left. Pirates came to make trades for leather and beef and alchemical goods. The many merchant ships carried glass or apples or rice or cheese. And mostly this was peaceful. They came to trade, and then they left, or they stayed. And that was that.

But the Colonizers were different. They did not want to trade. They wanted to take.

And they'd been taking for more than twenty years now.

The Colonizers fought cold and dirty, with guns and little care for collateral damage. It was the Wariuta way to respect even your enemies, but Kaia did not respect them; she hated them. She also did not know what life might be like if they ever left.

But the idea of keeping a Colonizer safe so she could help negotiate, to help haggle for what was rightfully the Wariuta's, didn't just irritate Kaia; it was like a wound, open and weeping and untreated by healers. Gangrenous and toxic.

Her father, Muteteli, had been killed by Colonizers. He had not even been armed, had been on the shore with his fishing nets and his canoe, simply seeing that the Wariuta would have trevally for the night meal. He was not a warrior, never had been. According to the other men who survived the attack, he had waved to the Colonizers, ever cheerful, before they shot him. The trevally he had caught rotted in the open sun, wasted, in the canoe Muteteli left behind.

Koa's father, Chimu, had been killed in the skirmishes that followed Muteteli's death. Though the Wariuta were more prepared this time, armed, at least, they still underestimated the Colonizers' blind disregard for life. They killed wantonly. Without thought or care. There was nothing holy in the way they snuffed out lives, nothing sacred. They pointed guns and pulled triggers, and Wariuta fell.

Chimu had been the greatest of the men—he loomed enormous over everyone, his body giant and his might met only by that of Ica. And so when he was killed—by a man crouched and hiding—shot in the back, the Wariuta knew the time of conflicts solved the old way had died, too.

The Colonizers looted alchemical stores, leaving behind all the healing ointments, the skin oils and protective creams. They searched only for the sticky black tar called kau, an explosive the Wariuta made that was ignited by water. The alchemists used it sparingly, made very little of it. It had been invented for terraforming but was used in battle to scare off enemies rather than kill them. It had been very effective at this for centuries. But the

68

Colonizers took every drop of it they could find, and the Wariuta knew they would use it for murder.

If they had not had such a singular goal, Kaia noted with disdain, they could have kept their delicate skin safe from the sun that ravaged them in the Wariuta land. There was an oil for that. But they left those jars behind or, worse, destroyed them.

And now Koa showed the girl, the Colonizer, Genevieve how to use that very same oil her people had almost entirely destroyed.

"Just put it on! This is why you people always burn," he said. He spread some on his own arm as an example. "Put it everywhere the sun'll touch."

"It smells," Genevieve said.

It took all of Kaia's self-control not to smack her.

"Not as bad as you do," Koa said, and Kaia laughed.

The girl, now with the Wariuta for several weeks, had still not bathed. Just looking at her made Kaia feel itchy. Koa's hut was thick with the smell of her.

Genevieve glowered and set about applying the oil to her filthy body. The skin on her nose and forehead was peeling. She looked disgusting, smelled disgusting. But Ica said they needed her. And so Kaia kept her safe. She could follow orders, even if they were mind-bogglingly stupid.

It wasn't only Kaia who hated her. Plenty of the Wariuta would see her punished for the Colonizers' many crimes. Kaia could feel the eyes of her people tracking the girl's movements as they walked around Yunka. She wanted to tell them all, *I know I know I know*, but she also knew she could not do that, could not defy or rebuke her mother in public.

Did Genevieve appreciate that her skin was now safe? Did she give thanks for the Wariuta healers who had mended her wounds? Was she grateful for her life?

No.

Koa ducked out of the hut to rustle up some food. It had become clear that Genevieve was a disruptive presence at the night meal, so the three had to eat away from everyone else, like pariahs. Like criminals. Another thing to hate the girl for.

Kaia sharpened her ax. She kept the weapon propped between her legs as she ran the whetstone along the sides. It was comforting work. She had been doing it a lot lately.

"You ruin that weapon," Genevieve said. "Sharpen too much."

Kaia glared at her. "If I could bury it in your back," Kaia replied, "I would."

It took a moment before Genevieve understood the drift of what Kaia had said, and when she did, she looked away. She did not seem afraid, exactly. Something else passed over her face. Kaia wished she could break her head open and read the scattered remains of her thoughts off the floor.

"I do a bad job," Genevieve said slowly. "Being a guest. I am sorry."

Kaia felt one eyebrow raise. "Colonizers are not guests. You are vermin."

This passed over Genevieve, and Kaia could tell she had not understood entirely. "My lady tells me that the strength of our Empire is there are so many *kinds* of us. It is stupid of me not to see that now."

"The Wariuta are not a *part* of your empire."

"You will be." And she had the audacity to smile. Not her normal snake's smile but a warm smile, a nice smile. As though she bequeathed Kaia with kindness. As if she were being generous. "The Empire of Nipran is the greatest Empire in the Known World. It always is. It always will be. This is not bad."

"We have very different notions of greatness," Kaia muttered.

She returned to her ax. Genevieve was right. She'd been over-sharpening it. She put it down and met Genevieve's gaze.

She was bigger than the Colonizer, taller. But she could see a kind of wiry strength in the girl's build. Could tell from the way she handled her own blade that she'd been trained. If it came to a fight between them, would Kaia's victory be certain?

"I do not wish to harm you," Genevieve said as if reading her mind. "Or your people."

There was a tenor of truth in the girl's voice, and it was not that Kaia did not believe her. It was that she knew that what Genevieve wanted to believe was separate from the truth. She picked up her ax again, let it rest against her legs.

If there was anything Kaia knew, it was that it was unwise to let your guard down around Colonizers.

When Kaia was small, she had overheard her mother discussing her future with one of the women who handled training the children who would become warriors.

"She is not fit," the woman had said.

Kaia had looked down at the stump of her arm and cried. The other children had occasionally asked questions about it, but mostly there was no difference in Kaia's life from those around her due to something as trivial as a single hand. That it could now, suddenly, bear such terrible consequences was crushing. All she had ever wanted was to be like Ica. And here was someone saying she simply could not, could never be.

But Ica did not accept that. And so Kaia did not, either.

Kaia began her training. When she was very small, it was mostly about mindfulness and balance, and having one hand did not hinder her at all. But still she practiced whatever she had learned in the day each night so that she would be better, she would be stronger and faster than all the other children who had nothing to work against.

As time went on, her determination to be the best only calcified. It was like a rock in her heart, and she loved it, loved the hard work and the practice and the discipline. It became such that the only competition she could truly look forward to was with herself.

Until the day Ica challenged her to spar.

It was not unusual for older warriors to challenge warrior apprentices. It was typically a friendly gesture. A generous thing an adult might do to help a teen they respected or wanted to encourage. Kaia was in her thirteenth year then and had plainly outstripped all her cohorts. So it was expected that, someday soon, she would be challenged by an elder.

But it was not expected that the challenger would be the leader of them.

It was not long after both Muteteli and Chimu had fallen. The warriors had sustained so many losses that it was whispered that the apprentices would be given familiars early to take their places. Kaia had heard the gossip and wished fervently for its veracity. She had been begging Ica for exactly this since her father's murder. And now, with the chance to spar against her mother, it felt like her moment to prove herself.

Ica normally fought with two axes, but for the sake of sparring, she replaced them with a long, thin sparring stick. And in an unorthodox move, she allowed Kaia to fight with her actual ax.

Kaia was so excited she could hardly breathe. After years of lessons, and faced with her first foe of consequence, she couldn't keep her mind clear. But she didn't let that stop her.

She lunged straight at her mother, the only person who stood between her and her chance for revenge against the Colonizers.

For a split second, Kaia saw the white of Ica's eye go wide and she thought, *I have her.*

She did not.

Ica parried her easily; with one graceful motion, she took a partial step back, narrowing her body, evading Kaia's ax, and leaving her daughter, having now accidentally overshot her target, on unsteady footing. Kaia whirled and attacked again, this time with the full strength she had developed from countless nights of practice. Her ax sliced through Ica's sparring stick, leaving her with two.

Ica raised one eyebrow, and Kaia knew she was done for—her mother was a demon with two weapons. Her only hope was attack. She could not possibly win in defense. And so she tried again and again, the ferocity of her attacks gaining in rage and futility. It was not long before her mother had knocked her weapon from her hand and had a shard of stick beneath Kaia's throat.

"You let your rage guide you." Ica did not move the shard but still held it to her daughter's neck. "And it will lead our people only to death."

"A glorious one, if you'd let me fight."

"There is no such thing as a glorious death," Ica spat. She let her hand drop and turned her back on Kaia. "If you don't understand that, then you do not understand anything."

She picked up Kaia's ax and handed it back to her. For a moment, Kaia did not take it. Her cheeks burned with humiliation and disappointment.

"You are not done learning," Ica said, kinder now. "That is all."

Kaia snatched the ax. Her mother held her gaze. She wanted her to see something, to change who Kaia was and how she felt, but Kaia could not, and the uselessness of it made her whole body restless with fury. She wanted to scream, wanted to hit Ica, wanted to throw her ax into the nearest Colonizer and watch the Imperial ships go up in flames.

"Life is precious, Kaia." Ica's voice was soft, almost pleading.

"What about Chimu's life?" Kaia could feel tears forming, but she ignored them. "What about Muteteli's?"

Ica's nostrils flared. "No better reminders exist for me of the precariousness and preciousness of life."

"You make decisions all the time that lead to deaths. Ours and the Colonizers'."

"Yes," said Ica. "And every one of those deaths rests on my heart. I do not close my eyes any night without seeing the faces of those whose lives I have stopped short. I hope to build a world where they need not rest so heavily on yours. That should always be the hope. To lead in peace."

"But that's not real!" Kaia shouted. "It never has been!"

"What is and has been is not what will always be." Ica heaved a sigh. Kaia could see she was angering her mother, but she didn't care. "You have so much to learn. I can only hope that you will before I am gone."

And with that, she left her daughter on the field of her defeat. They never sparred again.

· CHAPTER 13 ·

Thistle

At school, Dai did not act any differently, and so Thistle did not, either. There was some light teasing tossed their way—news of their betrothal had spread, naturally. All news spread quickly in Gia Dinh. But it wasn't even personal, really, just the kind of general teasing one had to expect, and that Thistle certainly had.

But after school, when he came over to the house and saw the Lady Minami's excess belongings being stored in the upstairs hallway, things felt different again. Stiff. The trunks were obviously Imperial—they bore her family crest. Only Imperials did that. Or rather, only the wealthiest Imperials did that.

Dai ran his finger over the three leaves that comprised the gilded crest. "Imagine having so much gold you can waste it on the boxes just to hold your crap."

"It must be nice," said Thistle.

This was, apparently, the wrong thing to say. Dai glared at her like she was willfully stupid.

"I guess," he said. Idly, he popped open the chest.

"Hey," Thistle said, a hissed whisper. "Don't do that!"

"I just wanna see."

The Lady Minami had unpacked in her room, but there were still some random bits and ends in her trunk. Despite her better judgment, Thistle peered in, too. A stray obi, embroidered with silver thread. A comb with pearlescent inlay that could probably pay for her stay in the Vo house for a month.

But then Dai pulled out a rolled paper, still loosely held by a broken wax seal. A letter.

They looked at each other. It was one thing to poke around the trunk. Another to read the Lady's correspondence.

"Put it back," Thistle said. But she did not say it with much conviction.

Dai unrolled the letter.

"It says . . . that Commander Niijima will find her in Gia Dinh. And that . . . she should stay at the Vo family guesthouse?"

Dai looked at Thistle as though he were seeing her for the first time. Commander Niijima was well known in Gia Dinh. Of course he was. He was the commander who'd sacked the city all those years ago and who now served as its acting lord. Thistle snatched the letter from him and read it furiously.

It was written in the most formal script of the Common Tongue, which was to be expected. But the seal bore the Imperial Lion. And the letter was addressed to someone named the Lady Ayer, not to the Lady Minami.

"It's not even addressed to her," Thistle said, as if maybe this could explain everything.

"I knew it," Dai whispered. He looked as if someone had rung a church bell right next to his ear.

"Knew what?" Thistle rerolled the letter, shoved it back beneath the obi, and shut the trunk a little louder than she'd intended to. Something like anger, hot and prickly, roiled in her belly.

"You father *was* a traitor," Dai said at last.

Thistle rounded on Dai, her friend, her best friend, the boy who was supposed to be her husband someday, and in that moment she hated him. "You can't be a traitor to something that doesn't *exist* anymore, Dai," she spat. "We're all Imperials now."

"No," said Dai simply, as though this could be simple. "Some of us aren't." And he started to back away from her like she were a dangerous thing, something aflame.

Thistle felt tears building, but she wasn't sad. She was furious. *He* was the traitor, not her.

"Your family lives on Imperial coin just the same as mine!" She stepped toward him, and he took a step back. She could feel a tear escape, and she batted it away. "Don't blame my mother for doing exactly what your parents do!"

"Why did Commander Niijima tell her to stay here, then?"

"But he didn't tell her; he told some other lady! It's the Lady Minami who's staying here."

Dai shook his head. "Thistle." His voice was soft, full of pity. "Is that even her real name?"

"Of course it is," she said. But she had no idea; she just didn't want to concede anything to Dai. He had called her father a traitor, and what did he know? He still had both his parents, who she knew served Imperials expensive food Quark natives could never afford.

"I . . . I don't think we can be friends anymore." Dai's voice was small. He took another step away from Thistle, toward the stairs, presumably toward the front door. "I'm sorry."

"What are you talking about?"

"We aren't all Imperials, Thistle. But you are."

"You're such a hypocrite," Thistle spat. "Look at your leather shoes. How do you think your parents paid for those? Where do you think they *came* from?"

"Your father was a traitor, Thistle. We all know that. And your mother—"

But before he could finish, Mrs. Vo came storming up the stairs. "Get out of this house this instant, Dai Phan." She grabbed him by his skinny wrist and pulled him down the stairs. "You," she said, her voice punctuating each step they took. "Are. Not. Welcome. Here." She flung the door open and tossed Dai out. "Anymore."

Thistle had never seen her mother so angry. And she had been in trouble loads of times. It was as if a whole new mother had come up those stairs, and a stranger had dragged Dai out of the house.

Distantly, she could hear Dai's voice as he shouted "Traitors!" at the house. Thistle looked out the window to see him running away. A few people stopped to watch him go. Mr. Bole peered at the house and caught Thistle's eye. He spat once on the ground and walked away with his wheelbarrow of fish.

Mrs. Vo came back upstairs, her cheeks flushed and her hair a bit askew.

"Don't you listen to that boy," she said. She grabbed Thistle by the arm, hard.

"Mother, ow—"

"Do you hear me? You do not listen to gossiping simpletons. Your father was a hero. Do you hear me? A hero."

"But Mother," Thistle said quietly, "the Resistance lost. *Quark* lost."

Mrs. Vo dropped Thistle's arm then and stood to her full

height. They could nearly see eye to eye, but she was still a bit taller than her daughter. For a moment, she did not say anything, just looked at Thistle appraisingly.

But then she raised her hand. And it was only in the moment just before she brought it down that Thistle realized what was going to happen.

The slap stung, bringing fresh tears into her eyes. Her cheek burned. Thistle put her hand to it, felt the heat from it as it throbbed.

"We may wash their clothes and fill their bowls, but remember this, child: We are not them. They are not us. And someday, this country will be free again. Do you understand me?"

"Yes," said Thistle.

But for the first time in her life, she knew her mother was lying to her.

• CHAPTER 14 •

Koa

After the messenger was sent and the meeting arranged, all the Wariuta, from the mountains to the shore, gathered in Yunka on the agreed-upon day. And so Koa was forced into the ceremonial headdress and cape that befitted his role as Ica's son. It did not fit him well. The headdress felt as though it was forever tilting off his head. Genevieve snickered a little under her breath as it nearly toppled off once more just as the Colonizer envoy approached. She had been teaching Koa the Colonizers' tongue, and Koa was surprised to find that he liked it, a little. It sounded much nicer when it wasn't being yelled at you amid bullets. It made his mouth take curious shapes, and it was the first thing in his life he learned quickly. And so now he knew he was what the Colonizers called a *prince*. The term fit him about as well as his headdress.

The Colonizers arrived with their armor glinting in the sunlight, sweat dripping down their faces in the heat. They were not dressed for the day's weather or the landscape or the season, and they suffered for it. One man, presumably the leader, since two other men had been carrying a piece of cloth to block the sun from him, approached Ica and bowed.

The Wariuta watched in silence, their faces uniformly pulled into masks of distrust. All had their weapons easily reachable on their backs, just in case, though now they stood behind Ica with their hands loose. The echoes of hyena giggles rose, but save for that, Yunka had never been so full or so quiet.

"*I am Commander Callum,*" the man said. This much Koa understood. The rest of what followed was garbled and confusing, and even if he understood some of the words, the context didn't fit, and Koa quickly lost the thread.

Genevieve stepped forward. "*I am Genevieve, maid to the Lady Ayer.*" At this, the look on the man called Commander's face changed. His eyes were only on Genevieve now, and if Koa was not mistaken, he was suspicious of her, too. There was a brief exchange between the two, but Ica quickly lost patience with it.

"Ask him if he brings us new terms," Ica interrupted.

Genevieve nodded. Another brief exchange. "He says it is the Emperor's will to own this land," said Genevieve. "But that, if it pleases the Wariuta, this can be achieved with peace. And all will benefit."

Commander snapped his fingers, and two men carrying a heavy chest came forward and dropped it at Ica's feet. As they did so, Commander barked words at Genevieve, who nodded her comprehension. Koa did not like the way she kept her eyes on the ground while Commander talked, as if his life were more important than hers.

"He does not expect Wariuta to trust right away. He comes with gifts. He hopes they will help the Wariuta see that the Emperor is generous. That to trade with the Emperor is good for the Wariuta. Good for everyone."

81

At this there was a ripple of laughter from the Wariuta. This was offensive. The Emperor must have known full well that his men did not trade with the Wariuta. That they came with guns and death and disease. But the laughter did not seem to bother the Colonizers. They opened the chest. Inside were many glass bottles, safely stowed in tidy cloth clasps that lined the chest in rows. Commander pulled up a bottle and handed it to Ica, who took it reluctantly.

"It is Kiyohime powder," said Genevieve, and her voice was reverent. "Enough to kill a thousand men, and each will die screaming. One bottle takes a year to produce in Iwei. This chest takes decades of work to make."

Koa did not need to see his mother's face to know she was disgusted. She handed the bottle back to Commander. "We do not have need of this," she said.

Genevieve translated, and Commander shrugged. His men collected the chest, and a new soldier came forward with a blood-red satchel. From within it, Commander removed a long, curved tooth the length of Koa's shin and offered it to Ica.

"This is a dragon's tooth," said Genevieve. "Very rare."

Koa waited for her to explain its use, but she did not elaborate.

Ica did not take the tooth. "What I am learning," she said slowly, "is that your emperor thinks we are simple people. That we can be bought with weapons and trinkets. He knows nothing of us, or our ways, yet he seeks to have our allegiance."

With a nearly invisible tilt of her hand, she gave Puka the command to join her. Puka giggled high and loud at Ica's side. Commander backed away a little from the hyena, his eyes fixed on the animal with undisguised disgust.

"The Emperor has one last gift," Genevieve translated. At Commander's words, her eyes widened. Commander pulled a chain from his neck, and at the end of it was a silver-hued glass vial the length of a finger. "This is mermaid's blood."

At this, even the Wariuta looked among themselves. Mermaid's blood was not favored among the Wariuta, but it was extremely valuable in the open market. The alchemists in Puno would be deeply interested in obtaining the blood for their experiments. Koa thought of the pirates who occasionally made port and knew that among them it was a highly controversial subject. Although they all knew that drinking the blood made them unsafe upon the Sea and some considered it a grave trespass, there were some who loved it. He didn't know what to think. But all his favorite pirates, the ones whose company he enjoyed, whose stories brought him joy, seemed to think it was bad. Koa was inclined to believe them.

Commander grinned with pride. "One drop on a wound, and soon all that will remain is a scar. Drink it, and you will see wonders you could never imagine. You will escape your life, if only for a few hours. Many believe it is holy and that the visions you see will bring wisdom and luck."

Commander handed the vial to Ica, who rolled it between her fingers. "How do I know this isn't just well-packaged wine?" She held the vial up to the sun and looked through it. "Or poison?" She gave it back to Commander.

Commander said something to Genevieve, and her face went white. But, doing as he ordered, she stuck out her hand. He pulled a dagger from his belt, and Puka took a step forward, but Commander did not aim at any Wariuta. Instead, he cut a gash in Genevieve's palm. She let out a small gasp of pain, but that was all. Koa looked to Kaia, who was less impressed with her stoicism.

Commander pulled the stopper from the vial, covered its opening with his finger, and, with the utmost care, upended it so that the contents just touched his skin. After corking it with painstaking slowness, he ran his finger down the cut on Genevieve's hand.

The Wariuta gasped as the wound stitched itself shut before their eyes. Genevieve rubbed her hand against her filthy dress. It came away with a smudge of blood but no other sign of her injury.

"Mermaid's blood does not keep," said Ica. "How do the Colonizers have so much?"

"The Emperor orders his navy to fish for mermaids as highest priority of the state. Their capture makes the Known World a safer and better place for all those who sail," said Genevieve.

Commander said some more words and put the chain with the vial on it back around his neck. "In his wisdom, he knows that this is in the best interest of all, and so he pays high prices for the blood. His alchemists learn to make it last. Vials like this one are from his personal stores. He offers a hundred of them to you. To the Wariuta."

"If we agree to let you on our land, you mean. If we agree to trade."

"Yes." Genevieve smiled. "It is a very generous offer."

Ica's face was impassive. She made a small motion with her hand, and Puka took two steps back, away from the Colonizer, Commander.

"I do not speak for the Wariuta lightly," she said. "We will discuss among our own and reconvene with you to go over our terms if we wish to agree to anything. Until then, you and your men will return to the shore, and no Wariuta will bother you."

Genevieve translated this, and Commander bowed, low and low-key stupid in the Colonizer way.

"He wants your reply in two days," said Genevieve.

Ica scoffed at this, which set Puka off, which set all the hyenas in Yunka off, and soon the Colonizers were running from the sound of the Wariuta familiars, who were laughing and laughing and laughing.

Koa looked at the blood in the sand from Genevieve's cut. She was not a soldier, not a warrior. She did not wear the Colonizer crest. But still, he had cut her. And if he would cut her, Koa wondered, what was he willing to do to the Wariuta?

• CHAPTER 15 •

Kaia

The Wariuta were not a nation the way the Colonizers were
a nation. There were factions by trade and location; and
while war had seen Ica elected as the leader, she still made
a point to consult leadership from each of the other factions.

Representatives from the alchemists, the cattle drivers, the
fishermen, the healers, and the potters all sat in the Canyon of
the Moon. Ica had led them and Kaia there to discuss the future
of the Wariuta and the Colonizers' offer. It was an unusual move.
For one, only Ica and occasionally Kaia were permitted into the
Canyon of the Moon. But also, Kaia had assumed—as most of
the Wariuta had assumed—that Ica would simply make the decision for them all.

But invite them she had, and now everyone sat in a circle
around the firepit. The ancient fire cast craggy shadows across all
their faces.

"Imagine what we could do with that blood," said the leader
of the alchemists. She was a tall, jittery-looking woman with a

reedy voice whom Kaia didn't trust. But then, Kaia did not trust the alchemists under normal circumstances. They had traded with the Colonizers even during the most violent times of conflict, until they were caught. And though Puno had been sacked years ago, Kaia was not the only one who remembered how little of a fight the alchemists had put up to stop them. And now the trade of enslaved people flourished in Puno. "If we could study it, it's possible we could replicate it, and then—"

"Then what?" said the leader of the healers tartly. This was Karal, and Kaia loved her. She was practical and kind and had helped Kaia as a child as she learned to navigate the world with a single hand. Kaia trusted her opinion intrinsically. "We become invincible? We take over the world? We become the Colonizers?" She shook her head with deep disapproval that Kaia decided she shared.

The alchemist bristled. "I cannot see how you would squander such a unique opportunity."

"I cannot see how you would be so myopic," Karal shot back.

"I'd hear from you," Ica interrupted. She gestured to the leader of the potters, Aya.

Kaia knew her distantly in the way that she knew anyone who lived in Yunka. It was a city, but a small one. Aya was old now, the eldest among the elected vocational leaders. Her stark-white hair was kept in three tidy braids, and the wrinkles in her face were deep and myriad.

Aya sighed and rubbed her thick hands together in worry. "The opportunity to trade without blood spilled is a good one," she said carefully. "But I don't trust the Colonizers to leave it at that. I fear if we let in their nose, their feet won't be far behind."

"And let's not forget," said the leader of the fishermen, "how many of my people they have killed! All for the crime of what, doing their job? On our home shore? Do you forget Muteteli already, Ica?" Her voice bore the tone of accusation.

But Ica did not rise to the bait. "I will never forget Muteteli," she said, her voice calm. "He was and is one of my great loves, and even if he were not, I do not let slip the memories of our fallen." She turned then to Kaia. "Tell us what you think, child. This is your future we discuss."

Kaia took a deep breath. It was the moment she had been waiting for since this meeting had been called. She stood and looked at each of the leaders. "I say we use what little kau is left in our stores and we burn their ships and kill their men." She met her mother's eyes, tried to discern what she thought. But, as always, the leader of the warriors was inscrutable. "Every life is precious. Let's give these Colonizers' lives value. To tell their Emperor the Wariuta nation is not his to take."

The leader of the fishermen stood to show her assent. "They will never leave unless we force them to."

And, to Kaia's surprise, Karal stood, too. "The healers will stand ready to treat our wounded." She gave Kaia a discreet nod of approval. Kaia could feel the pride build in her chest, roaring and billowing. She could lead these people after Ica, and she would do so fiercely.

But Aya shook her head. "Putting aside our anger, which is fair and righteous," she added with a nod to Kaia, "we must confront the reality that we may just be outnumbered and outmatched here—they have more soldiers than we have warriors, they have guns, and they do not blink before killing. I don't believe we can beat them. Not because we are not fierce enough, but because in order to win, we'd have to abandon everything that we are."

Kaia felt a little of the air in her chest deflate.

The representative of the cattle drivers, and the only man present, nodded his agreement with Aya. "What does victory even look like for us," he said, "if we lose half our people in the fight? I believe you'd fight bravely," he said to Kaia. "But I also believe you would lose. And I would grieve for you, and for my own daughters, too."

"The Colonizers have so much to gain from trade with us, and, frankly, we have so much to gain from them," said the alchemist.

A surge of dislike hit Kaia like a stone. Of course that was what she thought.

"You'd sacrifice everything that we are," Kaia shouted, "for some new toys to play with."

"Kaia." Ica's voice was stern. "We are here to discuss in good faith. If you can't, then you'll have to leave."

Kaia fumed. She glared at the alchemist but did not speak more. The vote was tied—the youth, the fishermen, and the healers on one side; the alchemists, the cattle drivers, and the potters on the other. Ica's vote would decide the future of the Wariuta. Ica's gaze drifted to the canyon walls, where the shadows cast by the firepit danced. It had not been long since Kaia and Ica had been down here, seeking counsel. Not long since they had both seen Ica's death in the flames. Surely Ica would fight—for her people and for her life. Surely Ica knew that was the only way. Surely.

But Ica did not stand.

"It is possible that we could stave off the Colonizers for another few years. But the cost would be unfathomable. Catastrophic. I do not believe that, ultimately, we can win. Choosing violence now means choosing violence for years, possibly decades to come. And as the leader of the warriors, I can't in good conscience and clear mind let that happen."

And that was that. There was no more argument to be had. Ica's words were final. The representatives all stood and left.

Maybe Kaia imagined it, but it seemed that the ancient flame in the firepit flickered out for just the blink of an eye.

Koa was not in the hut when Kaia returned, so Genevieve was alone.

Good.

The Colonizer sat cross-legged on the floor, braiding her filthy, greasy hair into two plaits. Her dagger was nowhere to be seen. "The Wariuta decide?" she asked, her voice all innocence and hope and ignorance. Cloying. Infuriating. "I hope you trade," she added. "It is good. Trust."

Kaia did not answer. Instead, she kicked the girl onto her side and, before she could scramble up, pressed her knee into her neck. Genevieve thrashed and gasped but could not free herself. Kaia snatched one of the braids and forced her to meet her eye.

"I do not trust," she hissed. "I will never trust you. You're a Colonizer, and Colonizers can*not* be trusted."

Genevieve's face was red and starting to purple.

"I don't care what my mother says," Kaia went on. "We may make this deal, but know this and know it well: I will kill you and all of those stinking, small little men you call your own if and when you betray my mother's trust." She leaned harder into the girl's neck, felt a sick smile stretch her face. She did not like herself in this moment, did not feel proud. But she did feel right. "Do you understand me?"

Genevieve's eyes fluttered.

Kaia opened her mouth to speak again, but before the words could come out, she was knocked, hard, onto the ground. Several things seemed to happen at once—the air was slammed out of her body just as she heard the Colonizer girl gasp for air. A great weight clamped over her arms. And she heard Koa's voice but couldn't make out the words he said.

She opened her eyes and saw her brother. Saw him anew.

He was holding her arms. He was the one who had knocked her down.

His own sister.

To defend *that girl*.

"Don't," he said simply. A few moments passed as they stared into each other, Kaia seething, Koa tearful. "Please," he added.

"She'd kill us all." She wriggled beneath his grip.

But Koa held strong. "She's a prisoner here," he said quietly. "And I won't let you beat prisoners. This one or any other. You are better than that. *You are better than them.*"

Koa was bigger than Kaia, always had been. But he had never leveraged his size or his strength against her. Against anybody, really, despite Kaia encouraging him to do so for basically his entire life. That he chose now to start felt wild, wrong. Against her. Against *her*.

"You're a traitor," she said through clenched teeth. To the Wariuta of course. But also to her. His sister. She was held down by her brother. She could feel tears falling down the side of her face and onto the floor.

"No. I'm not," Koa said. "I love you, Kaia. Please don't do this."

Outside the hut, Kaia could hear Tupac and Chima circling, panting, and giggling. She tried to imagine their familiars battling each other, tried to picture Chima's teeth tearing into Tupac's flesh, the yelps and cries and the whoops of pain and combat. It was a horrible vision, and it made Kaia's stomach turn. She let her body go slack, and as soon as she did, Koa released her arms and stood.

Slowly, Kaia sat up. Her arms were sore from where Koa had held her, but there were no marks on her skin. She wiped her face with her arm, ignored the slick of mud the floor and her tears had made. On the opposite side of the hut, Genevieve watched, her eyes darting between the siblings anxiously.

"You're lucky," Kaia said, "that my brother's got a soft heart. You don't deserve his faith." She pushed down the shame that itched in her throat and the urge to take it back. To make right what she had clearly just made wrong. She had been exactly the person her mother had wanted to guide her away from being. A person of might but not of honor. She should apologize, at least.

But doing that felt like a concession to the same empire that she would see burned to the ground. And she could not do that. She also could not meet Genevieve's eye.

To her surprise, Genevieve bowed her head. "Callum is a fierce man. I . . ."

"You what?" Kaia didn't yell, but her voice made the girl flinch all the same.

"She won't hurt you," Koa said.

"Do not feel . . ." But Genevieve could not finish her thought. "But he is a commander! The Emperor has chosen him. Yes. He is a man of his word. I am only." She looked at her hands. "I am nobody."

"Nobody," Kaia said. "And if he breaks his word, I will kill you. And nobody will mourn you." If she died, it would be a kind of justice.

"I mean—" Koa interjected, but Kaia put up her hand to silence him.

"No one," she said again, firmly.

CHAPTER 16

Thistle

The Lady Minami requested Thistle specifically to brush and braid her hair. Thistle was very bad at braiding hair, and she was not even sure she was much good at brushing it, but she did as her mother bade her anyway and went upstairs to where the Lady Minami's guest room was.

When she opened the door, she hardly recognized it as a room in the house where she had lived her whole life. There were throw pillows with silk cases embroidered with patterns. Lady Minami had hung a large piece of gauzy fabric over the window so the morning light came through in a pleasant, gentle way. And she had even propped her own mirror on top of the small table Thistle's father had built. It lent the room a kind of elegance the rest of the house did not have.

"Come," said Lady Minami warmly.

She was sitting before the mirror with her long hair down. It did not look like it needed brushing. It was smooth and perfect and clean. Thistle picked up a brush anyway—one of the Lady's, with delicate gold inlay in the handle—and started to pull it gently through the Lady's hair.

"I so appreciate your help." Lady Minami smiled at Thistle in the mirror.

Thistle smiled back. "Of course, my lady."

"You're a very fast learner, aren't you." It was less of a question and more of a prompt.

"Yes, my lady. Teacher says I'm too smart for my own good."

Lady Minami chuckled. "My tutors said the very same to me. Never seem to say that to the boys, do they?"

"No, my lady." Her hair smelled like the lavender shipped in from Iwei.

"I couldn't help but notice," Lady Minami said, "that someone had rifled through my trunk. The one in the hallway?"

Thistle kept brushing but averted her eyes from the mirror. Her heart beat very fast as she scrambled for the right thing to say.

"You're not in trouble," Lady Minami went on. "It's OK to be curious."

"I'm sorry," Thistle said. She did not know what else to say.

"Now, now. I've been staying here for over a month, and you never poked about my things before. It seems like something changed, doesn't it? Perhaps you weren't alone?"

Something like relief washed over Thistle. "Dai came over," she said, and fresh anger at him burned in her throat. This was all his fault. Everything was all his fault.

"Ah, see, that makes more sense. Dai Phan. Your betrothed."

Thistle pulled the brush through the Lady's hair, but it was rote. She hardly thought of what she was doing. "We'll see. I don't think either of us wants to be married to each other anymore."

"Oh, why is that?"

"He called me a traitor. Called my whole family traitors."

94

"Very harsh words. Why would he say such a thing? I was under the impression you two were good friends. Best friends, even. That's certainly not a generous way for best friends to speak to each other."

Thistle did not cry. "We aren't best friends anymore. We aren't even friends anymore. He said we're all traitors just for taking Imperial guests, even though his family owns a restaurant that only Imperials can afford to eat at. He's so stupid."

"That does seem quite hypocritical."

"Exactly!" It felt so good to be understood. "I don't see why wanting to make a good living makes us traitors."

"I should think not. It's perfectly normal. Admirable, even."

"Yes! If anything, he's the traitor for not reporting those guns he found."

As soon as she said it, Thistle wanted to shove the words back into her mouth in great heaping handfuls.

"Guns?" the Lady said. Her tone was one of forced lightness.

"They weren't his," Thistle added quickly. "He just found them."

"Well, that's hardly his fault," Lady Minami said.

"He wasn't even looking for them. He was looking for truffles. For his family's restaurant. They grow by the river."

"It sounds like he was just doing his job when he found them."

"Yeah," Thistle said. "They were buried beneath a tree, and he was able to knock off the lock."

"My, my. What a startling discovery."

"That's how I felt—you know? Because they're illegal, and I didn't want to get in trouble. I didn't want Dai to get in trouble, either."

"Of course not."

"I think it's good that no guns are allowed."

"That's very wise of you."

95

"Dai says they were there because the Resistance is coming back."

"What do you think?"

"I don't know." She thought of the Death shrine in their basement, of the sting in her cheek left by her mother's hand.

"Well, would you like to know what I think?"

Thistle nodded. The Lady's eyes found hers in the mirror.

"I think that a clever girl like you can only improve her lot in life by knowing what's really going on. I know we women are taught to keep our heads down and empty, but I disagree. I think the whispers only we are privy to make us powerful. It takes a lot of self-control to swallow our feelings and discreetly investigate, a lot of cunning. But if we can, then. Well, as I said. We can be quite powerful."

Powerful. It was not how Thistle would have ever described herself, but she liked it, liked the way it felt in her chest, liked the Thistle she could become if it was true. Powerful.

The words were out before she could help it. "Is Lady Minami your real name?"

The Lady smiled in the mirror, a full smile, her eyes twinkling. "Too smart for your own good, indeed," she said. "Tell me, Thistle, what is my true name?"

"Lady Ayer." She liked the way the name shaped her mouth, the sound of it.

"Very good," said Lady Ayer. "You know, I think you're far too smart to be a simple innkeeper's daughter. Such potential. I won't promise anything just now, but do you think you could be my . . . special friend? During my time here in Quark? To help me. To keep my secret. To collect those whispers that only the cunning can find?"

"Yes." She imagined herself like the Lady Ayer, elegant and

poised, full of powerful secrets and mysteries. She liked that version of herself immediately. Liked her much better than the Thistle who peeled carrots and got married off to Dai Phan.

"Well," said the Lady Ayer. "This must be my lucky day."

Thistle grinned as she continued to brush the Lady's long hair. The glint of the gold inlay on the brush caught the light, and Thistle looked at it again; she had not noticed when she first picked it up. Shining back at her was the Emperor's roaring-lion insignia.

This new Thistle was something to behold. A brave and clever girl, the finder and keeper of secrets. Much more impressive than the dead coward's daughter. She was fastidious in calling the Lady by her fake name, especially in her mother's presence, but she kept her true name, Lady Ayer, cradled close to her heart. The Lady had entrusted her with it, and she intended to protect it.

She had managed to smooth things over with Dai—she had told lies about how disappointed she was in her mother, and how much she hated the Lady Minami and all the Imperials who marched in Gia Dinh each day. How she hoped the Resistance *was* coming back, and that they'd make quick work of it, to boot. And when the guns were found by Imperial soldiers, she feigned despair.

And somehow that was enough to mollify the boy.

It had been so easy. He was so easy to trick.

Lying was easy.

She wondered how she had been best friends with him for so long without realizing how naive he was. How childish. How gullible. Not like her at all.

She had promised the Lady Ayer more information about the guns if she could find it, and so she was thrilled when, after school one drizzly, muggy day, Dai whispered that the Resistance was on the move. There were more guns, he said, even after those left by the river got rumbled.

"Where are they now?" Thistle asked.

Dai grinned, and she knew she had asked him the question he most wanted to answer.

"Come on," he said. And, like a fool, he led her to them.

Beyond the rice paddies, the Ó Baoill family kept an ironwood grove and lumberyard. Trees in varying stages of life and dismemberment grew in tidy rows or were stacked in neat piles. Thistle didn't like the grove or the yard much—both were full of large spiders that Dai knew the names of and Thistle did not care to ever learn. But she took her trepidation around the neck and stuffed it down, deep into her belly, where she hoped it would smother and die beneath her bravado.

The smells of sawdust and dying and dead underbrush were thick in the air. Dai, who had been walking a step or two ahead of Thistle the entire time, stopped in his tracks. He turned to look Thistle in the eye.

"Can I trust you?"

Thistle blinked at him, put on her best face of offense. "Obviously."

He smiled, wide and stupid. Trusting. "OK."

He knelt in the shade of a more established ironwood tree and, with his hands, moved some loose soil around until wooden boards were revealed. He pried these open to reveal a deep hole, at the bottom of which was another crate.

"Are those all of them?" Thistle asked.

"I dunno." Dai opened the lower box and extricated a large rifle. It was longer than the length of his arm, and it looked too big in his hands. "There's about ten different caches of them around the yard. This one's got all rifles, but I saw some other ones that were a mix of things."

Thistle picked up a rifle, too. It was heavier than she expected it to be. She didn't like the way it smelled. "How'd you know they were here?"

"Just digging," Dai said.

But Thistle could see him hiding something behind his teeth. She didn't push, though, didn't want him to get suspicious that she was mining him for information. She pointed the rifle at a tree, squinting to peer through the sight.

"Take your finger off the trigger," Dai warned.

Thistle put the rifle down. "Are they loaded?"

"I don't know how to check," Dai said. "But my dad says you should never rest your finger on a trigger unless you're ready to shoot."

"What does he know?" Thistle said. She hoped she sounded playful. "He's a cook."

But Dai didn't take the bait. He shrugged and put the rifle he'd been holding back in the box.

"We should leave before Mr. Ó Baoill sees us."

"Think he knows what's out here?"

"No idea, but I know he won't want to see *us* here."

That was inarguable. Mr. Ó Baoill was infamously cranky. But with so much land to cover, he could rarely find and stop the kids who played there and the teens who made out there.

They covered the rifles back up with the loose soil and snuck out of the grove. Despite her excitement to report what she'd learned to the Lady Ayer, Thistle could feel something cumbersome hanging between her and Dai. Once they cleared the grove, she took his hand. He flinched, surprised, but didn't pull away.

"Dai—are you mad at me?" She did not add *again*.

"No. Just." He squeezed her hand, held her gaze. His eyes were serious, and if she didn't know Dai better, she would have thought he was worried. "Don't tell *anyone*, OK? Not even your mom."

"Of course not," she said. And for a moment, guilt prickled her skin like mosquito bites. But certainly he wouldn't get in trouble after she told the Lady Ayer—the members of the Resistance would. Dai was just a boy, just a bystander, and the Lady understood that; she'd been very clear about that with Thistle. And so Thistle smiled at the boy who had been her best friend.

"I promise," she lied.

And she could tell by the way his shoulders dropped, the way his smile touched his eyes, the way he breathed out in a whoosh, that Dai believed her.

The raid on Mr. Ó Baoill's grove happened within the week. He was arrested, of course. The Imperials did not believe that the caches of weapons could have been hidden all over his land without his consent. And if Thistle felt a twinge of guilt when she saw Mr. Ó Baoill marched through Gia Dinh with his hands bound and his head down, she pushed it aside. She had found the information the Lady Ayer needed, and she'd found it fast. And anyway, it did seem implausible that Mr. Ó Baoill hadn't known. Sure, he had a lot of land, and he was old and walked slowly and with much effort, but it likely took hours to bury all those guns. He must have known.

The Lady Ayer had been so pleased with Thistle when the guns were found.

"What did I say?" she had told Thistle. "Too smart to just be the innkeeper's daughter."

Thistle glowed with pride.

But it wasn't until dinner some days after the raid that Thistle saw the true value of her contribution to the Lady Ayer. The Lady had requested to eat dinner with Mrs. Vo and Thistle together, which was odd. Typically, the Lady ate either in the city or alone, with Mrs. Vo or Thistle serving her. Thistle bristled with excitement. She brushed her hair with extra care and braided it in the best imitation of the Lady Ayer's style that she could muster.

Mrs. Vo was less excited, but that was to be expected, Thistle thought.

The Lady Ayer still sat in her typical spot at the head of the table, the seat with the most comfortable cushions. Mrs. Vo had steamed some fish and made a sticky tamarind glaze that was spicy and sweet. It was usually one of Thistle's favorite dishes, but somehow it felt cheap, or tacky, or too sweet, or too spicy on a plate before the Lady Ayer, who picked at her serving gingerly.

"I want to thank you, Mrs. Vo. For your hospitality these last months."

"Of course," said Mrs. Vo mechanically. "We are honored you chose to stay with us, Lady Minami."

"It has been my pleasure to get to know your daughter in this time."

Thistle smiled. The Lady smiled back. Mrs. Vo took a bite of white rice and kept her face placid and impassive.

"I will be returning to Crandon within the week."

At this, Mrs. Vo's eyes flittered up, and her face betrayed her relief.

Thistle's heart started to beat very fast. "Oh," she said. She felt as if her heart were breaking. "Do you have to?"

"Now, now, Thistle," said Mrs. Vo. "I'm sure the Lady Minami misses her normal life. We cannot force her stay here just because the two of you are friendly."

"Well, that's just the thing," said the Lady Ayer. "I'd like for Thistle to come with me."

"Really?" Thistle practically yelled. "You mean it?"

"I think she's proven to be an excellent assistant," the Lady Ayer went on. "Good help is so hard to find, even in Crandon. And I would ensure her a life of hard work and honor. Thanks to the Emperor." She kissed her two fingers in salute, and Thistle did, too. Mrs. Vo did not.

"No," her mother said simply.

Thistle felt her mouth drop open. It was the opportunity of a lifetime.

"What do you mean, 'No'?" Thistle demanded.

"Surely you'd like to think on it," said the Lady Ayer peaceably. "This would guarantee her financial stability for life. She may even find a suitable Imperial husband if she returns with me. To move up in the world. Certainly you wouldn't begrudge your daughter that."

"No," Mrs. Vo repeated. "I will not allow you to take my only family away from me."

"Ah," said the Lady Ayer. "What if we moved you, too? To Crandon. We could certainly find you some lodging in the Sty's End. Colorful district, lots of immigrants there."

This was better than anything Thistle could have ever imagined. She whirled to meet her mother's eyes, expecting to see her enthusiasm mirrored, but instead she found her mother's jaw set in anger. She was breathing very hard, and Thistle realized how pitiful she looked. How provincial. Her hair was messy, and her dress was worn down from being washed so many times. She hated her in that moment, hated how small she was, with her small guesthouse and her small dreams and her small view of the world.

"Absolutely not." And before there could be more argument, she pushed herself to her feet. "This is our home, Lady Minami. It may not seem much to you, Quark may not seem like much to you, but we aren't leaving."

"The thing is," Lady Ayer said, "I'm not sure you can stop her." She turned to Thistle then. "Thistle, would you like to come back to Crandon with me?"

"Yes!" Thistle yelled. She glared at her mother. "Yes, I would! And yes, I will!"

"You are my daughter," Mrs. Vo said slowly, clearly. "And you will obey—"

But Thistle jumped to her feet, too. Fury beat a song of resentment and fire in her ears. "You can't stop me," Thistle hissed.

"Thistle, dear, please take a seat. Mrs. Vo, you, too," said the Lady Ayer. Thistle obeyed immediately. Her mother remained standing for a moment, then reluctantly sat. "Now, Mrs. Vo, I'm afraid you've been outvoted here. But I would so prefer to have your blessing."

"We both know that you're not in the market for a lady's maid. Let's drop the pretense, milady."

The Lady Ayer quirked a smile. "I see where she gets it from."

"You have been using my home for the Emperor's business for three months now, and I have said nothing about it. I have guarded the Imperial interest, like a good citizen. But I will not see my daughter serve Nipran." She turned to Thistle then, and Thistle was startled to see tears in her eyes. "Your father died so that you might be free. And this is how you'd repay his sacrifice?"

"Careful, Mrs. Vo. You tread perilously close to treason." Lady Ayer's voice was heavy with warning, but Mrs. Vo did not acknowledge her.

"They killed him, Thistle. Your father, my husband. Took him in the middle of the night, without even the decency to return his body so that I could see him buried. He fought, so that—"

"He lost." Thistle felt her lip tremble. "He picked a losing battle, and I never got to know him because of his foolishness." She wiped away a tear and pressed on. "I won't mourn a man who chose a lost cause over his family."

"Thistle, please—"

"No." This time when she stood, the Lady did not stop her. "I won't make the same mistake he did."

And before her mother could argue with her more, Thistle left the room.

· CHAPTER 17 ·

Koa

The hyenas, whooping and hooting, circled the Wariuta envoys as they made their way to the shore. They had no reason to be anxious, but Koa did. Genevieve had promised him that all would be well, that this was good, and he really wanted to believe her. But there were times when her mouth would say this was the right decision and her eyes would say it was not, and Koa did not know which part of her to trust. Or if he should trust her at all. His mind would not let go of her words at the oasis.

Why not just kill her?

And he wondered if he'd been a fool.

It was an odd kind of day, one of the rare ones when the fog rolled in from the sea over the sand dunes. Koa did not like the way the mist hung in his hair, obscured his vision. Next to him, Tupac declined to run around with the rest of the familiars. Instead, he hung close to Koa, as though they were the only two nervous beings in all the world.

"Hold steady, pal," Koa said. Tupac growled his assent.

Ahead of them, Kaia led the group with Ica and the other leaders. Her ax was strapped to her back, and she had a great, heavy shield around her left arm. She didn't trust the Colonizers, that much she'd made abundantly clear. But she didn't seem nervous like Koa was. Didn't seem to feel the possibility of violence hovering over them all, ready to drop. Or maybe she did, and this simply did not scare her. She'd always been the better warrior. She was smaller than Ica, but she walked just as tall.

Next to him, Genevieve stumbled in the red sand, and Koa could tell that she'd rolled her ankle a little. He offered his hand to steady her, and she reluctantly accepted his help. For a long and silly moment, Koa was thrilled that she'd finally begun to regard him as a friend.

Though all the warriors were armed, Kaia had made the decision not to allow Genevieve her dagger. Just in case. And so her hands were empty, except for the sand that clung to her palms from bracing her fall.

"I am perfect," she said.

Koa was pretty sure that wasn't the word she meant to use. He buried his amusement behind a smile and was pleased when Genevieve actually smiled back. Maybe once the deal was done, Genevieve would stay. Maybe they could finally be real friends, the kind that did not need to keep up their guard around each other. They could take turns watching over Lilith's oasis. It would be nice, Koa thought, to have someone like himself around. The dream of not being so alone filled him with hope.

They made slow progress, walking only as fast as Aya could go, and it had likely been years since life demanded Aya make the trip to the shore. But soon enough, they could see where the Colonizers waited in a half-circle formation.

Koa watched Genevieve's face as she looked down at them.

Her brow was drawn in the middle. If he was not mistaken, she looked suspicious.

But all she said was "Odd formation."

And they followed the leaders toward the shore.

Once, when Koa was very young, his father had brought him to the shore.

The waves crashed around their feet. His father was so big. Koa wondered sometimes, Was he as tall as his father had been? As fat? He remembered his father as enormous, with shoulders like the rocks that built the mountains.

"Your mother will want you to be a warrior," said Chimu.

"OK." Koa did not have much of a sense of what that meant, just yet.

Chimu knelt in the sand, let the water roll over his legs, so that he could be at eye level with his son. Koa barely remembered his face now, could not recall what kind of nose he had or the shape of his father's lips. But he remembered the eyes and the lines around them.

"You will have a choice," Chimu said. "Always remember that. You have the choice. You do not have to be what Ica wants."

"Ica's in charge," Koa said.

Chimu laughed, and even though his laugh was big and booming, it was lost in the crash of the waves.

"And for good reason. She is the greatest of us." He put his giant hands on Koa's little shoulders then. "But Koa. She will not always be right, and that is especially true when it comes to deciding who you should be. Do you understand?"

Koa watched the water rolling away, watched the sand gather between his toes.

"No," he said.

Chimu sighed and stood. Koa had the sense he had done something wrong and wanted to take it back. But he *didn't* understand.

"You're going to be big and you're going to be strong. You already are big and strong," his father added when Koa frowned. "But that doesn't mean you have to be a warrior. You are your own person. And I suspect your heart is too gentle to be like me."

"Is that bad?"

Chimu smiled, and so Koa smiled. "No, my love. No, that's a wonderful thing. And I hope, even as you grow and become your own man, that never changes."

When they reached the Colonizers, all the Wariuta except for Aya—who was just too old—took a knee in the sand. A show of respect, of their peaceful intent.

"We agree to trade with you," said Ica. "On the condition of peace, and the cessation of any further encroachment by Colonizers onto Wariuta land."

Genevieve translated this in the staccato rhythm of the Colonizer tongue. Commander nodded and bowed, but it was not the low bow of respect Koa expected. It was hurried. Next to him, Genevieve made a small hiss. She met Koa's eye, and fear dropped in his belly like a stone. She looked panicked. Something was wrong.

But before he could raise his voice—to say what? he didn't know—the leader of the alchemists stood and stepped forward to where Commander waited, and she raised her hands skyward. A signal.

At once, there was chaos.

Explosions of kau went off all around them, enclosing all the non-alchemist Wariuta with the Colonizers. The Colonizers raised their guns.

"No!" Ica shouted, and she stood with her hands up.

But the Colonizers fired.

Koa's mind went silent. There was so much noise, but it all rose into nothing in his ears as he watched, horror-struck, what unfolded. Aya was the first to fall, her body still on the ground, her legs crossed at the ankle as if she were just dozing in a hammock, as if she could stand again at any moment.

And then Ica fell.

Her hands were still above her head when the bullets found her. For a terrible moment, her body seemed to dance, but Koa knew this was death, this was death finding his mother and taking her from this world, with what seemed like a thousand bullets that tore through her body and left the woman who was their leader, was his mother, an empty shell upon the sand.

All around him there was death, death, death, as if life didn't matter at all, as if there was nothing sacred about the breath in their chest or the thoughts in their heads. Just blood and fire and smoke.

A burning in his arm told him he had been shot, and he looked down, detached, to see blood pouring from his biceps. Nothing had penetrated; it was just a glancing blow. He blinked down at the wound, trying to understand it, trying to understand what was happening, when he was knocked to the ground, and it was a moment or an hour before he realized that Genevieve was lying over him, trying to protect him with her tiny body.

"Come on!" she screamed. And her voice pushed open the gates for all the other sounds to come rushing in at once, a cacophony of screaming and gunfire and kau. His eyes searched wildly, and he saw Chima's body. His heart stopped, but Kaia was still alive, and she felled a Colonizer with her ax, her face covered in blood that dripped down her neck and her chest. He hoped, he hoped, he hoped that it was not her blood, but he couldn't look longer to decipher it before Genevieve pulled him and they were crawling away from everything. Koa was hyperaware of the feel of the sand on his knees, of the fog and its chill, of Genevieve as she led him away from the massacre.

She was still tugging at his arm when they cleared the explosions of kau, still yelling "GO GO GO" when Koa turned back to try to understand what had happened. From a distance, it was hard to see anything except smoke. There were bodies strewn about the shore, the Wariuta and their familiars, but a spattering of Colonizers, too. Just death, death, and death. He looked at it as if it were something happening to someone else, saw that they had set all the old crab traps and fishing canoes on fire, too.

But then there was a snuffling at his side, and Koa couldn't help it; he let out a howl that boomed across the dunes. Tupac sniffed his hand. His reluctance to join the other familiars had saved his life. Koa hugged his familiar close to him, and Tupac panted, his breath hot on Koa's wet face.

"Not now," Genevieve said, and her voice was quiet but urgent. She guided Koa back to his feet with her hand soft on his uninjured arm. "We warn Yunka."

Koa's eyes went wide with fresh horror. "No," he whispered. "They wouldn't."

But Genevieve only pulled him along. She did not need to tell him that if they would massacre the Wariuta on the shore, they would certainly massacre them in their homes as well.

They ran.

They did not have weapons, and there were only two of them. But still they ran. If they could just warn the others in time. Koa could lead them to the oases, no Colonizer would ever find them there, the trail was too long, too difficult, too circuitous for them.

There was fresh water there, and frogs, they could survive there if they must, could wait out the occupation if they had to. They could be safe; he could keep his people safe.

He smelled Yunka before he saw it. Smelled the smoke, not of the cook fires but of the fire of destruction. Yunka was a scene of disaster, of apocalypse, as it rose over the dunes. Fire engulfed it in its entirety, the thatched roofs of the huts uniformly ablaze, casting the late-morning sun into darkness. Ash fell from the sky like rain.

Koa made to run into Yunka, and Genevieve tried to hold him back.

"Koa!" she yelled.

But Koa did not listen to her. He ran, as fast as he could, his long legs carrying him faster than he would have believed, Tupac at his side, giggling loud and scared. There could still be Wariuta left. There could still be lives to save. And Koa would not let some smoke keep him from finding them.

• CHAPTER 18 •

Thistle

Mrs. Vo didn't knock, she just pushed the door open into Thistle's room. Thistle lay on her bed, her eyes focused on the little crack in the plaster of her wall. She did not stir at her mother's entrance but held her body as rigid as her fury would allow. She felt rather than saw her mother sit on the bed, but still she did not move.

"I know you're disappointed," Mrs. Vo said. "I know you think . . . hm. I know you think the Lady Minami is very glamorous."

"That's not it," Thistle groused. "That's not it even a little bit." If her mother thought a nice outfit was all it took to impress her, then she didn't know her own daughter.

Her mother lay a hand on Thistle's back. Thistle tensed away from it. "You can't trust her, my dear." Mrs. Vo sighed. "You can't trust any Imperials; they—"

"Killed my father, so you keep saying." Thistle sat up and glared at her mother. "But how do you know it was them and not the Resistance?"

Thistle could tell she was trying her mother's patience, but Mrs. Vo held her composure. She took a deep, steadying breath. "I know because I'm in the Resistance."

Thistle blinked. This was not the answer she had been expecting.

"You are . . . what?"

"Mm. I always have been. Always will be."

Everything felt very still. Outside, Thistle was dimly aware of the normal sounds in Gia Dinh—the fruit vendors closing up shop, the clop of horse hooves now and again. But it all seemed so distant.

Before her sat Mrs. Vo, in her endlessly mended dress, with her messy dirt-brown hair. Thistle, she knew, must have looked much more like her father than her mother, whose family had emigrated from the Cold World some generations back. She had his face and his hair and his build—must have, anyway, because she scarcely looked like the woman she was seeing anew. Mrs. Vo's jaw was clenched, her eyes serious.

They had the same eyes, though.

"I've never told you because just knowing is dangerous. And I . . . I wanted to keep you safe. You're my baby. I never expected you would want to leave with one of them, one of—"

"She's not like the old Imperials, Mother," Thistle said. Heat rose in her cheeks. Between the Lady Ayer and her mother, only one had lied for Thistle's entire life, not trusted her with the truth. As though she were a *child*. "She thinks the Empire is strongest when it honors its diversity."

Mrs. Vo let out a loud snort. "Sure. Once they've killed and conquered us, they're willing to say it's nice that we have a few dinner dishes they enjoy. That's not the same as freedom, Thistle; you've never known it, you've never—"

"I could, though," Thistle said. Her voice was louder than she meant it to be. "If you'd let me go."

"Not with her. Not ever with her. It's not a coincidence that Mr. Ó Baoill's grove was raided while she was here."

Thistle's face burned a deep and traitorous red. She tried to look away, but Mrs. Vo was not fooled.

"What have you done." It was less a question and more a demand.

"What was right." She still could not meet her mother's eyes, but she could feel the heat of them boring into her. "Guns are illegal and—"

"Laws made by tyrants are not laws worth following," Mrs. Vo spat.

It was, Thistle could tell, something she had said many times in her life. Never to Thistle, though, never before this horrible night. All around her she could feel the comfort and normalcy of her life crumbling down. Maybe they had never been there at all. Maybe her whole life had been a convoluted lie her mother worked daily to uphold. A facade.

"What do you know?" The contempt in Thistle's voice boomed like cannon fire. "You're just the widow of a coward with dishpan hands and no power. Of course I told the Lady Ayer; she's actually a person of consequence, someone who matters, someone—"

"The Lady who?" Mrs. Vo's face was shrewd, her eyes focused on her daughter.

Thistle shriveled inside. "Minami."

"That's not what you said. You fool child, you're toying with forces you couldn't possibly comprehend." She stood and made to leave Thistle's room, but Thistle lunged for her, catching hold of her mother's wrist. The force of her grip startled Mrs. Vo, who whirled on her, her whole body rigid with fury and disappointment.

"Don't tell them!" Thistle pleaded.

Mrs. Vo wrenched her arm from Thistle's hands.

"You've made your choice, Thistle." And with rising horror, Thistle could see the new reality of her life cresting in her mother's eyes. Regret. She could see her mother's regret, and in that instant, she knew her mother would choose the Resistance over her. Was choosing the Resistance. "I can't change what you've done."

"Please!" Thistle cried. "They'll kill me!"

"Why could you not have just minded your business like I told you?"

"You would let them kill me?" Thistle's voice was hysterical, Thistle was hysterical, could feel her breath leaving her, her vision narrowing so that all she could see at the end of a long tunnel of blurred nothingness and dark was her mother, her mother leaving her, her mother leaving her for dead. "I'm your daughter!"

Her mother moved to the door and did not turn. Without facing Thistle, she murmured: "I have no daughter."

And she closed the door behind her.

Thistle heard Mrs. Vo's footsteps quietly padding down the hall.

Thistle was dead asleep when she was shaken awake and a hand was clamped over her mouth.

"They're in the house." It was the Lady Ayer. It was the middle of the night, so she was in her nightclothes, which was the only thing that made any sense. Everything else was off, wrong.

"Who—" Thistle tried to ask, but the Lady's hand only clamped down harder.

A clatter of dishes breaking downstairs made it clear to Thistle that whoever was in the house wasn't making much effort to be quiet. Who would be in their house, and why they'd knock dishes onto the ground, was beyond Thistle's imagination. She felt very much as if she were still in a dream, except that the pain in her arm where the Lady's other hand gripped her was very real.

"I don't think we can hide," whispered Lady Ayer. Thistle could hear the door to the cellar being opened and boots clambering down the stairs. "So we're going to make a run for it."

Thistle nodded, fear just starting to creep along her spine like a spider crawling upon a branch. She thought wildly of the spiders in Mr. Ó Baoill's grove, of the guns that had been hidden there, of the smell of the gunpowder, of the weight of the rifle in her hands. It had been so heavy. She couldn't imagine hefting one, let alone aiming it in earnest. Having one aimed at her.

The Lady Ayer's body was rigid against hers but not, Thistle realized, afraid. Her movements and her breath were steady, sure. She let the Lady's courage bolster her own. She was not alone. There was no need to be afraid. She gulped down a hiccup of fear and focused.

Down the hall, she did not hear anything, which was odd. Why wasn't her mother responding to the clatter?

She met the Lady Ayer's eyes, and understanding passed between them.

Her mother didn't respond because her mother must have known this was coming.

"Are you ready?" the Lady asked.

"Yes."

Lady Ayer carefully, slowly, silently twisted the doorknob and pressed the door open. After a quick dart of her eyes, she gave Thistle a brief nod. Thistle kept her own eyes trained on the Lady as she led her at a run out of the house. When they were half-way down the front stairs, Thistle distantly heard a man's voice call "HEY!" but neither she nor the Lady stopped. Thistle's heart drummed in her ears like the Emperor's own taiko, loud, loud, loud, as she and the Lady Ayer spilled out onto the street, and the Lady flagged down an Imperial patrol that happened to be passing.

"In there!" she shouted. "They're trying to attack us!"

Three of the men who'd been casually patrolling ran into the house, their rifles drawn. The Lady and Thistle remained on the street with one of the soldiers, who put himself between the two and the house. Lady Ayer clutched Thistle close, and Thistle watched the house as though she could see through the walls, as if somehow the stone walls would reveal what happened within.

Then there was yelling inside the house. Indistinct but urgent.

Then a gunshot. A scream.

More yelling.

"It's OK," the Lady Ayer whispered into Thistle's hair. "It'll all be OK."

It felt like days had passed by the time the soldiers emerged from the house. One led a cuffed young man Thistle did not recognize—his handsome faced half-obscured by new bruises— and the other led an openly weeping Dai.

The part of Thistle that was still a child evaporated at the sight of her erstwhile best friend, blood dripping from a wound in his scalp, his face wet with tears and what might have been vomit. They were supposed to have been married, Thistle and Dai. Dai and Thistle.

"What has happened?" the Lady demanded.

"Found these two inside," the first soldier said gruffly. "This one"—he shook his captive, the young man, who seemed too dazed to fight back—"shot the woman."

"No, he didn't!" Dai wailed. "No, he—" But the other soldier hit him with the butt of his rifle, hard, on the back of the head, and Dai cried out in pain but did not speak more.

Thistle felt as though she were watching it all from very far away.

The woman, the soldier had said.

There was only one woman in the house. She and the Lady Ayer were outside.

There was only one woman.

The woman.

"She's dead," the other soldier said.

"Take these men to the Consulate and have them interrogated immediately. Let them see the Emperor's justice," Lady Ayer said. If the men were surprised to be given orders by a random woman in her dressing robe, they didn't show it. "And send back at least two men to stand watch over us," she added. "There was an attempt on our lives tonight, and I don't intend to suffer a second."

"Yes, my lady." The soldiers each held up two fingers, and the lady kissed two of hers and touched them to her heart in response.

"Thanks to the Emperor," she said, and the men echoed her. They led Dai and the staggering young man off to be interrogated. And probably, Thistle realized, hanged. Perhaps Dai would be spared for being a child—perhaps not. He was nearly a man.

The Lady Ayer turned to Thistle then and put her hands on her shoulders so that Thistle had nowhere to look but into the Lady's eyes. They burned into Thistle's.

"I know that this has been a terrible, terrible night," she said. "That there will be no salve for your wounds except time. But I think you should come with me to see your mother, one last time. Come and see what those men, this *Resistance*"—she spat the word—"have done to your family."

118

Thistle did not speak, did not argue. Lady Ayer led her into the quiet house, the too-quiet house, to where her mother's body waited.

They found her in the kitchen. There, on the floor just next to the stove, was the body, crumpled and wet. The smell of copper and sick, and a terrible smell Thistle did not recognize hit her just as the realization did. The smell was blood. There was a split second of madness in which Thistle thought she saw the body move, the gentle stirring of a breath. But that was just her imagination. There was too much blood, pooled and terrible, beneath the body that had been her mother.

"Look," said the Lady Ayer. "Look at what those men have done. Thanks to the Emperor, his justice will find them. Thanks to the Emperor, they will pay for this."

Mrs. Vo was facedown so all Thistle could see was the familiar shape of her body, in a horribly unfamiliar position. She could not look into the face of the woman who would have seen her own daughter dead, the face that had betrayed her and then been betrayed. Instead, she turned from the body and stepped past Lady Ayer out of the kitchen and then out of the house, as if in a trance.

There was nothing left for her there.

Thistle and the Lady Ayer left for Crandon only a few days later. When the Lady asked her to pack her things, Thistle did not. Not because she was disobeying the Lady—she would never, not on purpose, for the entirety of the time they knew each other. But because there was nothing of her old life she wanted to keep.

The Lady understood this and helped Thistle buy an entirely new wardrobe for Nipran. As they sailed into Crandon's port, Thistle looked up at the statue of the Emperor that loomed enormous over the city. It was the grandest thing she had ever seen in her life, which felt right. She felt grander, too. Bigger. She had a purpose now, as the Lady's maid.

She was dressed in the new clothes the Lady had had made for her, a fine silk kimono in the Imperial style. The Lady had braided Thistle's hair herself, so that she might learn the newest Imperial style. When Thistle had seen herself in the mirror, she'd looked like a whole new person. And Thistle liked the new person.

"It is a shame you're from Quark," Lady Ayer said. She said this without feeling, without any regard for the insult it did Thistle. Rather, she said it like a fact as simple and true and objective as *lousy weather today*. She was right, Thistle knew. "But you could pass as at least part Imperial if it weren't for your name. We should change it before we return to Crandon."

"What to, my lady?"

"Something Imperial but maybe not Nipranite." She paused thoughtfully, considering her options. "What do you think of the name Mary?"

Despite herself, Thistle crinkled her nose. The Lady Ayer laughed.

"Right you are, far too simple a name for a girl like you." She lapsed into silence once again, and Thistle could feel the air growing thick with opportunity. She had a whole new life ahead of her. She could be anyone she wanted.

"What about Rose?" Thistle asked. There was a Princess Rose from a book of Nipranite fairy tales that Thistle enjoyed very much. But the Lady Ayer shook her head.

"No, no. Too fussy. Too precious. You've outgrown the garden fence now, my dear. You're thinking too small." Thistle smiled at this. A big name, then, for her new self. "What about Genevieve?" the Lady Ayer offered.

"Like your nanny."

"Strong woman. Good woman. She'd have liked you, I know it."

Thistle felt her face crack into a grin. "Yes," she said. "I like that name very much."

"Good. That's a very good name for my apprentice."

Apprentice. The word felt warm and good and important in Thistle's heart.

Before they left Quark, the news had come that the young man had indeed been sentenced and executed by hanging. Dai's trial still had not happened, but Genevieve could hardly muster curiosity about his fate.

They were not Thistle and Dai anymore, and she was not even Thistle.

And if sometimes, late at night, when sleep would not come, she would see her mother's body on the kitchen floor, crumpled and wasted and gone, well. That was something from Thistle's life, too. And Genevieve did her best to leave it all behind. She had a new life now.

Thanks to the Emperor.

CHAPTER 19

Koa

There were only a handful of survivors, and they were all children, small enough to have hidden during the attack or lucky enough to have been inside a hut that kau had not hit. Koa swallowed the bile that threatened to rise again. This was no moment for weakness. He carried Kalei in his arms. She was a baby, still nursing, still so delicate and small. Her mother's body was right outside their hut, Kalei inside, somehow, miraculously, asleep. He did not know how he would see her fed, did not know how to care for a baby, but he held her close all the same.

He would learn. He'd have to.

The children did not want to walk with Genevieve, and so she walked at the very back of the group as Koa led them to the oasis, his oasis, the hardest oasis to find. The Colonizers would not track them there, and they were too young to be affected by the siren's song.

When they arrived, he counted them.

There were only twelve.

All of Yunka contained only twelve children. Babies. The weight of the loss stood beside him, but he couldn't bear it yet, could not look it in the eye or it would crush him.

Lilith poked her head out of the water and then emerged, her face unusually soft.

"What is this?" she asked.

"Nipran attacks," said Genevieve. Her voice was thick with tears. "They kill Yunka."

Lilith's eyes snapped to Koa, who only nodded. In his arms, Kalei stirred, and then her face crumpled into a wail. Looking for her mother, Koa thought. Her mother who was dead and gone.

Just like his own mother.

He could not save Ica, he reminded himself.

But he could save these children. He could honor her in this way, by protecting the children she couldn't.

He shushed Kalei, bounced her in his arms the way he had seen mothers do, but she kept on wailing, high and plaintive and piercing. Her crying set off more crying from other children, and it seemed that soon the oasis would be nothing except the sound of their grief.

"And this is all that is left?" Lilith asked.

"Yes," said Genevieve. "Bodies. Everywhere." She was weeping. *Good*, thought Koa. She had told him to trust them. She should weep.

"They do not change," growled Lilith.

Koa did not respond to this; he just did his best to soothe the baby. Some of the children had already gone to sleep on the warm sand, exhausted, no doubt, by the trauma in their wake. Koa's body felt the drain, but he couldn't sleep, not while he needed to guard the children, not when he needed to decide how best to proceed.

"You must get that baby some milk," Lilith said. "Goat is best, until you find another woman. Cow will work, but not forever."

Koa sagged with relief. There were cows nearby, and goats in Puno. But would they be safe in Puno? He didn't know. But he did know he could steal a goat. And for the first time since they made the trek down to the shore, Koa felt some ounce of resolution, of control. He was so relieved by it that it took him a moment before he realized that Lilith—*Lilith*—was being helpful.

"Thank you," he said.

Their eyes met, and he was surprised to see something like anger thrumming in the siren's gaze. It was not her usual bitterness, it was something different, something raw and fresh and burning.

"I can help," she said.

Koa couldn't resist, he laughed. "Eating the children is not help."

"When have I *ever* preyed on a child?" Lilith snapped. Koa flinched, abashed. "You think that not one has ever come to the edge of my waters, curious and unafraid? You abandon your post too often to believe that."

"I'm sorry," said Koa, and he was. But, he thought, Lilith was still a monster. He knew this, just as she knew this, and though nothing was said aloud, that understanding passed between them.

"How can you help?" Genevieve asked. Her voice was ragged, and her words bore the weight of her effort. "You are stuck."

"My blood," said Lilith plainly. Koa tilted his head, confused. "My blood carries the memory of a weapon that can destroy the Empire."

For a few moments, no one spoke. Kalei's wails punctuated the otherwise quiet that had fallen over the oasis. Koa let his eyes drift to the distance, where the smoke of what was once Yunka rose into the night. He wondered if Kaia survived, then pushed the thought away. There was no way. And there was also no space in his heart to grapple with that just now.

"I do not understand," said Genevieve finally.

Koa snapped back to the present, to Lilith, who was glaring at Genevieve.

"One of you must drink, and I can show you," said Lilith, as though Genevieve were very stupid. Which, Koa thought, she wasn't. The idea was as appalling to him as it clearly was to her. They exchanged a look of suspicious bemusement.

"What, like. Cut you open?" Koa asked. He couldn't imagine doing this, for one, but also, nearing the edge of her water was a death wish. She was stronger than a human, by far, and her offer could easily just be a trick to lure one of them close enough to drain.

"If there were a less painful way, I would take it. But I lack the words." Lilith looked as frustrated as Koa felt. "My wrist would be easiest." Lilith reached one elegant arm out of the water like a gift. And a gift from the Sea, Ica had always said, was not to be trusted. *Ica.*

"Why would you give us this?" Koa asked. "Is this a trick?"

"I would see Nipran fall."

Koa looked to Genevieve but couldn't catch her eye. Her gaze was fixed on the siren, her jaw set. There was soot smeared on her sunburnt face, except in clean tracks forged by her tears. She took a breath.

"I will help."

Koa's brow furrowed. "Help with what?" None of the children wanted to be near her. She did not know the land. From what he'd seen, she did not know how to cook, or forage, or cast pottery, or herd, or fish.

125

She locked eyes with Koa. "Make Nipran fall."

Koa wanted to laugh, but the look in Genevieve's eyes was too bright with fury, too incendiary to be stoked with mocking.

"I will fight," said Genevieve. "Lady Ayer promises me . . . promises me Nipran means justice. Order." She motioned to the children, most of whom were deeply asleep. "This is not order. This is not what she promises. This is murder."

And before Koa could stop her, she pulled her dagger from where she must have secreted it away on her leg and went to Lilith. Koa felt his stomach roil as he watched her drag the dagger across the skin on the siren's wrist. Lilith barely flinched. There was a pause in which Koa wondered if Genevieve had cut deeply enough, but then the siren's blood, thicker than he expected, redder, began to spill.

Just as Genevieve's lips closed over the open wound, Lilith grabbed a fistful of her hair. Koa drew a shocked breath, Genevieve made a sound between a gulp and a shout, and Lilith pulled her under the glassy green water.

PART TWO

The Song

CHAPTER 20

Alfie

Alfie had never eaten so much butter in his life. Or meat. Or vegetables. Or fruit. Or cheese. Or rice. Or bread. But the butter. The butter was the best.

He looked better for it, too. His cheeks were full; the bags under his eyes were gone. He slept more soundly, and without the drink to help him get there. Working in the Emperor's kitchen was easily the best gig he'd ever held down in his life. Not a lot to compete with, honestly—pickpocketing was brutal, and pirating was . . . Well. It'd nearly killed him. He wasn't cut out for that kind of life. And the older he got, the more he thought that probably no one was. That no one should have to be.

The fact that he'd been placed in the kitchen as a spy for the Pirate Supreme wasn't exactly the life of ease and safety he might have hoped for. It meant that just as with every other job he'd ever had in his life, his survival depended on not getting too comfortable.

Which was hard. Because the Emperor's palace was *so* comfortable.

The servants' quarters were so lush they made the Nameless Captain's cabin look dim. Alfie could hardly imagine what the Emperor's chambers might be like. Heaven, or some such. The nursery gave a small glimpse, and it had initially been so dazzling that he'd rather forgotten what he was supposed to do upon arriving there with a plate of cold sliced plums and delicate mochi stacked on porcelain dishes for the Emperor's many children.

Or, it should be said, many daughters.

The Emperor had only recently sired his first and only male heir. After decades of daughters, of discarded wives. The palace was abuzz with relief and excitement.

Alfie was on his way to deliver some freshly smooshed berries and ice milk to the child when it occurred to him that—even knowing he was there to bring death to literally everyone who lived in this palace, probably and unfortunately including his coworkers and the many princesses he often served—this was the happiest he'd been in his whole life.

He pushed open the door to the nursery—opulent red lacquer with gold inlay, a door more expensive than Alfie's life was worth, surely—and was delighted to see that Keiko was there.

"You!" he boomed. Keiko laughed, and it was somewhere between embarrassment and delight. She was his favorite of the nurses who worked in the palace. Alfie put the tray of treats for the Crown Prince and future emperor down on the table. "Light of my life! Fire of my loi—"

"Not in here," Priyanka interrupted. Priyanka—the head nurse—was old, and Alfie liked her even if he didn't like her in the same way or quite as much as he liked Keiko. Apparently she had been a nurse to the Emperor's children since she was practically a child herself, which, Alfie figured, must have been at least

130

a hundred years ago. She gave him a beleaguered smile before returning to the little princess whose hair she was braiding. "You know better than to talk your nonsense in here, Philip."

Ah. That was the other thing. He had to go under a fake name, a fake life story, a fake . . . everything, basically. So even if he liked Keiko, she couldn't like him, because she didn't know who he was.

But that was a thought for another time. "I've got the same question I have for you every day, milady," he said grandly.

Keiko rolled her eyes. "I'm not going to marry you."

Alfie feigned taking a shot to his heart and staggered theatrically. One of the princesses (Alfie could never keep their names straight, and anyway they were all named some variation on Jingū) giggled behind her hands.

"No matter!" Alfie crowed. He gave a long and unnecessarily deep bow. "Tomorrow will come and perhaps it will bring me a better reply."

"Hmm." Keiko pulled the Crown Prince from his golden crib (solidly gold—how was this lifestyle sustainable?), and he immediately started to wail in protest until she managed to get him to take a bite of the ice milk from his (again, literally solid) golden spoon.

"How is our majesty today?" Alfie asked.

"Oh, you know," Keiko said. He saw her eyes dart around the room, but the princesses and other nurses were all uniformly distracted with their many toys and books and instruments and impending toddler disasters. "Majestic."

Alfie was just opening his mouth to make a joke about royal diapers when the door to the nursery burst open with a crash. Several of the princesses cried out, and all others looked toward the threshold fearfully. Seven of the Imperial Guard were there, hands on the hilts of their swords.

"Princess Jingū," said the captain. Alfie suppressed a laugh. He really needed to be more specific. "Daughter of the Emperor's Eighth Wife, the Disgraced Lady Michiko."

Ah. There it was. As of earlier that morning, Lady Michiko had not been disgraced. Alfie and Keiko shared a look. He wondered what she had done—or, more likely, what slight the Emperor had perceived from her.

Alfie watched as one of the princesses, maybe eight or nine years old, stood shakily. She was, he thought, being rather brave about it. Here were seven men with deadly weapons ready to collect her, and she acted with more courage and grace than he had the last time he'd been assigned to clean the staff latrines.

Another princess, maybe four or five, tried to pull the Princess Jingū in question back down by the hand, but she shook her off. She met the men halfway, and Alfie was stunned to see them grab her by her arms, hard, as if she were a criminal and not a scared little girl in a pink kimono.

"Where are you taking her?" Priyanka was on her feet now, her face taut with worry. Alfie had never seen her look anything other than sanguine. And it was her fear, he guessed, more than anything else, that made the rest of the nurses scared, too.

"Away," said the captain. His men hauled the little princess out by her elbows. Several of the other princesses were weeping now, but the men paid them no mind. "Thanks to the Emperor," he said with an almost sarcastic bow.

"Thanks to the Emperor," all—even those who were crying—echoed.

The door slammed shut behind the men, and Princess Jingū, Daughter of the Emperor's Eighth Wife, the Disgraced Lady Michiko, was gone.

The arrests and executions had been ramping up lately, that was undeniable. Alfie knew from his sporadic correspondence with Rake that rebellions in the colonies were mounting, with the help of the Pirate Supreme. The unprecedented amount of dissent was, clearly, making the Emperor angry. And though Alfie had seen his anger exercised on the streets of Crandon throughout his whole life, he'd never imagined he would see it within the walls of Emperor's own palace.

Directed at the Emperor's own child.

Keiko wiped a tear. Alfie reached out to comfort her, then pulled his hand back. There were rules about the palace staff, about men and women, about touching. It felt so inhumane to watch her crying and not try to comfort her.

"She'll be all right," he lied. He tried not to think of his sister. She was happy, at least, but she was also gone.

"She's just a baby."

He could hear the strain in Keiko's voice, the worry. She bounced the Crown Prince in her arms, his giggles ringing incongruously.

Well, thought Alfie. *No, she's not strictly. And her life has been literal gold and peaches and butter, and so what's a touch of bad luck now after a lifetime of such fortune?*

As if reading his mind, Keiko glared at him. "Children shouldn't pay for their parents' mistakes."

"No," said Alfie ardently. "That's true."

Alfie woke that night in a mess of wet sheets and cursed.

It had been so long since this had happened! Shame bubbled hot and humiliating in his throat. As quickly and as quietly as he could, he pulled the sheets from his bed. He would die of embarrassment if Juan or Charles—the other kitchen boys he shared a room with—awoke to see him covered in piss. Again. He'd been able to bury the first incident in a tall tale of sake and bad choices, but he hardly thought he could pull that off convincingly for a second time.

And though part of him was silently carrying his soiled bed linens to the laundry, one foot remained firmly in his dream. In the world where Fawkes was still alive, his hands looming enormous, like the Emperor's statue over Crandon. Rake had seen the body, had assured Alfie that Fawkes was well and truly dead, but for some reason that did not provide Alfie the peace he hoped it would.

It wasn't like Rake was an expert in lending comfort, though. He was about as soft as a pistol's barrel.

As he crept back from the laundry, the evidence now buried deep within the enormous daily load of linens the palace produced (anonymous and gone), he heard men's voices in hushed argument in the atrium, which was—as a rule—empty at night. He stepped silently to the edge of the door frame and listened to the two figures who stood beneath the rib cage of the articulated dragon's skeleton that hung from the ceiling; it was longer than the room was wide, curling back on itself in a neatly arranged spiral, and visitors from all over the Known World came to witness it. It was, they said, the last of the dragons, killed by the 900th Emperor's own naginata.

A man with an accent Alfie recognized as from Iwei but trained in Imperial tongue was saying, " . . . because now Callum is headed back here for some kind of girl savage show-and-tell, and frankly I don't think the Senate will—"

"When has the Senate ever done anything?" the second voice interjected. That voice, Alfie realized, was not a man's but rather

Senator Tsujima's, rasping and harried with xyr age. A chance to listen in on xyr conversation was a rare and ripe opportunity. Senator Tsujima knew everything that happened in the court. Xe had spies everywhere xe was not. "We are hamstrung by bureaucracy. All the true power lies with the Emperor, thanks to him. You must be patient. Men like Callum are always barking about wars and new lands."

"But if we send men to the Red Shore, then—"

Ah. Alfie listened hard for information that could be passed back to the Pirate Supreme.

"—who will tend to the Resistance in Quark? Or the rebellion in Sty's End for that matter? The Guard is stretched thin as it is, what with the assassination attempts on the constabulary, and morale is dwindling. I fear the Empire will lose the battle for our men's hearts, which will lead inexorably to loss of our land. *My* land."

"Dissidents come and go," said Senator Tsujima, xyr voice dismissive. "You should worry more about your wife's reputation than about skulduggery abroad."

"And what's that supposed to mean?"

"That you should cut her allowance. She has been drinking too much of the mermaid's blood, I hear. So much, in fact, that she shames herself in public with her intoxication."

The argument mounted from there, but Alfie slipped away, his heart hammering with pride. He would have to find time tomorrow to get to the docks, where several of the Supreme's men were tucked away, undercover and ready to receive intelligence from their many operatives scattered throughout Crandon.

For once, he'd have something to report.

But as he scurried back to his room, he felt something catch in his throat. If the Supreme found out that the Guard was already onto the plans for picking off the various constables around Quark, then surely they'd switch targets.

And the other target under consideration was the Crown Prince.

Alfie tried to push the imagining away, but he could not—his mind treated him to various terrible and bloody scenarios, all ending with a dead baby and worse: a dead Keiko. She was his nurse, after all. If anyone made an attempt on the Prince, she would need to stand in his defense. If the assassins didn't kill her, the Imperials would. He knew what it was to fear for his life, to have a pistol pressed against his temple. He could remember, always, with startling clarity, the feel of Fawkes's hands on his throat, of the world going gray and wrong around him.

It was nearly morning.

He stopped at a window and looked out at Crandon. The orange and flickering lights of blazing lampposts shimmered as far as he could see, tiny fires that begged to spread. The city deserved to burn. The Empire deserved to burn. But the collateral. He had not considered the collateral when he first made his promise to the Pirate Supreme. To serve them faithfully.

To help destroy Nipran.

He shook away his discomfort. It was fine. It would be easy enough to distract Keiko, to pull her away when the time came. She was not some Imperial lady who'd never seen a bad day in her life—she'd worked, been cheated, and still worked some more. He pushed the memory of the Lady Hasegawa down and away. Flora may have loved her, but Alfie didn't. She was just like the rest, and even if he was happy that Flora was happy, he still missed his sister.

But Keiko. Perhaps, his mind whirred with the possibility of it, Keiko could be recruited. Perhaps she could help.

He smiled into the horizon. Already the sun was just beginning to glow in the distance, dimming the orange lanterns as it rose.

He would send the message to the Pirate Supreme. He'd be useful. For once.

The Sea

Her mind is slipping.

So many of her daughters have been taken; mankind's thirst for mermaids has always been greedy. But now it is something else, something mechanized, weaponized. She cannot remember so much now. Where there ought to be a memory, there is only emptiness, and she is angry, but at whom? She cannot remember anymore.

Mother, please, *Evelyn calls. The Sea tries so hard to listen. Evelyn's voice is an anchor, and she bends toward it.* Mother, how can we help?

This is something the Sea remembers. How much Evelyn wants to help. How willingly she gives of herself for others.

But it is not Evelyn's help she needs.

She searches. Off the Skeleton Coast in Tustwe, a crabber checks xyr traps. In a kelp forest, a sea otter snags an abalone and returns to the surface with her bounty. A shark finds a whale carcass and feasts until he is sated enough to find a mate. An eel curls into her cavern.

They are not who the Sea needs.

She needs them. If only she could remember how to find them, if only she could pick through the deafening noise of her awareness and hear their call. Surely they search for her, too.

She does not find that chosen person, the person she plucked from all the humans of the world to be her champion; she cannot remember their name. But she does find a rock. A smooth lump of quartz. She rolls over it again and again, listens to its story. It is a story she has heard before, a story she can still remember now that she is reminded of it. This rock has had secrets whispered into it, ugly and hopeful and full of love.

Flora's story.

If the Sea cannot find her chosen one, then perhaps her children can. At least one of her daughters has met the person she seeks.

Flora, *says the Sea.* I need you to find the Pirate Supreme.

· CHAPTER 21 ·

Geneviève

She watched it as if it were a dream—visions that flashed devoid of sound or smell or taste or touch. Down through the purple depths of the sea, below where the light existed, down, down, down she was led, deeper than mountains were tall, deeper than the sky was high. There was no life here, no darting fish or swaying sharks, past even the strange glowing creatures that dwelled in the darkness.

She heard it only once they reached the Sea's floor—like a clicking at first, far away, then a creak, then a groan, like an ancient ship treading water but bigger, louder. It shook the blood in her veins, rattled the bones in her ears and her feet.

She saw it only once her heart felt as though it had stopped. A shadow in the shadows, black in blackness, but there as sure as she was of anything. It was enormous, as big as the Emperor's statue in Crandon. It exhaled a puff of blue flame, and for an instant, its face was illuminated: craggy, iridescent black scales and curved teeth, as long as a man was tall.

A dragon.

She opened her mouth to scream, but no sound emerged.

Instead, her lungs filled with water. She fought against it, tried to find breath, but for a time she could not comprehend, a time that felt like infinity, no breath would come to her, just the burning pain of drowning.

She thrashed but could find no purchase.

And then, finally, the light came back, dazzling and blinding, burning and bright. Fresh air hit her lungs like a punch of relief. She gagged, spat water, felt herself being dragged from the oasis and onto the hot sand. Her body recoiled in shock at the violent change in temperature.

A shadow loomed over her, blocking the sun. "Are you OK?" asked Koa's voice.

Genevieve rolled onto her side and retched bile.

"Imperials," came the siren's voice. "So fragile."

Genevieve had seen the dragon skeleton before in the Emperor's palace. The last dragon's skeleton. After what may have been an hour or ten minutes, Genevieve turned to the siren.

"You tried to kill me!" She meant to shout it, but it came out as more of a wheeze.

Koa slapped her on the back, and she nearly vomited again.

"If I wanted to kill you, you'd be dead," said the siren, her voice sanguine.

"You're OK," said Koa, but Genevieve ignored him.

"Why did you show me this?" she spat. "The dragons are all dead."

"Idiot child. That's an Imperial lie. The First Dragon remains. She always does."

Another lie? Genevieve could barely stand the anger in her chest. How many lies was the Empire built upon? Wariuta bodies still littered the shore. How many times had that happened? How many bodies lay on the shores of nations all over the world, lured under the pretense of peace? She tried not to think of Dai, of the young man who'd been hanged. Of her mother. Dead, and for what?

Another lie she'd believed. Humiliation burned in Genevieve's throat.

"Yeah. A thousand miles beneath the sea. Maybe a million. Great," Genevieve said. "What good does that do anyone?"

The siren rolled her eyes, impatient now. "The Nipran Empire has more soldiers, more resources, and more footholds around your world than any other humans have ever had. You will need what only the First Dragon can offer in order to beat them."

"Dragons," Koa marveled. Then, looking thoughtful, he said, "I don't actually really know what they are, other than large."

"Creatures from the Sea," said the siren. "But not *of* the Sea."

Genevieve folded her arms. "You talk nonsense."

"Where mermaids are bound to their mother, dragons are not. They make their own choices. They can fly, they can breathe fire, and their song brings justice to the world."

"That's neat," said Koa.

"Indeed," said the siren.

"Nobody has time for songs; we need weapons."

The siren looked at Genevieve with something like pity before taking a deep, steadying breath. "Yes. And that's precisely what a dragon's song is. Convince one to fight alongside you, and you can win. If you intend to take your fight to the Emperor, you'll need something more than your pluck."

That was true. Genevieve wiped her nose on her sopping-wet sleeve and tried desperately to get her mind around the issue. Nipran was not what it seemed. The Empire and its justice were lies. It had to be stopped. There were still dragons. Perhaps the dragons could help. She would need to tell someone who could help her find the dragons.

"Koa," she said carefully, "I know . . . I have no right to ask for anything. From you. From. Any Wariuta person."

"Correct."

"But. Can you take me to Puno? So that I can find passage back . . . to Quark, maybe?" The Resistance could still be there; it was possible. Dragons were still around, so perhaps anything was possible. She had to fix the infinite mistakes she'd made in her short life, and going back home seemed like perhaps the only way to do so.

Koa did not appear to be listening anymore. His eyes were on the baby he'd been cradling since they'd left Yunka. She was asleep now, her long eyelashes resting on cheeks that bore the salted tracks of dried tears.

"Koa?"

"I suppose we have to go to Puno anyway," he said after a time. "I need to find additional carers for the children. They need proper food and shelter, not just frogs and milk."

"Thank you."

"I'm not doing this for you." He met her eyes then, and she could see that they had closed off to her, gave her none of his normal, characteristic warmth. "You're on your own. But I won't stop you from coming along with us."

"Koa, I—"

"No. I'm not interested in what you have to say. I don't think you mean to, but with every breath, you lie. You're a—" And here he said that word she did not recognize. "A well-intentioned one, maybe, but an ignorant one. And I won't see more dead because of you."

Genevieve watched as he cradled the baby with one hand and,

with the other, assembled an additional makeshift lean-to with fallen palm fronds so that a couple more children could rest in the shade. It seemed impossible that only hours ago he'd been silly and smiling.

Next to her, his hyena rumbled a quiet growl. Startled, she pulled her skirt closer to her body. The animal watched this with its black eyes. Watched her and did not blink.

Puno was nothing like Yunka.

Genevieve felt as ignorant as Koa had said she was. She had assumed, despite any evidence or reason, that the cities along the Red Shore would all be identical. But this was not the case at all.

Yunka was set into the sand dunes, with homes perfectly suited for the brutal desert sun and winds. Little huts that kept in the warmth at night and the cool in the day. Puno was wildly different. Carved out of the west side of a set of craggy mountains, it seemed both ingenious and a little precarious. Most of the land had been cleverly terraced so crops could be farmed along the slopes. What buildings did exist were made of the same dark-gray stone as the mountains and the terraces, slick from fog and moss. But there was something about it that lent the sense that it could all come tumbling down. It made Genevieve a little nervous.

The Lady Ayer may have taught her the language, but she hadn't thought to mention that the society was enormously varied. Pink people, Black people, even some she could tell were from Quark. In this way, it looked, she thought, rather more like Crandon than the insular, savage culture the Lady had prepared her for. When studying up for this mission, the Lady had described vicious battles to the death between highly skilled warriors, strange ceremonies, and superstition. What Genevieve saw here was just . . . a city. With people minding their business.

144

More lies.

Koa had not spoken to her once since they left the oasis, but now he turned to her. "You'll find more"—that word again—"on the south side of town."

Genevieve gulped. She did not want to ask anything else of Koa, but she was also, suddenly, so afraid. What else didn't she know? How else could she ruin everything? She paused, unsure of what to say, what to do. Behind them, one of the little boys pointed excitedly at a baby goat and giggled.

"Go on," said Koa. His face didn't look certain, but he did not falter.

This was fair. Genevieve knew that, knew the blood of his family was on her hands. She had not seen Kaia fall, but she had seen Ica. Dead and broken. Heard the howls of hyenas gunned down. Smelled the blood and gunpowder.

"OK," she said. "OK."

But as she turned away from Koa, she felt a horrible yank on her hair, heard Koa's cry of anger.

"You," hissed a familiar voice. She could not quite place it. Genevieve tried to thrash, but her every movement only exacerbated the pain in her scalp. Koa stepped forward, but the click of a safety being released on a pistol stopped him in his tracks. She could see the war in Koa's face—he seemed bothered by the use of violence, though perhaps not bothered by whom it was being used against.

"It's OK," she said in Wariuta through gritted teeth. "Go."

But Koa didn't move.

The hand loosened its grip just enough so that Genevieve could see who held her. Her eyes widened. Red hair, a face leathered by years at sea.

Rake.

The Pirate Supreme's operative aboard the *Dove*. The man who had killed the Lady Ayer. Who had beaten her. Who had essentially told her—correctly, she now realized—that she did not understand the violation of the Nipran Empire in Quark. Only a day ago, she would have given anything for a chance to kill this man, to avenge the death of her mentor. But now. She didn't know what to feel as she looked into his hardened face.

"I . . ." She tried to find her words again, to find purchase in her own mind.

Koa stepped forward carefully. "You cannot—"

"You were right," Genevieve said to Rake. "You were right about Imperials. I just saw . . . They killed them. They killed them all."

Rake's eyes narrowed at her suspiciously. "Killed who?"

"The Wariuta," she said, her words tumbling now. Koa watched, bewildered, unable to follow enough of the Common Tongue to understand. "They lured them to the shore with mermaid's blood and the promise of peace, but then they shot them all down. Old people, women. They burned Yunka to the ground, killed the children. These ones here, they're all that's left."

Rake's eyes darted to the dozen kids, then back to Genevieve.

"Mermaid's blood," he repeated.

"They're all dead, Rake. They killed them all."

"Mm. Imperials will do that." He let go of her hair but kept his pistol trained on her. He looked to Koa then, and in a strangled kind of accent said, "Sorry for dead," in Wariuta. "But girl come me."

Koa raised one eyebrow. "You know this man?" he asked Genevieve.

"Yes."

"He doesn't like you," said Koa.

"Most people don't."

Rake's hand encircled her arm and started to pull. "You'll need to come with me," he said.

"Yes," she said distractedly. Seeing that she was being pulled away, one of the little girls had started to cry. Not, Genevieve thought, because she liked her but because another change was simply more than the little girl could bear.

"Tell me where to find you," Koa said to Rake. "Once I've found a safe spot for the children."

Rake blinked at him, clearly out of his depth.

"Tell him where we're going," Genevieve translated. "He doesn't trust you. Or me."

"Then why's he care?"

"Just. I think he's not so keen on murder?"

Rake shrugged. "Fair enough. Tell him we're staying in a guesthouse on the southeast side of town. By the alchemists' lodge."

Genevieve translated this, and Koa nodded, mollified. Without another word or look to Genevieve, he led the children in the opposite direction.

"You've got some explaining to do," said Rake as the children trailed away.

"I know." It was, she realized, quite lucky that Rake had found her. Not lucky if he murdered her outright, but then, if he was going to do that, he would have done so already, right? And anyway, she had information to share. Certainly he wanted to destroy the Empire. She could pass the knowledge the siren had given her on to him, and through him to the Pirate Supreme. "I have so much to tell you."

"This isn't a campfire," he said coldly. "We are not friends."

Genevieve rubbed her scalp, which was still sore. "Yeah, clearly."

He did not release his grip on her as they moved through the crowded roads. Genevieve's stomach roiled with hunger she had not noticed until she smelled the cookstoves that seemed to be going everywhere.

"Is the Pirate Supreme there?" she asked. "I want to talk to them."

"I'm sure you do," said Rake. "But I wouldn't let you anywhere near them if my life depended on it, you traitorous little snake."

"But—" Genevieve wanted to explain; she'd changed! She knew better now! She'd learned! But how to say that without sounding like an operative. "I can help."

"Yeah, sure. I'm taking you to the Fist. You can tell that to her."

"The Fist?" Genevieve scoffed; she couldn't help it. "What kind of stupid name is that?"

Rake turned, and the smile he gave her robbed her of what little bravado she had left. "She doles out the Resistance's justice here," he said. "You can plead your case to her."

"The Resistance?"

Genevieve's blood ran cold.

"Like I said," Rake said, his voice barely containing his amusement now, "you've got some explaining to do."

· CHAPTER 22 ·

Tomas

Tomas Inouye knew he'd fallen out of favor with Commander Callum when the Lady Hasegawa had escaped her imprisonment on the Floating Islands. If the commander had known how intimately involved Inouye was with that escape, Inouye would have kissed a noose for sure. But it was enough that it'd happened on his watch. And so now, while the rest of the soldiers enjoyed the first pass of rations in the galley, Inouye was trapped in the moldering, stinking brig, watching over the barred and locked cage that held an unconscious one-handed girl.

The slaughter of the savages on the Red Shore had not sat well with Inouye. Seemed ugly. There'd been so many women. Old people. Children. If the Empire could be brought down by girls and kids, then it wasn't much of an empire, was it? Or at least it certainly wasn't the Empire he'd been brought up to believe in. He hadn't said this aloud, of course—not to anyone. You could never tell who was a snitch hoping to curry favor. Hadn't Tomas ratted out a fellow before in the hopes of promotion? And when he was outed, Callum'd see him whipped for impertinence. Big fan of whippings, Callum. Inouye was not such a fan of Callum for this, and several other reasons. Chiefly his haughty demeanor and frankly prickish attitude.

The girl stirred a little in her sleep. Inouye watched her. She was still filthy with dried blood, but without her ax, she didn't seem so fearsome. He'd seen her in battle. Seen her take down Lieutenant Bisset with one swift swing of that ax. Had watched as she buried it into his back, his body, once whole and breathing, suddenly cold and gone.

"You'll see death," his father had told him when he enlisted. "And you'll never be the same."

His father had served for nearly all his life until he lost several fingers to frostbite on an exploratory mission that had yielded nothing of value to the Empire. Had set their family up passably if not comfortably for Tomas's whole childhood. His father's words had not been a warning so much as a statement of fact. He believed in the duty of good Imperial men to serve in the Guard. And though his father had never amounted to much in his many years, he believed, despite their family's low standing and Tomas's lack of any real martial talent, that his son would make it further than he had. Seeing death was, by his reckoning, just one of the many ways boys became men.

Inouye did not feel like much of a man. But again, this was not something he spoke of aloud.

The boat creaked, and above him, Inouye could hear the heavy footsteps of his brothers-in-arms heading off to their cabins to sleep. His watch was only just beginning.

The candle that illuminated the dingy brig flickered in its lantern mutinously.

Bringing the girl back to the Emperor was, Inouye thought, stupid. What'd the Emperor care that a one-handed girl could wield an ax? Surely, as a god, he would be unimpressed. Surely he'd seen more amazing things. There was a dragon skeleton in his palace! But Commander Callum seemed to believe this would entice the Emperor into sending troops over to more fully colonize the Red Shore, and it wasn't Inouye's place to argue.

Bored, Inouye kicked at the iron bars that separated him from the savage girl. She startled awake and was on her feet with frightening speed.

"What's your name, anyway?" asked Inouye.

But she only glared at him and sat back down on the cold, damp floor. She didn't speak Common Tongue, that much was clear.

"I'm TAW-MUS," he said loud and slow. "TAWWWW-MUSSSS."

The girl just stared at him as though he were the stupidest person she had ever seen.

"My NAME," he shouted, "is TAW-MUS."

She blinked. There was a chamber pot in the corner of her cell, which she regarded suspiciously. It had not been well cleaned since the cell's last inhabitant, Inouye knew. He knew because he was supposed to have cleaned it and had not. Not that he had disobeyed orders so much as he had edited them down somewhat. And anyway, she was likely used to squalor, so what was a musty chamber pot to her?

Without shame or hesitation, she sat on the chamber pot and took a long, loud piss. Inouye looked away at first, but when he looked back, she was still glaring at him. What a wild thing she was, unconcerned with his gaze even in this private moment. She was pretty, in an odd, savage way. The tilt of her eyes above her jutting cheekbones. Not pretty like a lady, but beautiful like an animal, maybe.

Distracted by the search for the most apt comparison, he realized a moment too late what she was doing. She had stood and picked up the chamber pot, and as he scrambled—seemingly in slow motion—to get clear of the way, toppling over backward and hitting his head on the floor, she swung the chamber pot at him.

He felt the hot splash of her piss all over.

Soaking into his uniform. In his hair. In his mouth.

And even as he spat and yelled abuse at her, as he banged his rifle against the bars of her cage, she only stared at him, impassive and unflinching except for a shadow of a smile in her eyes. The piss had gone cold, and he shivered in the gloom and the chill of the brig.

"Unbelievable," he muttered once he had yelled himself hoarse.

He righted his stool and sat back down, using his handkerchief to try to scrub some of the mess from his face and hair. If the other men figured out what had happened to him, he'd never hear the end of it, and the shame, preemptive and scalding, burned through him in a blaze. Just once, he'd like to guard a prisoner and not have his life ruined over it.

The girl sat back down on the moldering pile of straw that was her bed and said something in the strange staccato language her people spoke. He couldn't understand, of course, but he could still hear the impertinence in her voice. The hatred. That was fine. He hated her, too.

And then, in what sounded like a curse, a malediction, she spat one word he did understand:

"Tawmus."

• CHAPTER 23 •

The Pirate Supreme

The Pirate Supreme did not like Barilacha, the capital city of the Floating Islands. That is to say, they did not like what Barilacha had become. Everywhere, Imperial Guards stalked about like loose dogs, teeth bared. The Pirate Supreme wanted to comfort every person they saw, to whisper: *Someday these men and their guns and their boots and their ignorance will be gone, I'll see to that; the Floating Islands will be free.* But they couldn't, and so they didn't, and they swallowed the disgust they felt when they saw two soldiers leering at a local girl, no more than fourteen. Pushed down the urge to pull the pistol they had secreted away in their coat and ensure that the Imperials would never enact their violence upon her, or anyone else, ever again.

The Pirate Supreme had to be discreet.

They rode the rickety and unsettling elevators away from the shore, from the Sea, and toward her. Their skin crawled. Every step away from the Sea felt like a mistake that compounded itself. Every step toward her felt like a mistake best left in the past. She would not be happy to see them, they knew this. They had to seek her out regardless.

It had been years. Decades, now.

Her door was the same, with its golden-hand knocker that they knew had been pilfered off the captured ship of a Cold World slave trader. They knew this because they were the one who took it, who brought it back from the Sea and gave it to her. It was a gift to her as much as a punishment to that slaver, and they had both delighted in its duality. A perfect present. They wondered if she still had the slaver's head, too.

They knocked. Their hand reunited with the gold one if only for a moment.

Why did they feel anger already, annoyance that billowed, when she had not even yet opened the door? She had stopped begging them to return long ago. Stop writing, stopped calling out to them. So why did it feel as though she had made them come back? Why did they feel manipulated?

She opened the door, and for a moment they regarded each other like strangers. She had aged. So had they, they knew, knew the creases in their face had become deep and permanent, knew their muscles had gone wiry and long beneath their sun-worn skin. And yet it was still startling to see her, her black hair laced with white, the skin on her neck loose and puckering. But Xenobia was still beautiful.

She gasped.

"Kwizera." She did not speak their old name so much as she breathed it.

"No one calls me that anymore."

She stepped aside, and they wordlessly followed her into the home they had known so well for so long. Little of the house had changed, not the darkness, not the cramped ceiling. Not the tea she served them in a small ceramic cup. At least the cup was new.

They knew better than to unquestioningly drink the witch's tea.

"I wondered—I hoped, I mean—that you would ever—"

"I'm not here for us," the Pirate Supreme said. "I am here for the Sea."

"Ah." Xenobia sat down opposite them at the little wooden table, and her face would have been a blank wall if they did not know her better, did not see the flicker of fury in her eyes. "Were we so bad for each other, Kwizera? Truly?"

"You tried to kill me."

"Only the twice."

"The situation is the same. I've got just enough room in my heart for one tempestuous bitch, and it isn't you."

Xenobia smiled her shark's smile. "How is your lady love these days? I hear she's been very testy."

The Supreme pushed down their irritation. Xenobia knew, of course; they could tell, could see the smug victory in her eyes. The Sea had been alternating between furious and distant. With her mermaids disappearing at such a terrible pace, she couldn't help but blame the Supreme, whom she had charged with their protection. Their bond wore thinner and more strained each day. They wondered if she could even hear them when they called anymore. Or if she would listen. They had resolved to call upon her less, telling themself that it was best for the Sea, when really it was their own fear that the Sea would not respond.

"I need your help."

Xenobia fingered the string of pearls at her neck. "Of course you do."

"If I had any other ideas, literally anything, even the inkling of another plan, I wouldn't be here."

"Don't go whispering sweet nothings into my ear or I might get too full of myself."

"I need you to help me find the banished mermaid."

Xenobia's face fell, and they could see it in her eyes. Fear.

"No," she said simply.

"The Sea will not listen to me. And I . . . I suspect that the memory the banished mermaid holds is the essential one to defeat Nipran. For once and forever, Xenobia. Imagine it. A world without the Emperor's shadow looming over us all. A free world. You used to believe in such a thing."

"I also used to have tits up to my chin. I'm sure you remember them."

They pushed away the memory, which was crystalline and bothersome in its clarity.

"It's possible now. There are Resistance cells all over the Colonized World ready to fight at my word. We just need your—"

"Why would I help you? Help the Sea?" Xenobia interrupted. "She has taken everything from me. And you." She did not finish that. She didn't need to. *Chose her over me*, she could have said. *Left me*, she could have said. *Abandoned me. Betrayed me. For power. For the Sea.*

"This life here. It can't be safe. There are Imperials all over the place, and we both know what they'd do if they found out about your business. About what you are."

"Not everyone needs to be a revolutionary, you know. Always so grandiose. We don't have guns secreted away, but that doesn't mean we don't have power. It's quiet rebellion, so I'm not surprised you don't understand it. No one in Barilacha would ever betray me."

Unlike you, she didn't say, did not need to say. The words hung between them anyway.

"Your safety is precarious here, and you know it." They picked up the cup as though they intended to drink, but at the hungry look in Xenobia's eyes, they put it back on the table, their suspicions confirmed. Whatever was in that cup—poison or potion—couldn't be trusted. "As long as the Imperials have unfettered power, no one is safe, especially not you. And the Emperor's appetite for new subjects is ever growing. Just a week ago, his men committed slaughter on the Red Shore—"

"What do I care of that ill-begotten trading post?" Xenobia muttered, but the Supreme pushed on.

"And captured the near entirety of the Wariuta stores of kau. I can't imagine you need me to explain that it is objectively bad for the Emperor to have large stores of deadly explosives."

There was a pause, and the Supreme could feel Xenobia's mind churning. She didn't like the idea of the Emperor developing weapons of mass destruction any more than they did.

She stood, poured more tea from a different kettle. Whereas the tea in their first cup smelled of linden flowers and dittany, the new tea smelled of clove and something else savory, woody. She took a conspicuous sip of her tea before she placed the cups down for herself and the Supreme and then left the room for a moment.

When she returned, she carried the mirror that had always hung in her bedroom. It looked the worse for wear, the frame around it cracked. But the glass was still whole. She placed it on the table between them, and it reflected the mud ceiling back at them.

"I'm only doing this," she said tartly, "so that maybe one day I can poke my toe in the Sea without fear of her sending a tidal wave to murder me on the spot. I assume that's something you'll communicate to her?"

"Of course."

"I'm not doing this for you."

"Of course not."

"Because you're an asshole."

"Well—"

But before the Supreme could argue that point, Xenobia closed her eyes and began to murmur the words of a spell. Kwizera felt a twinge of nostalgia in their chest, for nights spent watching Xenobia hone her craft. They brushed it away.

The ceiling flickered and then faded from the mirror face, and the Supreme watched it intently as green water slowly became visible. Green water that rippled, then splashed violently. Xenobia kept murmuring, more urgently now. The green water was surrounded by red sand. The banished mermaid must have been in one of the many oases of the Red Shore.

But then they saw why the water was thusly disturbed.

The siren was hauled onto the sand by several men. Several men of the Imperial Guard. She thrashed and spat and tried to bite them, but they were unhindered by her fight. The dead guardsmen that floated facedown in the green water told the Supreme that the mermaid had not been caught easily. Each of them had been smart enough to plug their ears. They were immune to her best weapon. She was pulled onto the sand and then dropped.

As she tried to drag herself back to the water, the men of the Guard raised their pistols.

They could not hear the bullets, but they could see their effect. The life drained from her eyes.

Xenobia stopped murmuring. Only the mud ceiling remained in the mirror.

· CHAPTER 24 ·

Alfie

Keiko would tell him about it after. Alfie was not so foolish to pretend that he would have been brave enough to
watch it unbothered. He had been fortunate that he was
off reporting to his contact for the Pirate Supreme at the Crandon
docks when the entire palace was gathered into the great courtyard to bear witness to the executions.

No one was surprised that Lady Michiko was sentenced to
death. She had lain with a senator while married to the Emperor.
This had happened before in history, and—Alfie thought, given
the Imperial predilection for taking on many wives even well past
the time in the Emperor's life when he was likely able to perform
any husbandly duties—it would happen again and again and again.
And again. And just like every other time it had ever happened,
the wife was sentenced to death and the senator, too, for betrayal.
They were hanged in the courtyard before all who knew them,
a warning.

But this time, so was Princess Jingū.

They'd had to stand her on an empty shipping crate so that the noose could reach her neck.

It was not enough to simply punish the criminals. Their families must be punished, too. The senator had been a young man, not yet married or father to any children, his parents already gone. But their graves were exhumed and their remains thrown into the sea.

And still, the next day, the three bodies hung in the courtyard as all tried their best to pass them without seeing them, trying to ignore the smell of them as they went about business that invariably took them through the courtyard, which was at the center of the palace grounds.

Alfie secreted a bottle of sake from the kitchen. It was easily taken—there were so many bottles, and everyone was a little distracted. And he took it to Keiko, who had a rare day off from watching the Prince. A kindness from Priyanka, no doubt.

Alfie knocked on Keiko's door. There was no answer.

"Come on," Alfie said as kindly as he could. "I know you're in there. And I've got a present for you."

Silence.

"Keikooooo," he crooned.

He knocked again. "Beautiful Keiko, if you don't open this door, I'll have no choice but to serenade you from the hallway. I have been practicing my finest Iwei opera voice, and I think both you and everyone who happens to walk by will simply—"

There was a shuffling, scurrying sound, and Keiko opened the door. Her eyes were narrowed in annoyance, her hair disheveled, and Alfie could see that she'd been crying. A lot. He lifted the bottle of sake and two glasses with a smile, and, after a perfunctory glance down the hallway to ensure no one saw, she let him in.

The nurses got their own rooms, and Keiko kept hers very tidy. Her bed was made, and there were a few books stacked in a neat pile on the small tansu where she presumably kept the rest of her belongings. A tiny window let in the last bit of red light from the dwindling sunset. It was a sparse room and a small one, and Alfie's heart wrenched in envy at the idea of space of his own.

"Your room is as lovely as you are," he said instead.

Keiko gave him a withering look. "Honestly, Philip, stop. I'm not in the mood." She put a couple of flat cushions on the floor, and they both sat down, Alfie chastised, Keiko miserable. He poured them each a glass of sake and was a little shocked when Keiko downed hers in one gulp and held out the cup for more.

"I'm sorry," Alfie said as he poured. And he meant it. He was sorry that Keiko had seen a child she'd helped care for killed. He was sorry it made her so sad. He was sorry that it would probably happen again.

"She was a very sweet girl," Keiko said mournfully. A fresh tear rolled down her cheek, and she ignored it.

Alfie, thinking Keiko was too lost in thought to notice, rolled his eyes.

"What." It was less a question, more a demand. *Explain yourself.*

Alfie sighed. "Easy to be sweet, isn't it? When you have every-thing you want all the time."

"Except her life," Keiko spat.

Alfie wanted to help, but he couldn't help it, couldn't help himself. "One bad day," he said. "She never had to wonder when her next meal would come, never lived without adults to care for her. It's sad she's dead, but so are countless other kids that didn't get to live in the palace and died too early as well."

Keiko laughed. "You live here, too, you know."

"But I haven't always, have I?" Alfie could feel the heat on his neck. He wanted so badly to shut up, and he just couldn't seem to do it. The memories of his own childhood, not far from this palace, scrounging for food, begging for anyone to care. A set of cold, dead ears in his hands. Fawkes. "And anyway, I work here; that's different."

"Yes," Keiko took a solemn sip of her sake. "I suppose it is."

They sat together in silence. Alfie did his best to drink his wine slowly. He could feel the bad mood, the anger swelling inside him, and if he drank too much, he'd unleash it all on Keiko, which was the last thing he wanted. He was supposed to be comforting her, he knew that; why was he so bad at everything?

"They're not all cruel, you know," Keiko whispered. "There are good ones."

"I've heard that before." He could not keep the bitterness from his voice.

To his surprise, Keiko's hand found his and squeezed it firmly. "I don't know where you've been. I don't know what you've seen. But I'm sorry it hurt you."

Their eyes met, and Alfie was too taken aback by her kindness to notice that he was crying. Wordlessly, he leaned toward her. It could just be exhaustion, if she wanted. It could just be a gesture of friendship. She gave him a rueful smile, reached her hand up, and cupped his cheek. She did not kiss him. She also did not need to speak to the sorrow they shared. How strange it was to know just from this that she had lost someone she loved, too. How strange to have a friend.

Alfie knew the plan to have the Crown Prince assassinated was likely speeding along the docks, careening toward the time when Keiko's life could be imperiled. And Alfie recognized two things at once. The plan must go forward. And Keiko must not be hurt. He would have to get her out of harm's way, have to remove her from the bloody path that would find its way to the tyrant's heir.

And he'd have to do so without Keiko knowing it.

It was risky, Alfie knew, to return to the docks so soon. One trip out of his way was reasonable as a kitchen boy. Maybe he'd saved enough for a visit to the whores who prowled there. But two so close together would be harder to explain. Still.

Funny how, after all the years he had been on the *Dove*, the streets of Crandon were still indelible in his mind. He could find the fastest route at any time of day, knew how to dodge the constabulary patrols. So even if it was risky, he could do it; this was one thing he could do.

He'd failed to keep his baby sister safe.

He'd failed to keep himself together.

Failed to be strong. Failed to be brave.

But he wouldn't fail this time. And not just to keep Keiko safe—to keep all the nurses safe. Priyanka. The irritable one. That one he'd caught looking at his butt several times. She deserved clemency for her good taste at the very least. All of them. There was no reason for any of these women to suffer because they, too, lived under the boot of a tyrant.

The sun was high, and the air was thick with the dust and grime kicked up by the horse-drawn carriages. The tang of sea salt in the air found him, and he knew he was close.

His contact worked as a crabber and would not tell Alfie his name. But he was easily spotted—fully a head taller than everyone else who worked on the docks and tattooed from brow to toe with the blue ink so popular among men from the Cold World. His pink skin was mottled with scars.

He was taking a break, leaning against one of many stacks of shipping crates, smoking a pipe. The smoke curled above his bald head in great winding tendrils. All around them, seagulls called and the men of the docks went about their business, hauling crates and yelling to one another. Alfie ran to his contact.

"Hey!" He nearly tripped over his own stupid feet as he neared him. "Hey, man, I gotta tell you—"

But before he could finish, before his contact could even turn to meet his eyes, several men from the Imperial Guard emerged from behind the great shipment, their pistols drawn.

"Carden Moi," their leader barked. To Alfie's horror, his contact startled. "You're under arrest for collusion against the state."

Alfie immediately made to run away, but one of the guards called, "Hey!" And Alfie knew he was cooked. He turned slowly and gave an obsequious bow. Carden was being cuffed, none too gently, and hauled off, but the leader and one of his underlings remained.

"You'll be needing to come with us for questioning." The underling grabbed his arm.

"Wait, hold on, then!" Alfie said quickly, his mind racing. "I was just . . . he sold us bad crabs!"

The two men of the guard exchanged a dubious glance. "What's that?"

"That man—his crabs." Alfie's mouth couldn't quite catch up with his mind. "They were spoiled. Got them to the palace, and they were no good."

"The palace," said the leader.

He gave Alfie an appraising look. Alfie did his best to look respectable.

"Easy enough to check," the other said, and Alfie's stomach dropped. It was a lie, of course. The palace hadn't bought any crabs. He was hoping the invocation of the palace would have been enough to keep him safe.

No such luck.

They tossed him in the back of a barred carriage with his contact and headed off to the city jail.

"So," said Alfie, conversationally. "Your name's Carden?" After all their time in contact with each other, Alfie had never known his name. He'd called him Cranky McJerknuts in his thoughts, but that wasn't something he could say aloud.

The man whose name was apparently Carden glared at him with his unsettlingly blue eyes. He reminded Alfie a bit of Fawkes, so Alfie looked away. Carden was not Fawkes, and this was not the *Dove*. He needed to keep his head about him if he was to wriggle out of this.

"Don't tell them anything. Not a thing," Carden said as they slowed to the jail. "Remember, there are fates worse than death, and cowards always find 'em."

"Right." Alfie gulped.

Carden was dragged out of the carriage first, and then more men came for Alfie. He smiled at the men, trying to look innocent and compliant, but the men did not smile back.

"Right."

CHAPTER 25

Genesieve

She wondered what the Lady Ayer would do. She was smart, had taught Genevieve everything she knew about manipulation and guile. And yes, maybe she'd fought for the side Genevieve now wanted to see defeated, but that didn't mean everything she'd taught Genevieve was bunk. She'd been an excellent mentor.

And Rake had killed her. Shot her through the neck during that terrible battle aboard the *Dove*.

The Lady Ayer's murderer led her to a small stone house, where a ragtag group of people milled about. Pirates, no doubt. Too many piercings and tattoos and strangely flamboyant clothes to be anything else. Didn't even try to look respectable.

But then, Genevieve thought, maybe that was the point.

Inside, the house was small and dank and smelled faintly of mold. Rake bade Genevieve sit on a small wooden chair, and after she did, he cuffed her to it. Genevieve did not struggle against this and did not even argue. She did not need to like Rake to know that he could serve as an effective conduit to the person she so desperately needed to reach.

And even as deep dislike, possibly hate, bubbled in her chest, Genevieve stayed still, stayed obedient. She was a better person than he was, she reminded herself. She could be a better prisoner than he'd been as well.

Rake set about making a fire in the hearth.

"So why's he called the Fist?" she asked conversationally.

"She."

"Why's *she* called the Fist?"

"I suppose due to her predilection for knocking out Imperials," he said. He fanned the small flames he had made. "And those who lick their boots." He gave Genevieve a meaningful look.

"I didn't know," she said solemnly.

"Bullshit. You're from Quark." The fire was stable now, so he backed away from it, pulled up a stool, and sat down. He took his pistol from his boot and started polishing it with a greasy rag stowed in his other boot.

"The Resistance killed my mother, you know," said Genevieve quietly. She'd done her best to push the sight of the blood, the body that lay in the kitchen, down, down and away, but still it rose, in the quiet of the night and in the stillness of the morning.

Rake stopped polishing his pistol for a moment, and their eyes met. He looked so much like the men Genevieve had grown up with—wiry and weatherworn. She wondered what his childhood had been like in Quark. If he'd gone to a school like hers, known boys like Dai. How odd it was, to have started in the same place and then taken such wildly different paths.

"I'm sorry," he said. "It's no small thing to lose your mother."

And for a moment, they were just two orphans, alike if not identical in their loss.

But then he looked away, and the moment of empathy, of sameness, snapped out of existence. He squinted down the sight of his pistol and resumed polishing it.

They sat in silence for what felt like hours. Genevieve's hands went numb in her cuffs, her arms sore from being stuck in the same position. The fire crackled and danced, and Rake had to add more wood to keep it going. Whoever the Fist was, she was sure taking her time.

At long last, the door creaked open, and Genevieve heard the footfall of someone behind her. Trying to maintain what little dignity she could muster as a person handcuffed to a chair, she did not strain her neck to try to see the person.

"Rake." It was a woman's voice, low and rasping.

Rake stood, and—was he blushing? He straightened his coat and squared his shoulders. Genevieve suppressed a laugh. He had a crush on the Fist, that much was blazingly and immediately obvious.

"Got a prisoner for you here. Says she has some information that could help fight the Empire. Be warned, though; I've met her before. An Imperial bootlicker if I've ever met one. Was working beneath an Imperial operative, so I suspect she could easily be a spy."

"I'm not," said Genevieve.

"That's what a spy'd say, though, isn't it?" said Rake coolly.

Genevieve could hear the Fist take off her coat, throw it on the floor. "Either way, information is information," she said. "We can dispose of her after, if need be."

"Ah," Rake said. "Not so sure on that count. There's a Wariuta boy who seems to be watching out for her."

Genevieve wasn't convinced Koa would be all that mad if she got killed, but decided against mentioning that.

"Hmm." There was something familiar in the voice, but Genevieve could not place it. The vague Quark accent, maybe. "We'll cross that bridge when we get to it."

The Fist circled around, and when their eyes met, Genevieve felt the breath catch in her throat. They stared at each other, both too dumbfounded to speak for some time. Very distantly, Genevieve was aware that Rake was still talking, but for the life of her she had no idea what he said.

"Thistle," said her mother.

Her mother, who was not dead. Her mother, who was very much alive. There was a puckered bullet scar on her throat that explained the change in her voice, and she wore a patch over her left eye now, but that was her mother, that was Mrs. Vo, the same woman who'd taught her to peel carrots and braid her hair.

"Mother?"

"What?" Rake practically shouted. "You little snake, you *just* told me your mother'd been killed by the Resistance!"

Mrs. Vo laughed, and it was a bitter laugh. She made no effort to undo her daughter's binding but rather sat down on an empty chair as though Genevieve's presence had knocked the wind out of her. "Is that what she said? Well, not quite. Was the Imperial Guard that shot me that night, not the Resistance."

This time it was Genevieve's turn. "What?"

"Mm. Came in, guns already pointed. Could tell they felt bad, shooting a woman. Said 'Sorry, ma'am. Lady Ayer's orders.' Left me for dead. If it hadn't been for the Resistance, I would've died, but they came and found me. Nursed me back to health. And you"— she gave Genevieve a venomous look—"were already long gone."

"The plot thickens." Rake's voice was like ice.

"I . . . She told me—I saw your body! You were dead!"

"Thistle." Her mother motioned to herself, still quite alive.

"She said that the Resistance had shot you, said—"

"And you believed her."

The memory of that night came back in a rush. The Guard had gone in first, hadn't they? Then the shots had rung out. Dai had tried to say something, but a soldier had hit him. And as she sat, a new, clearer picture of the night came into focus. Of Imperial troops shooting without question. Just as she had so recently seen them do. And yet, unlike the Wariuta on the shore, somehow her mother had lived.

"Mother, I . . ." She could not find the words that would suitably explain the rush of realization that was still tearing through her. "I'm sorry."

And then she wept. For herself, and for her foolishness, and for the loss of the Lady Ayer all over again, and for the Wariuta who likely still lay on the shore because of her idiocy, her naivete, in believing in an Empire of justice that had never truly existed.

"Uncuff her," her mother said.

Rake did as he was told.

And then she was folded into her mother's arms again. And even if now they were laced with muscle, even if the voice that soothed her was damaged and strange in her ears, she was in her mother's arms once more.

And so she wept.

The Sea

Has the Pirate Supreme called for her? She does not know. She cannot hear them anymore. She can hardly hear her own daughters, their voices overlapping and minute as the echo of waves in a seashell.

There: A daughter has found a cool bed of sand in the mangrove lagoons of Tustwe. But she is not calling to her mother; she is simply lolling, her body languid and her eyes closed. At least she is safe.

And here: Another of her children fights against an abandoned net that she has become accidentally entangled within. The Sea is distracted by her panic but cannot attend to her just now. She will survive.

But where? So many of her daughters are gone, gone, gone. Once she knew them each by name, knew their hearts, held their memories close. But when she reaches for them, there is only the nothingness of loss, the infinite void that grief has left her.

Over there: Florian and Evelyn move together. She does her best to guide them, but she is so scattered now, so confused that often she is not sure that her own guidance is true anymore. She is glad there are two of them, glad they can depend on each other if not on her, though it rankles her not to be dependable to her children. What is she, if not a mother?

If she could just reach the Pirate Supreme.

Why have they abandoned her in her time of gravest need?

So arrogant, humanity. To kill her daughters as if she did not encircle their world, as if their food and their lives and their safety did not depend upon her whims and her serenity.

In her fury and her frustration, she raises a mighty hand and lets it fall on a small fishing ship off the coast of a nation whose name she can no longer recall. Who are these men to her? No one. She fills their lungs and lets her grip wind around their little kicking legs until they are still. As gone as her memories.

In a moment, she will forget them.

CHAPTER 26

Genevieve

When Genevieve woke the next morning, her body stiff and creaking from the thin mattress she had slept on, she was only a little surprised to find that, in her sleep, her hand had been cuffed to the bed frame.

The cuff clanked against the wooden frame as she sat up and rubbed her puffy eyes with her spare hand. They were sore from crying, from exhaustion that felt like no amount of sleep could cure.

"You're up," said Rake, which. Yes, clearly. "Your mother had some business to attend to. She'll be back shortly."

"Business?"

"None of yours."

Genevieve suppressed the desire to groan. He may have been a double agent under the Nameless Captain, may have been a Resistance fighter, may have kicked the ever-living crap out of her and murdered her mentor, but he was still corny.

"Was it your decision or hers to cuff me?" She tried to make her voice sound impassive, blandly curious.

"Hers," Rake replied with obvious amusement.

It stung, but Genevieve kept her face still. "There anything to eat?" Her stomach ached with hunger.

"Later."

"So. Just you and me, then?"

"And you'll remember how that went last time. So no funny stuff."

"To be fair, last time it was you who did the funny stuff."

Rake made a sound between a laugh and a growl. "I can't believe you're her daughter."

"Make you feel at all guilty for kicking me in the head?"

"No."

The door opened then, and there stood the most improbable trio. Her mother, who was wearing a highly suspicious-looking cowl and hood. And Koa, with his enormous hyena by his side chittering a high giggle. Koa looked exhausted, his face drawn. She'd nearly forgotten about him in all the shock of the previous night. But there they both were, two figures from such different times in her life.

It was a moment later that Genevieve realized her mother had a vise-like grip on Koa's enormous arm.

"Do you know this one?" she asked in her new, rasping voice.

"Koa," said Genevieve quickly. He'd noticed the cuff on her hand and looked a bit alarmed. "I'm OK," she added in Wariuta.

"You speak their tongue?" her mother asked.

Genevieve nodded. Her mother let go of Koa's arm and showed him to a seat. He looked so out of place perched on a small wooden stool, the hyena sitting by his side. He regarded Rake dubiously.

"Always a prisoner," Koa said, more to himself than to anyone else. "Are you really OK?"

"I'm fine. Koa, this is my mother."

Koa looked at Mrs. Vo with such clear surprise on his face that her mother laughed. "I see he's just as surprised as you were."

"Not quite." She turned back to Koa. "Are the children safe?"

"With some carers. Found a woman with milk for Kalei."

"What's he saying?" her mother asked.

"That he's found care for the children orphaned by the Imperial attack." And the horror of what she had seen, only two days ago now, hit her anew. She swallowed it down. "Yunka was decimated."

"Must want revenge," said Mrs. Vo. "Must want to make the Imperials pay, no? Ask him that."

Genevieve did, but Koa shook his head. "No more blood," he said.

When Genevieve translated this to her mother, she scoffed. "Blood's the only language they speak, boy. And they didn't just kill everyone; we hear they also took at least one captive, maybe more. A warrior girl to show the Emperor."

Genevieve's heart set to racing. "With one hand?" she asked her mother, hoping against hope.

Mrs. Vo's eyes narrowed at her. "How did you know that?"

"They have Kaia," she told Koa, and Koa's whole body reacted, suddenly taut. He looked from Mrs. Vo to Genevieve desperately.

"Tell her to let her go!" he demanded.

"No, not my mother. The Imperials."

"I have to get her."

"Does that girl mean something to him?" Rake asked.

"His sister." Genevieve did not like Kaia, exactly, but the idea that there were any survivors from that massacre was so heartening, so wonderful, she could barely contain the bubbling hope inside her.

"Big boy like him could be useful," said Rake. "Warrior, that's why he's got the animal."

"Hmm. Tell him they're taking his sister to the Imperial Palace. In Crandon."

Genevieve did.

"I have to go get her," Koa said. "But . . . the children. I have to protect what's left of Yunka. What little is left."

He cradled his face in his hands. He looked much older than he had even a few days earlier, his face and body carrying the weight of his grief and his burden. Genevieve was hit with the desire to hug him, but of course she could not.

"He's conflicted because he wants to guard the children and also rescue his sister," Genevieve translated.

"I see." Her mother bent and whispered into Rake's ear then, and he nodded, whispered back. Resentment that somehow her mother trusted this pirate over her rankled Genevieve, until she was reminded, forcibly, by the bullet scar in her mother's neck, that she had little reason to trust her own daughter.

Her mother did not look at her but rather at Koa as she spoke. "Tell him we're going to Crandon. And that he can come, and that we will help him find his sister. If he's willing to fight."

Genevieve translated this, and she could see the visceral, physical pain the idea of more bloodshed cost Koa. He regarded his hands sadly.

"I'll have to get the children sorted first. I can find them temporary care, at least," he said, more to himself than to Genevieve. "But then I'll go. For Kaia."

"He says he'll go," said Genevieve. "If I come, too."

Rake and her mother's eyes met. "Why should we trust you?" Mrs. Vo asked.

"I . . ." She looked down at the cuff on her wrist, the cuff she'd earned. "I know I haven't given you a reason to trust me."

"You worked for one of the Emperor's worst operatives," Rake added for good measure.

"Abandoned your own mother for her," said Mrs. Vo.

"But I." Her mind spun. She knew if she simply told them the truth, that she had changed, that she had seen what the Empire was now, had seen that it was all lies, she would sound like a liar. Like a spy. "If I step out of line, I swear I will put up no fight if I'm to be killed."

"We could kill you now," Rake muttered. "Save ourselves the trouble."

But her mother put up a hand to silence him, and he resumed glowering.

"And I swear if you do," her mother said slowly, meaningfully, "I'll be the one to kill you."

• CHAPTER 27 •

Tomas

Commander Callum led the procession through Crandon to the palace on the back of a great gray horse. And even if Inouye was relegated to the back, on foot, he could still appreciate the looks of awe that greeted the men as they paraded through the city. Several yards ahead of him, the girl was carried in a prisoner's barred carriage, and the people gawked at her.

If the intention of the procession was to humble her, it was not working. She held her head high and met the eyes of those who stared. More than a few looked away, cheeks red with shame. Having been the recipient of more than a few blistering glares over the voyage, Inouye understood entirely.

Inouye had never been inside the palace before, but he'd seen it from the outside, all gleaming gilded details and great tall walls. The grounds, he was thrilled to see, were beautiful, with koi ponds and bridges and trees and flowers in nearly every direction he looked. A great white peacock waddled just beyond a copse of cherry trees. He had never been so proud to be Imperial. Truly,

Callum's replica in the Floating Islands had been a farce by comparison. All of the architecture, none of the grandeur. There was simply no imitating royalty.

When they reached the throne room, it took all of Inouye's self-control not to crane his neck to take in the many details of the walls, the ceiling, and the painted columns. Everywhere, painted and sculpted Imperial lions looked down from plinths and alcoves. It had a slightly claustrophobic effect—the walls felt close against them even in the vastness of the room.

The entirety of the palace had been gathered to watch Callum's reception. Senators and maids, lords and guards, stood lined against the length of the room. The Emperor's many wives and many children all sat on their knees at the base of a great dais, their faces and bodies completely still. And on the dais, beneath a stately, ornate octagonal pergola, enshrouded with heavy black curtains save for the space just in front of him, the Emperor sat on his golden throne, flanked by large jade lions.

It was an honor, of course, to even look upon the Emperor. And though Inouye was relegated to the back of the procession, he could still make him out clearly. He wore red robes embroidered with black and gold and green threads. He was old, Inouye realized. His head looked slightly bowed beneath the weight of his enormous jeweled crown. His small pale hands were folded on his lap.

Callum stayed on his horse even into the throne room as his many men marched in after him, laden with the goods of his exploits. The cases of kau. Strange fruits from the Floating Islands. Vials and vials of mermaids' blood. And of course the girl, who had been removed from the cage and was flanked by four men, who held her at sword point.

"Thanks to the Emperor," Callum boomed.

"Thanks to the Emperor," Inouye and the rest of the room shouted back.

"In your grace and in your name, I have gone to the farthest reaches of the Known World, and thus your wealth grows," Callum said. He enumerated the many treasures as his men hustled forward to display them to the Emperor, who showed little interest in any.

But then the girl was presented, marched to the front of the procession by her guards. Many of the wives and ladies gasped at her bare feet and bare muscled legs. One senator ignored all decorum and pointed at her missing forearm.

"And this creature," Callum said, his voice thick with disgust, "is a savage warrioress from the Red Shore. When we, thanks to you, defended our ships against her attack, she managed to kill four of our men before she was subdued."

More gasps, and murmuring now. Callum was making his case for sending more men to take the Red Shore entirely, and all knew it.

"The vile chieftainesses of the Red Shore castrate their males to subdue them. They leave their baby boys in the sun to die, either by exposure or eaten by the mad, frothing hyenas they keep at their sides. And then they teach their females, like this one"—he motioned to the girl, who stared, seemingly unafraid, up at the Emperor—"with one single purpose. Murder. Trained since birth to kill, bloodthirsty and cruel, the females of the Red Shore practice in dark magic and bloody sacrifices."

Callum looked around the room meaningfully. Every breath was held in anticipation of what he would say next.

"And so, if in your wisdom and your beneficence you will it, I will lead your men to destroy the scourge of their savagery. I will bring order and justice and civilization to the Red Shore." He bowed his head in practiced deference, somewhat dampened by his refusal to get off his damn horse. "Thanks to the Emperor."

"Thanks to the Emperor," the room echoed.

When the Emperor finally spoke, his voice was reedy, thin. "She will make a lovely addition to my menagerie," he said.

This was not an answer to Callum's call to arms. Callum seemed a little taken aback. His horse shifted, likely uneasy to be so surrounded by human bodies, and the sounds of the hooves on the great marble floor were so loud against the hush of the room that they shook the room like gunshots.

But the Emperor did not say anything more. And so after a few minutes of strained and confused silence, Callum saluted him, turned his horse around, and led the procession back out of the throne room and into the palace grounds.

Inouye tried not to think of the bitterness and the bile he could taste in his throat. All their work, all their fighting, all the blood— and the Emperor didn't even care.

Inouye could tell he was still in bad standing with Callum when, as soon as the demonstration was over, he was ordered to take the girl to the menagerie rather than joining the feast with all the others.

"Will you need extra men?" Commander Callum had asked. This was a barb, of course, an insult. Some of the other men chuckled.

"No, sir," said Inouye. He was an Imperial soldier, after all. His pride rankled at the very notion that she could get the better of him. Without a piss pot to throw, anyway.

She'd be kept in the menagerie, along with the other strange and wonderful creatures from abroad. At least there would be that, Inouye reflected, a visit to see, if only briefly, the jaguar and the oryx and the great white bear.

"There's no unicorn," Windsor said as he looked about the many gilded cages.

"Can you try and focus?" Inouye snapped. He couldn't believe he'd been paired with this buffoon. Windsor shrugged. The evening was waning, and Inouye hoped they could complete their task with enough time to join the other men for dinner.

The girl was proving to be much more docile now than she had been with a piss pot in her hands, her eyes downcast. This would be easy work.

Windsor picked his nose absently. "Don't think she'll run for it here, do you?"

Inouye looked around. The palace gates were tall, unscalable. There were guards posted all around them. They were mere feet away from the golden cage in the menagerie she would call home. In the cage next to hers, a tiger prowled. Where would she go?

"Probably. Grab her as soon as I open the cage, hear me?"

Windsor nodded, but not as attentively as Inouye would have liked.

"Windsor," he admonished.

Windsor flicked whatever he'd found in his nostril into the night.

The girl watched all this, her eyes darting between the men. Inouye felt a twinge of unease but then reminded himself she was bound. She had no weapon. There was only one of her. They were in palace grounds. They were Imperial men. They would not be bested by some wild and savage girl who was born in a hut.

He opened the door.

The girl burst over the threshold, and she was more blur than body. In the instant that Inouye registered she was moving, she'd kicked Windsor in the groin, and he was down, rolling on the ground, and the girl was moving again, and too late, Inouye put up his hands to guard his face, but she had already rammed him with her shoulder, knocking the wind from his lungs and possibly breaking one of his ribs. He tried to call out, but his voice would not come to him, and Windsor, useless Windsor, just cradled his balls and whimpered.

Inouye staggered to his feet.

As she ran, the girl wriggled from her bindings, and Inouye knew with a sinking feeling that she would be free of them in moments, that they had not tied her tight enough, that she'd put up enough of a fight as she was bound that she had effectively rendered the ropes useless. That he was about to lose another prisoner. Another girl.

"Guards!" he called, but his voice was just a rasp. And anyway, they'd mostly be in the courtyard, wouldn't they? For Callum's reception. He needed his breath, and so he shut up and ran as hard as he could.

He had not run so fast in his whole life, and it was no easy feat in the heavy leather boots he wore. They were like stones on his feet he had to drag along as the girl sprinted ahead of him. He'd never been jealous of someone with bare feet before in his life.

It was only because he was so much taller that he was able to catch up to her, just shy of the outer palace walls. He leapt for her as she ran, and with a stroke of luck caught one of her feet. They both landed hard, and then the true fight began. Despite his size advantage, he could not seem to keep a hold of her, could not seem to pin her down.

When he landed one good punch across her jaw, he thought he had her. But she blinked past the pain and used his momentary distraction to punch him back, in the throat. She would have

183

wiggled away then, but he managed to throw his body on top of hers and use his weight, if not his hand-to-hand combat skills, to stop her.

As they wrestled, his hands trying to find purchase, her thrashing wildly but silently, the shame of his continued failure began to eat at Inouye's resolve. He was not the Imperial man he'd been promised his whole life he would be. All his life he'd been told he was strong because of who he was, and yet here he was. Losing to a girl.

It had all been a lie.

As if she could hear his thoughts, the girl wrapped one leg around Inouye's neck, her thigh and her calf pressing on his windpipe. He clawed at the bare skin of her leg but could not loosen her grip. She bore down harder.

"Sh," she crooned as she squeezed. "Tawmus, shh."

When the darkness started to contract around him, Inouye knew at least one thing he'd been told was not a lie. He saw death then, just as his father promised him he would.

He reached for death.

And death reached back.

CHAPTER 28

The Pirate Supreme

Even when they were young and in love and unable to keep from touching each other, Kwizera had known Xenobia was not necessarily trustworthy. That she would see to her own interests first. It was something they had loved about her, and a source of respect—she was a survivor, and always would be.

But it felt different now. It was one thing to survive at all costs as a young person, so new in the world. A different thing altogether to do it now. Selfish.

"I wish it weren't true, either," Xenobia said.

Their eyes met, and they could see that she had divined their thoughts.

"It's your fault she was there," they said. They knew they were being cruel just to exorcise their own anger, but that did not stop them. "If you hadn't—"

"I know." Xenobia's voice was firm. It was many years ago when Xenobia had promised the mermaid a spell to unite her with her human lover—and just as many since the Sea had punished them both for the betrayal, banishing the mermaid and cursing Xenobia with a loveless life. "But there's nothing I can do about that now, is there." This was not a question. It was a plea for clemency.

The Supreme stood, needing to move, needing to control something, even if it was just their own body. They had been so sure that the banished mermaid was the key. That she held the memory of the legendary creatures who lurked in the Sea's depths, who could be called upon for aid. But without the confirmation of her memory, that was just a legend. And what good could stories do them now?

Xenobia's eyes were downcast. "Someday maybe you will see that I was just trying to give that mermaid what we had."

She did not say the word *love*, but it hung between them anyway.

"Today is not that day." The Supreme did not want to talk of love with Xenobia, didn't want to be reminded of what they had been. They wanted to save the Sea, to free her from the grip of the Emperor. And with the death of the banished mermaid, it felt as though there was little hope left for that.

"I trained a new witch, you know," Xenobia said. "And my understanding is that she has joined your great love as a new daughter."

The Supreme's mind whirred. Only two people had joined the Sea recently, and they had seen them go with their own eyes. If Xenobia had a connection to one of them . . . "Florian?"

"That was one of his names," said Xenobia. "Perhaps he can be of some assistance?"

"How did you know—"

"I have my ways." And when it was clear that this was not enough to mollify the Supreme: "Our connection has been lost. But I could feel him submerge."

"Can you call to him?" Mermaids had a direct line of

communication with the Sea, a line that had all but been severed for the Supreme. If they could just reach her, if they could just beg her for help.

"Possibly."

They did not want to ask for help, but already the Emperor's men had taken the Red Shore. Already his ships prowled the waters near Tustwe, growing ever more bold. Tustwe had not yet been colonized, but it was the lone holdout among nations in the Known World. And it was only a matter of time before those many ships found the Forbidden Isles.

They were desperate for any edge. They did not need to say this aloud; the witch could see it in their face.

"They're the ones, I think," said Xenobia. "From the song. True love's might, and all that." She did not say what they each remembered.

That there had been a time when they both believed that song was about Kwizera and Xenobia.

"I think so, too," said the Supreme, to themself mostly, remembering what Florian's brother had told them—that the girl had died. That she had been, apparently, reborn as a mermaid. And though they could smell the taint of mermaid's blood on his breath, they knew he had told the truth. This once, Xenobia was not lying.

"We have to call to him," said the Supreme. "You have to."

"I can try," says Xenobia. "For a price."

"Always a price with you."

"I'll do whatever is needed, whatever you ask of me. For you. For the Sea. But when we are done, you must step down as her steward. You must return to Tustwe, with me. We go home."

If we survive, the Supreme thought.

If we win.

We can't win. But we have to try.

Heartened that the tea was not poisoned—Xenobia had had plenty now to be sure—Kwizera took a sip. The last place they wanted to go was Tustwe. Tustwe had stopped being home years ago, even before Xenobia stopped being home. Word had reached them that their father had died, and their brother, too. There was nothing left for them there. They were no one in Tustwe. They were the Pirate Supreme on the Sea.

But without the banished mermaid's help, they needed Xenobia. Memories of Xenobia, her arms wrapped around them, rose unbidden in the Supreme's mind. They tried and failed to push them back down. They had made their choice years ago— between Xenobia and the Sea, the Pirate Supreme had chosen the Sea. They had chosen power. But power did not make one feel safe. When was the last time they had felt at home, anywhere? Maybe it was time. Maybe.

"Come with me to the Forbidden Isles. We're convening Resistance leaders there."

"And our deal?"

"I'll honor it."

Xenobia pulled a small shining dagger from her cleavage and cut a jagged line in her palm. She held the dagger out for the Supreme, who took it with some trepidation. A blood bond. A powerful magic. No going back now. They would have to trust Xenobia.

They cut their hand.

・ CHAPTER 29 ・

Alfie

Alfie was tossed in a holding cell along with a very emaciated elderly man who looked just a little too excited to have some company. He made a great show of having Alfie sit, as though he were inviting him into his house for dinner, not having him crouch on a boulder in the dark.

"Haven't had a cellmate in years!" croaked the man. His voice was like paper on paper, it was so strained and quiet. "Was starting to think they forgot about me."

The smell was overpowering. As his eyes got used to the dank, Alfie realized the boulder was next to the corner the man had clearly been using as a designated toilet area.

"They . . . they feed you, though, right?"

"When they remember, I suppose." The man scratched his scraggly white beard. Even in the dim light of the jail, Alfie could see that he had a number of sores along his neck and chest. "What're you in for?"

"Wrong place wrong time," Alfie said. He wasn't sure what could be overheard by the guards, and he wasn't keen to tip his hand to a stranger, nice though he seemed. "Was just trying to contact our crab vendor, let him know that he'd sold us some bad goods," he added for good measure. It didn't hurt to practice your lies. "Had no idea he was wound up in some mess."

"Whoring?" the man asked, and Alfie startled.

"What?"

"Was he into whoring?"

"I . . . I don't think so."

"I was."

"Oh."

"Yes," said the man seriously. "Was damn good at it, too. Half the Guard came to me in my time. Wouldn't know it now, but I was a real looker. And a real wizard with—"

"That's nice," interrupted Alfie. He didn't really want to know about the man's sexual exploits of yore. "Seems unfair to lock you up just for being good at your job."

"Oh, that's not why I'm in here."

"What are you in here for, then?"

"Murder."

"Did you do it?"

"Oh, yes."

Alfie laughed; he couldn't help it. "OK."

Alfie tried to conquer his unease. Being locked in a cell with a man who was clearly only sporadically fed and mostly left to rot and forced to defecate in a corner was not, he thought, a great way to get in the right headspace for what promised to be a brutal interrogation with the Imperial Guard. One wrong answer and he'd be stuck in this jail forever, like this poor old man. Poor old murderer. Whatever, no one deserved such a fate. He knew the constabulary were bastards, but their cruelty seemed to know no end. Fear and anger pricked in his chest and his eyes, and he wondered if he was crying because he was caught or because he was furious or if it even mattered which.

"I'm sorry they did this to you," Alfie said. He didn't know what else to say.

"There, there," said the man. He squeezed Alfie's hand. "You'll be OK. Chin up."

Alfie squeezed the man's hand back, oddly bolstered. "Thanks," he said. "I'm Alfie. What's your name?"

"My name?" The man seemed to be shocked by the question, and it was several moments before he answered. "Jung Hoon."

"If I get out of here," Alfie said, "I'll try to get you out, too, Jung Hoon."

"OK." Jung Hoon laughed, a dry-leaf sound. "Sure thing, Alfie. I won't hold my breath, though." And, still chuckling, he eased himself onto a pile of rags that he was clearly using as a bed. In the hours that passed, Alfie tried to sleep but found that he couldn't. If he tipped off the Guard, he was dead. If he didn't cooperate with them, he was dead. No matter how he sliced it, he couldn't imagine an outcome that didn't leave him dead.

He thought of Flora, stepping into the Sea. He wondered if she ever thought of him. He hoped not. She had done enough worrying over him for a lifetime. At least he got to see her happy before he died. That was something. Maybe that was everything.

Jung Hoon was snoring softly when a guardsman came down to their cell and unlocked it. "Philip Boucher?"

Alfie sprang to his feet as Jung Hoon stirred awake.

"That's me."

"You're free to go."

"What?"

"Do you want to stay here?" the guard asked, impatient.

"No, I—I'm not going to be interrogated?"

"Nope, palace vouched for your story."

"'Course." Alfie's mind raced. He'd been lying, so who had covered for him? Who had risked their neck? He prayed it wasn't Keiko. "'Course they did."

"Told you you'd be just fine," said Jung Hoon warmly.

Alfie smiled at him in the darkness. "Thanks, man," he said. "I—"

"You wanna leave or not?" the guard interrupted, and Alfie stepped to.

"Chin up," Jung Hoon called after him.

"Philip Boucher," said his rescuer. Alfie knew that voice, but it didn't make any sense; why would that voice be here? Perhaps he'd lost his sanity in the darkness along with his hope.

"Senator Tsujima?" he asked the light. His eyes had not adjusted, and he felt as though he were losing his senses.

"A simple misunderstanding," xe said, xyr voice apologetic. "The Guard has to be so vigilant these days. But I was able to confirm that you'd gotten me some crab from that terrible man." Alfie's eyes started to make sense of the senator, who was smiling at him with a crocodile's concern. "You know how the Guard is. Ever zealous, but perhaps a little hasty at the price of accuracy. Thanks to the Emperor, I heard the news and could clear it up."

Alfie didn't move. It seemed a trick, a prank, but one with terrible consequences should he fall for it. He imagined stepping out of the constabulary only to be bludgeoned to death for doing so.

"Come on, then," Senator Tsujima said. Xe stepped into the light of the Crandon street and reached out a manicured hand to Alfie. Xyr nails were painted with a green lacquer and inlaid with gold details. Alfie was mesmerized by them as they glinted in the torchlight. "Unless you'd rather stay here?"

"No," he croaked. His body ached from lying on the cold stone, so standing was painful. But he shook life into his feet, happy to take them as far from that cell as he could go.

"I should think not," the senator said. Xe proffered xyr arm to Alfie, and xe led the way back toward the palace.

"Go along then, Jiro," Senator Tsujima said, waving xyr hand dismissively toward a waiting servant. "Ready my carriage, won't you? It'll give me a moment to check in with poor, beleaguered Philip here."

The servant bowed and was off. Soon just Tsujima and Alfie stood together Once xe was sure they were alone, the smile fell from xyr face like a mask.

"What is your real name, Philip?" xe asked. "You don't sound like someone from Iwei; surely that's a fake name. You sound like you grew up here. In Sty's End, if I were to be precise, I can hear it. From the look of you"—xe pinched Alfie's cheek, hard—"I'd guess you grew up with not enough to eat, but that you've gained weight, a lot of it, and recently. So who are you?"

"I—"

"I mean, I know you're a spy for the Pirate Supreme. But curiosity bedevils me—my most favorite vice, you know. I do love to gossip." Xe smiled beatifically, and there was a glint of cruel, sharp teeth. "What is your name?"

"Alfie," he blurted. He could feel his cheeks burning. He'd been in the palace for only a few months, and he was already blowing his cover; if that wasn't proof he was a shit spy, he didn't know what was.

"See? What'd I say? I know a Sty's End boy when I see one. I grew up there myself, you know. Don't let anyone tell you that your birth is your destiny." Xe examined Alfie's face closely. "You don't look like a pirate, Alfie." Xe said his name with a dagger's sharpness.

"I wasn't a good one," he said truthfully. A bad brother, a terrible pirate, a worse spy.

Senator Tsujima cackled. "A pirate turned spy," xe said with an air of being impressed. "I'd have you make one more turn, young Alfie. As recompense for your freedom."

The senator had a reputation for manipulation, and Alfie was starting to see why. Xe did not need to say that if Alfie did not grant xem this request xe would see him thrown right back in the cell from whence he'd come. That was obvious. And so Alfie gulped and nodded, already dreading whatever task he was about to be dealt.

"You were already privy, I think, to a plan to assassinate the Crown Prince?" Tsujima whispered. Xe did not wait for a response. "I would see that done, if I had my druthers, and expediently."

Alfie blinked, stunned. But before he could answer, both he and Tsujima startled. In the distance, the sounds of cannons firing could be heard.

"Now, don't disappoint me. Bad things happen to boys from Sty's End who disappoint me," Tsujima hissed. And xe turned on xyr heel and stepped into the ornate carriage that awaited xem.

CHAPTER 30

Genevieve

After all the time the Lady Ayer had spent searching for clues as to the whereabouts of the Forbidden Isles, it seemed mad that she, Genevieve, was headed there now. The voyage was a short one, and mostly she was not allowed abovedeck—her mother did not trust her enough to let her see which direction they sailed, and it didn't escape Genevieve that she'd clearly been assigned a rotating schedule of guards.

Koa, who had never been on a ship before, was magnificently seasick. Pallid and sweating, he lingered abovedeck out of necessity, so that he could vomit overboard rather than in his berth. This meant Genevieve was usually alone. Which was fine. She had been mostly alone since she'd started informing for the Lady Ayer. She was used to it now.

Still, she could have done without the constant dirty looks from the various pirates, especially Rake. He seemed to yearn for another chance to kick her in the head. And, if she was honest about it, she wouldn't have minded a chance to repay the favor.

It was only week later when they reached the small cluster of islands where the Pirate Supreme held court.

Whatever she'd been expecting of the Forbidden Isles, it wasn't this. They were neither forbidding nor grand. Just very small islands clustered together, with a number of mooring points for a great variety of ships. The one thing that made them unusual was that each island seemed to be entirely unique. The largest was dense with fragrant green trees Genevieve could smell even as they sailed past it. One of the smaller ones seemed to be entirely made of starkly black rock that jutted from the clear blue water. At first she thought a trick of the light made it appear as though the rocks were moving, but as they neared it, she saw a great number of enormous black lizards perched all over the rocks, heads bobbing as they sunbathed. Some of the lizards bobbed in the water that lapped against the rocks.

"Iguanas," said her mother. She had crept up on Genevieve as they sailed on toward an island composed almost entirely of sheer cliff faces. "Taste like chicken."

Genevieve scowled. "Doubtful."

"Mm. There are enormous tortoises that live here, too. Bigger than the dogs in Gia Dinh. They say they live for hundreds of years."

"That can't be true."

"I believe it. Their meat is very tough."

"Is there anything on these islands you haven't eaten?"

"Pirates."

Genevieve smiled. "I am sorry, you know. For." She did not know what she should apologize for first, and the breadth of possibility winded her.

"I believe that," her mother said.

"But you don't believe I've changed my mind."

"Did the Lady Ayer give you that name? Genevieve?"

Genevieve looked back at the water. She could see a school of very large fish passing beneath them. Everything around these islands was so alive, teeming. How odd it was, to consider all these lives being lived with no concept of empires or operatives or betrayals.

Her mother put her hand on Genevieve's back, and the warmth of her touch spread through her whole body.

"I'll always love you. But you're not my Thistle anymore, are you?"

Genevieve met her mother's eyes, which were soft and sad.

"No," she said. "I suppose I'm not."

Several feet away from them, Koa sprinted to the side of the ship and vomited spectacularly over the rail. A few of the pirates chuckled, and Rake brought him a bottle of something clear that Genevieve hoped was water but could just as easily have been rum.

"Everything's different now," said Genevieve. The world felt like an ever-shifting place beneath her feet, and she could not seem to catch her balance.

"Yes," said the Fist.

The pirates had brought down the sails and were tying the ship to one of the few vacant moorings. They had reached the Pirate Supreme's stronghold, which was built into the side of the island, mostly hidden from sight. It was a smaller island than some of the others, but Genevieve could see why it had been chosen as the stronghold almost at once. The natural rock formations that defined it yielded innumerable caves and crevices. Exploring it would be difficult. One would need to know where to go upon approach.

But there, moored just before the island, was the ship that had changed Genevieve's life. That had seen her mentor dead and her shipwrecked on a distant shore.

The *Leviathan*. Her black flags with the white mermaid rippled in the light wind.

A prickle of hatred, but Genevieve pressed it down. She could still hear its cannons booming in her ears, could still see the great tentacles of the sea bashing men into the cold depths, never to rise again. The Empire was a lie, Genevieve could see that now; the Emperor had to be stopped. But those many, many men. They didn't all deserve to die—they had believed, just as she had, in a lie they'd been told their whole lives. In order and justice.

But then, did that excuse matter? When the lies spilled so much blood? She thought of the dead on the Red Shore. Of the children orphaned by the Nipran. Surely those men who had fired upon those women, those men who had sacked Puno, had believed the lie, too.

Genevieve didn't know what to think anymore. And the uncertainty of it churned in her stomach.

She did not speak of any of this, but she felt her mother's hand fall off her. And before she could say more to her, she saw the Fist walk away, barking questions and orders to the pirates with whom Genevieve had fought. Rake joined her, and the two shared quiet words that Genevieve could not hear, their heads tilted together.

"I don't know how you people stand it," Koa wheezed. He sat on the deck, looking exhausted, with his legs spread, as if he'd just run a very long way, very fast. His hyena nuzzled against him, offering his own kind of smelly comfort.

Genevieve sat down next to him. "I promise, you'll get used to it."

"I never know when to believe you." He petted his beast, who lolled onto his back so that Koa could scratch his belly.

Genevieve winced a smile. "No one does these days." They sat together for a moment in silence. "I never meant you or any of your people any harm. I hope you know that."

"Well." He looked at his fingernails. "What you meant doesn't really matter, does it? My people are dead."

"Not Kaia."

"No." And he smiled, a ghost of the big smile he used to have. "Not Kaia."

Genevieve had been to the Imperial throne room, and the Pirate Supreme's was like a storage closet in comparison. Treasure stacked against the walls like it didn't matter, wasn't precious. A wooden chair at the head of the room, not a proper throne, as if the Pirate Supreme themself wasn't that important. It was all much less reverent than she had been expecting.

Maybe, she realized, that was the point.

She had spent so long looking for them with the Lady Ayer, this supposed villain. And here they were. Whatever she had been expecting, this wasn't it. Maybe she had expected someone bigger. Or an Imperial. But there they were, small boned and Black and grinning as if everything was a joke only they were in on.

The Supreme was sitting on their chair, one leg hanging over an armrest. Less regal, more drunkard in posture. They were alone save for a tall, ample-bodied Black woman with her salt-and-pepper hair stacked high and messy on her head. She stood next to the Supreme, looking haughty. Rake led the Fist, Koa, and Genevieve to them, and their footsteps echoed against the plain stone walls.

"I know them," Koa said, and his voice was happy for once.

Genevieve did not need to wait for confirmation. Tupac lolloped forward, tackled the Supreme, and licked their face as they laughed.

"The Supreme comes to Yunka to trade now and again. Always has the best stories!" Koa waved. The Supreme grinned, standing and brushing themself off, scratching Tupac behind his pointed ears. "Had no idea they were so important."

"The name didn't tip you off?"

"People call themselves all kinds of things," Koa said with a shrug. "I don't verify; I just call them what they call themselves."

The Supreme stood and, in flawless Wariuta, addressed Koa with their arms outstretched. "My friend! I can't tell you how happy I am to see you." They wrapped Koa in a tight hug, and the two laughed a little with pleasure at the reunion. The Supreme was about a foot shorter than Koa, but they held on to his shoulders and met his eyes seriously. "I am so sorry for what has been done to the Wariuta."

Koa bowed his head. Genevieve wanted to hug him but held back. The burden he carried now was too great for one person, and yet there he was. She wished she could fix it for him.

"I will see justice done for your people. Know that."

Koa did not respond to this.

"I have important information I must give you," Genevieve blurted in Imperial. She felt as if a thousand years had passed since she had seen Lilith's memory, and she wanted to share it directly with the Pirate Supreme before there were any more cataclysms in her life.

The Supreme looked a little offended that she'd interrupted. They looked at Rake with raised eyebrows, and Rake glowered at Genevieve.

"This child was the charge of the late Lady Ayer," he said with hardly disguised disgust. "She claims to have had a change of heart and wishes to help us now."

"She's also my daughter," the Fist added, but she did not elaborate.

"Do you trust her?" the Supreme asked Rake.

"No."

"Then why bring her to me?"

"She's a child who's just awoken from years of lies," her mother said. "And while she has not yet earned back her trust with me, I still know my child. Whether she's right or not, she believes what she's saying is the truth."

It was not, Genevieve thought, as much respect as she deserved. There was a part of her, the part that had pushed Dai down in the mud in Gia Dinh all those years ago, that wanted to shout at her mother for undermining her at such an important moment. But if she wanted to prove herself, squabbling with her mother like a baby probably wasn't the way. So she clamped her mouth shut and fumed.

"I see. Xenobia," the Supreme made a little motion with their hand, and the woman who had been staunchly ignoring the visitors turned to them. "Any way to tell if she's lying?"

"I'll know once she tells her story," said the woman casually.

"Go on, then, child. Tell me your tale." The Supreme sat back down on their chair and looked at Genevieve expectantly. With all eyes on her, Genevieve shifted uncomfortably.

"There's a dragon," she said. The Supreme tilted their head, probably thinking she was stupid or mad or both. Genevieve pressed on. "There's a dragon at the bottom of the sea, and if you can call to her, she will come and fight for you."

"All the dragons are dead," said Rake.

"So are all the witches, supposedly," muttered Xenobia.

"I . . . the siren said—"

"Siren?" interjected the Supreme.

"At the Red Shore." She switched to Wariuta then, so Koa could vouch for her. "Koa, tell them. Tell them about the siren."

"Lilith?" Naturally he was confused. He'd understood very little until now. "She lives in the oasis. I guard her. She's been there for longer than I've been alive."

The Supreme and Xenobia exchanged a meaningful look.

"Guarded her," Xenobia said. "She's dead."

Koa grimaced. "Was it them?" he asked, and Genevieve did not need to ask whom he meant. "So much death," he added, to no one really. He looked older than he should, older than he had even two days earlier.

"Yes," the Supreme replied. And then, in the Common Tongue: "But. Before you came here—she told you about the dragon?"

"Showed me," Genevieve clarified.

"She gave you her blood?" asked Xenobia. "Willingly?"

"Yes." Genevieve took a deep breath. "Or, really, she offered Koa her blood, but I was worried she'd kill him and so I took it instead, and she dragged me underwater and it was so terrible, and I saw the dragon in the depths, and she was telling me, or showing me, I suppose, that her song can still be sung, whatever that means, and she showed me her teeth, and they were huge, and anyway she didn't say so, but I got the impression she meant to offer her aid for the Pirate Supreme, which sounds silly, but I could feel it, could feel who she meant to fight for, and I know the Emperor is bad now, and so that's why I'm here."

She had not said it all aloud since it had happened, and she realized how bizarre she sounded. So much had been told. Nothing had been said. Somehow she needed to communicate all that, urgently. So much was riding on her competence. She looked around at her audience.

Silence.

And then: "She's telling the truth," said Xenobia.

"How do you know?" asked Rake.

"When you spend your whole life crafting magic, you can hear the construction of an untruth in a story. Hers has none. She has told us what she has seen as best she remembers it."

On the one hand, Genevieve was glad to be believed, but on the other, she did rather wish the witch had given somewhat more substantial evidence. She could sense more than see the glance exchanged between her mother and Rake.

But the Supreme whooped and clapped their hands in delight. Everyone except Xenobia watched, bewildered. "I knew it!" they hooted. "We have to find those mermaids!"

"Whaaat," Rake said, looking between Xenobia and the Supreme, "is going on?"

"We've got a chance," the Supreme crowed. They shook Rake by the shoulders and planted an exuberant kiss on his cheek. Rake blushed a flaming red. "We gather the coalitions now. It's time to move."

CHAPTER 31

Florian

They were lost.

Once Florian had known the stars in the sky like a map, but that felt so long ago. All the little bric-a-brac of his life above had started to run together, to fade or even disappear. And so he knew some little fraction of his mother's suffering. It was so painful to forget.

In one hand, he clutched the quartz that knew his secrets. In the other, Evelyn's hand gripped his reassuringly. She could not find her way any more than she could make the Sea catch fire, but her constant company and encouragement staved off hopelessness. He squeezed her hand back, an unspoken thank-you.

Distantly, Florian could hear a humpback whale's song echoing, mournful. A calf had been lost to a whaling spear. He could feel the whale's grief as though that spear had hit his own chest. They stopped to listen, to bow their heads, to honor the pod's loss.

And it was then that Florian felt it. The quartz grew warm at first, just warm enough for Florian to take notice, before, in an instant, it turned so hot he nearly dropped it.

"What's wrong?" Evelyn asked.

"I . . ." Florian looked at the quartz. Was he imagining things, or did it glow? He felt a tug in his chest to the east, as if he were being called. As if he were being summoned. As if he were being demanded. He could not hear the voice that shouted his name, but he recognized it all the same "Xenobia?"

"The witch?"

"She's calling me."

"Do we go?"

"I think I have to."

Florian gripped the rock, and once again he whispered his story into it. He told the rock of his love and his mother and whom he needed to talk to in order to save her. He told it of Xenobia and her lessons and the trades he had learned to make and the bond they shared, whether he wanted it or not, of teacher and student.

"I will give you my memories of my birth mother," Florian said. They weren't all bad; Florian knew that. But he could not bear to part with any that might include Evelyn. Nor, he realized, could he bear to part with any memories of Alfie. And so the spell was cast. "Let me speak to her."

There was the sound of rending, of tearing. Florian cast an arm protectively across Evelyn's chest. Before them, a hole in the Sea opened. But it opened not into nothingness or sky or land. It opened into a narrow room with treasure stacked on each side of it. Florian squinted as the room came into focus.

There were people in the room, talking to one another. They did not notice the window that had opened between them just yet. Florian's eyes fell on the girl from Quark first.

"Genevieve?" Evelyn asked.

The whole room whirled at the sound of her voice. And that's when Florian saw him. Rake. He fought the sudden and powerful urge to throw himself through the window, to hug the man who had once been like a father to him. And from the look on Rake's face, he suspected the pirate felt very much the same. Rake ran to the portal and tried to reach his hand through. But he could not touch Florian.

"My boy," Rake whispered. "Look at you."

"There you are," said Xenobia. She tilted her head. "Have you missed me?"

"No," said Florian truthfully. "But I'm glad you called me. I need your help. I need you to find the Pirate Supreme."

There was a chuckle from the back of the room, and that's when Florian saw them. The Supreme stood and walked to the portal, their eyes alight with curiosity.

"Mother needs your help," Florian said in a rush.

"Too many of her daughters have been taken," Evelyn added. "And she wonders why you have abandoned her."

The Pirate Supreme's face fell, and Florian could see the pain as clear as the moon. "I will never abandon her," they said. "I keep calling to her, but she must not be able to hear me . . . Our connection has grown too weak."

"She can barely hear us," Evelyn told them. "Though I know she's trying."

"You can help your mother and us all if you will listen," Xenobia said curtly. Clearly she had grown weary of all the emotion. "There is a dragon. Deep in the trenches of the sea. We need you to go and beg her to come help us."

"To help you what?" asked Florian.

"Destroy Nipran," Rake replied.

"Save the Sea," said the Pirate Supreme.

"Set us free," Xenobia added.

"Of course," Evelyn said. No hesitation.

Florian whipped his head around to look at her, bemused. "We will?"

"Yes. We must do whatever we can to save our mother. And if saving her means stopping the Emperor, well." She shrugged a merry little shrug. "That's just a bonus."

"Doing this will keep you safe," Rake added. "And Alfie, too. If we can stop the Empire, then the mermaids will not be under such constant attack. You will finally have the life you've earned." To Florian's shock, there were tears in Rake's eyes.

Florian reached out a hand to him. "Thank you. Father."

This was apparently more than Rake could stand, and so rather than letting anyone witness him weeping, he simply turned and walked out of the room, the balls of his fists pressed into his eyes. A woman Florian didn't recognize followed him.

"Go," Xenobia said not too kindly. "To your mother's greatest depths. The dragon rests there in a great cavern not even the light can touch. The rock will light your way; I will see to that. Now go. You're our only hope."

And before there could be any more discussion, the window closed.

"Come on, then," Evelyn said cheerily. "Let's go save the world."

◆ CHAPTER 32 ◆

Kaia

I f she kept moving, the pain would not find her.

In every quiet moment, she would see it all again. Watch her mother fall, arms in the air like a child rather than the legendary warrior she was. See Chima, her familiar, her shadow, cut down by bullets she could not outrun. She would imagine Koa's corpse, and her whole body would curl into itself trying in vain to protect itself from grief so immense she could not stand it. Her own obvious failure would pummel her with its truth again and again. She had failed to protect her people, and now her people were gone.

So she kept moving.

Escaping had been easy. She'd taken the measure of Tawmus early on, and knew it was just a matter of time before he made some crucial and fatal error. She did not regret his death, even if she had been taught to honor life. He did not deserve her mourning. None of the Colonizers did.

Now that she had escaped, she didn't have a plan other than to get out of the palace. But where the palace ended was hard to say.

She'd done a good amount of slinking about at night to know that it continued outside the buildings. And hiding had told her that hundreds of people walked past her single vantage point during the day. Escape would not be easy.

But the other thing she noticed was that, for the most part, people kept their eyes down. They attended to their own tasks and nothing more. And so if she could just blend in. She needed to hide her arm. The palace seemed to have some kind of law against anyone with any sort of disability. No crutch, no cane, and everywhere stairs that proclaimed their indifference to those who might struggle up them. She needed clothes like the clothes these people wore. Her skin was not nearly covered enough to possibly blend in.

Luckily, the dresses the women around here wore all had long sleeves. If she held the pretentious posture they held all the time, shoulders in, eyes downcast, as if they were trying to make themselves disappear, she could probably carry it off.

And so she lurked.

It was not long before she found a small window to a bedroom that belonged to a pretty girl. Kaia wondered where she was from—she was pink-skinned, with wide hips and cow-like eyes. She looked to be one of the workers, perhaps; her clothes were not ornate and excessive like those Kaia had seen in the great and terrible room where she had been marched before all those staring eyes. She was lovely the way a hot bath was lovely, and Kaia did not mind watching her.

There was something in the way the girl moved. The gentle way she folded the blankets over her bed. She reminded Kaia of Koa. Like a person who would do whatever it took to do no harm. She felt the lightning strike of loss and clenched her jaw. She did not have the luxury of wallowing.

And anyway, this girl's clothes would be the perfect size.

Kaia waited until the girl had closed the door behind her, and slipped in through the window.

After a quick dig in a wooden box at the foot of her bed, Kaia found what she thought she needed—a long-sleeved thing and a thing to go around the waist. But how was it assembled? That was more complicated. Why was it so complicated?

She was trying to figure out how best to secure the things so that she was as covered as she could be with her one hand, when the door burst open and the girl entered, looking back at a boy. They were both laughing but stopped upon seeing Kaia there, half in and half out of the clothes she had stolen.

The girl's eyes were wide with fright. But Kaia could see that the boy was not unaccustomed to danger. He cast an appraising look over the situation, his eyes darting across Kaia's arm and her pathetic attempt to dress herself.

"You're the girl," he said. In Sky Tongue. Her tongue. Kaia was so shocked that she actually felt her jaw go slack, felt her mouth make a big, stupid O. He held up his hands in the universal signal of good intent. "I'm not going to hurt you."

He did not look like a typical Colonizer, though the Colonizers looked many different ways. He looked as though he might have family in Tustwe, just as she did. But that was not enough, Kaia knew from experience, to create solidarity. This boy was not her brother. Her brother was dead.

"How—" the boy started, a question he did not finish.

The girl seemed to ask the same thing at the same time, and the boy looked back and forth between the two, speaking as quickly as he could in both languages.

"She recognizes you from the procession. Your arm . . . makes you pretty distinctive. We heard you'd escaped, the whole palace knows, everyone's looking for you. And—I've traveled a lot, and I've been to Puno a bunch of times. She wants to help."

"Puno? Are you a merchant? Or a pirate?"

"Does it matter?" So he was a pirate. "I want to help you."

"Why should I believe you?" Kaia ached for her ax, a dagger, anything so that she would not feel so naked. She could easily get past these two, but if they raised an alarm . . . To say she was outnumbered was a farcical understatement.

The boy looked to the girl and then back to Kaia again. He had translated for the girl up to this point, but he did not translate what he said next.

"Because I'm only here to help destroy this empire from within. And I can't imagine that's something you'd take issue with. And besides, maybe you can help me. My name is Alfie. It's nice to meet you." He tried to hold out his hand to shake hers, but Kaia ignored the gesture.

"You're a spy?"

"Yes."

"A pirate and a spy."

"I sound pretty impressive when you put it like that."

"I don't know if *impressive* is the word I'd use."

The girl looked at the boy called Alfie, confused. She, of course, had understood none of this. Kaia eyed him shrewdly.

"She doesn't know?"

"No."

"So you do not even trust your friend, and yet you ask me to trust you."

"Listen, I could have called the Guard ages ago instead of chatting here nicely with you." He sounded a little annoyed. "And I still can. Get in their good graces. Would help my cover, wouldn't it, to be a good little citizen? Maybe even the Emperor would give me a smile. But I don't give a shit about that." He took a steadying breath. "I will help you if you'll help me. Does that seem like an arrangement you can trust?"

Kaia looked at the girl. "What's her name?"

"Keiko," Alfie said.

The girl bowed in the manner Colonizers considered polite. It did not become her, even if she was beautiful.

"She stays with me until you've made good on your word."

"She has nothing to do with this," said Alfie.

"If you have nothing to hide, then she has nothing to fear from me."

"Hurt her, and I will see you hanging from the Emperor's gallows."

"Give me reason to, and she'll be in too many pieces to watch me hang."

Kaia held Alfie's gaze. She had little interest in killing Keiko, but her patience for the people in this land was gone. They had taken everything from her, taken everything she had once been. There was no room left for honor, or pity. She looked at Keiko and tried not to think of Koa, of the way their spirits were clearly of a kind. No, she would not be able to kill her. But Alfie needed to think she would. And who knew? Maybe this Kaia, the Kaia with no people and no family, the Kaia who had lost everything, even her own familiar, wasn't a Wariuta warrior anymore. She was just a life, adrift in a sea of pain. Why not cause a little, too?

"OK," Alfie said. "We have an accord."

CHAPTER 33

The Pirate Supreme

She smelled the same. After all those years. They caught a glancing blow of her scent, and they were back in their youth, their body entwined with hers, bodies and breath moving as one. They remembered the sound of their name on her lips, the roll of her tongue as she whispered *Kwizera*. And even now it was like they could feel her standing next to them, even when they weren't looking at her.

Rake cleared his throat.

In their throne room, representatives from each of the many coalitions of the Resistance stood gathered. They surveyed the attendees with pride. The Sisterhood of Widows. Chieftains from the Cold World. Koa stood in for the Wariuta, shifting on his feet, unused to authority. From Iwei, Quark, and the Floating Islands, guerrilla leaders. Xenobia for the few remaining witches. The Fist and her daughter. And even an ambassador and her attendants from Tustwe, the last free nation in the Known World.

The Supreme called everyone to order. Thirty or so heads turned to face them, and they grinned. The time had finally come.

How long had they waited for this moment? Too long. They pushed Xenobia's scent from their mind as best they could.

"Friends," they said. "We are here to destroy the Empire of Nipran. To watch the palace in Crandon crumble and to burn their nation to ash."

The ambassador from Tustwe darted her eyes toward Koa's hyena, clearly a little unnerved by the animal. The hyena rumbled a friendly growl, and she looked away.

Abebi was the first of the representatives to speak. She was an older woman with her hair in dreadlocks. Her arms bore the scars of battle, and her hands were gnarled from years of hard labor. "The Sisterhood stands with you. We have several operatives in place in the Imperial Palace, as well as within the Crandon constabulary. They await my orders."

This was no surprise. The Sisterhood of Widows was a nationless, ever-growing army of women whose husbands or wives, lovers or partners had been killed by the Empire. They existed in every known nation, even Tustwe. Xenobia's mother had once been in the Sisterhood of Widows. And once, long ago, Xenobia had fretted that she, too, would be a member if Kwizera did not make more effort to keep safe.

The Supreme nodded their approval. "The Sisterhood has long been a powerful member of our coalition. I thank you."

"The nationless stand with you," said the Fist.

"And Iwei." Iwei was the first nation to be colonized so many hundreds of years ago. Their representative was young, more child than man still, named Gavroche. The Supreme had met him before and was immediately fond of him. A creature of spit and spite.

"The tribes of the mountain stand with you," said one of the Cold World chieftains. He was pink-skinned and covered—even on his face—with blue tattoos, as was the way of his people.

"As do the tribes of the bogs," said another.

"And the forests," said another.

"And the wastes," said the next.

And so it went, down the line of the representatives until they reached the ambassador from Tustwe. The room hushed, all eyes on her. She wore the traditional garb of a politician, a green umushanana with a yellow sash, a thin gold circlet around her shaved head.

Tustwe had refused to participate in any kind of direct action against the Empire for decades now, and Nipran had not so much refused to colonize them as been unable—the Skeleton Coast precluded invasion by merit of its terrible sailing conditions. The name was earned by the carcasses of ships too foolish to heed warning that littered its shore. It was said only those from Tustwe could master the routes in and out of that nation, and so far that had been true. Kwizera had sailed from that very shore, so many years ago, with Xenobia, their hearts open to a new life. How could they have known what was to come?

"And what of the Sea?" asked the ambassador. The Supreme's heart fell into the pit of their stomach. One of the many reasons for leaving Tustwe was, in their opinion, the national lack of grand ambition. Of course they'd find an excuse to balk at the last moment. "In Tustwe we hear wild stories. Of waves as tall as gods. Of ports devastated, whole towns obliterated throughout the Known World. Of even pirate ships that sink, men consumed by sharks. Do you no longer have her allegiance?"

"It is I who stand in allegiance to her, not the other way around." This was not an answer, and they knew it. The Supreme had hoped no one would ask about this. Their connection to the Sea was all but lost, and though two mermaids had enlisted to hopefully find a dragon, that was hardly the same as the might of the Sea.

They held the ambassador's gaze.

"Tustwe offers a fleet of our ships," she said. Her tone was firm, her cadence slow. She was speaking very carefully. A true politician. "And a small retinue of soldiers who have volunteered. However, Tustwe will not officially raise arms against the Empire of Nipran."

Murmuring. The Supreme and Xenobia exchanged a look. They had both thought that if an ambassador from Tustwe had been dispatched to attend at all, Tustwe was ready to finally bear arms. Still. The ships would be welcome, as well as any soldiers.

"Hedging your bets," Rake said. Not rudely, exactly, but not politic. The Supreme suppressed a smile. They had always liked Rake, especially for his rough edges.

The ambassador smiled in that way that politicians do. "We have long held a policy of nonintervention. While we do not condone the behavior of the Empire, particularly the recent invasion of the Red Shore, our queen cannot commit to any acts of direct aggression against them. She has her people to think about. And besides"—she looked to the Cold World chieftains with contempt—"Tustwe will never ally with slavers."

In response, the chieftain of the bogs spat on the ground.

"Anything her majesty has to offer will be gratefully accepted," said the Supreme. "Our coalition is broad. It has to be to win." There was nothing of their disappointment in their voice. The ambassador was not the only politician here. They turned to speak to the rest of the room now. "Already in place are plans for various assassinations. We will not speak of them here. The fewer who know the particulars the better. These are operations of incredible delicacy and secrecy, and they must stay that way. However, these plans cannot be depended on for victory. And so we are here. To set a day of attack. To plan as best we can."

"Coordinated attacks across the colonies, ramping up until the invasion of Crandon," said Rake. "Assassinations of high-ranking officials. The destruction of consulates. We can spread their forces thin if we do these things simultaneously. Create chaos."

"If we're lucky," said one of the chieftains.

"That's the thing about luck," said Gavroche, smiling. "We each have to get lucky only once. They've gotta be lucky every day."

"And that is where the witches can help," said Xenobia. "In Quark, the Red Shore, and in the Cold World, anyway. There aren't many of us, but those who remain are powerful. We will craft the tales of your heroes and help to make them true."

"Separately, we have all been forced to live beneath the Emperor's heel," the Supreme said. "But together. Together, we will see him dead and his colonies freed."

The room erupted in cheers.

Reflexively, the Supreme looked to Xenobia, and it was as if no years had passed at all. They were still just Kwizera and Xenobia, and together, the two of them would bend this world away from the Empire. They reached out their hand, and Xenobia took it.

Death had come for safer targets. Best, Kwizera thought, to give him a grand one.

· CHAPTER 34 ·

Alfie

Kaia did not look like a maid, even with her hair combed and in a kimono. Maybe it was the way she held herself, like she was ready to fight, her legs flexed and eyes roaming. Or maybe it was just because she was missing one hand. It was hard to say.

Keiko pulled a corset around her waist and yanked the ties back. Kaia called out in shock.

"What is she doing?" she demanded. She whirled on Keiko, who backed away as though from a wild animal. "Is this some kind of Imperial torture device?"

"Of sorts?" Alfie said. When Kaia looked as though she might only punch him out, he added: "It's called a corset. All the women wear them here."

"Barbaric."

"Sure. But you have to let Keiko work, OK? She's trying to help you."

Kaia closed her eyes as if to gather herself, then reached her hand out to Keiko and touched her shoulder gently. It was as good an apology as she could make directly without the Common Tongue, and Alfie was glad to see it.

"Can it be a little looser?" she asked when it was tied and done.

Alfie asked Keiko, who shook her head. "It's as loose as I can make it without calling attention to her."

Corseted, and with the obi on, Kaia looked somewhat more in place.

"Remember to keep your head down," Alfie said.

"Tell her to keep her hands together," Keiko reminded him. Then, realizing what she'd said, she added, "Or, to make it look like her hands are together."

Alfie translated this, and Kaia rolled her eyes.

"I have never hidden my arm before," she said. She sounded angry, but not at him. "It seems this place is determined to squash out any speck of dignity I have left."

"I know. But the palace would never hire someone who . . ." he scrambled for something polite to say.

"I know." Kaia straightened her shoulders and then bowed her head experimentally. It was, Alfie had to admit, a passable impression of the proper posture of an Imperial girl.

"One last touch," Keiko said. She grabbed a bonnet and fastened it over Kaia's hair. "She'll look like a laundry girl this way."

Kaia examined herself in the small mirror Keiko had propped on her tansu and shuddered. "I look like a complete fool." She touched the bonnet, a look of disgust on her face, but she didn't disturb it.

All in all, it wasn't a bad disguise. The bonnet hid her dirty hair. Alfie smiled at both Keiko and Kaia. "This is going to work," he said. And he believed it. He had to.

Keiko had done the best she could. Now it was time to test her labor.

"I don't know," said Keiko. She looked at Kaia, her brow crumpled in worry.

"It'll be fine," said Alfie. "Trust me."

Keiko looked at him then, and he sensed he had said the wrong thing. She seemed troubled, and not about Kaia. About him.

"You told her my name is Keiko," she said.

Alfie laughed a little, bemused. "'Course I did. Would you rather her call you something else?"

But Keiko was deadly serious. "You gave her my real name," she said pointedly. "Why didn't you give her yours?"

Alfie's heart stopped. What name had he given? He racked his brain, trying to remember what had happened. He'd been so stunned, so confused by Kaia's presence, and it'd been such a scramble to make sense of the situation, to defuse it. He didn't remember what he'd said. "Didn't I?" he said stupidly.

"No. You said. You said the name Alfie." She tried to hold his gaze, but Alfie looked away, cursing himself inside. "Is that your real name?"

There was no point in lying. And anyway, he couldn't think of one. "Yes."

"If you want me to trust you, you need to trust me," said Keiko.

"Are we going?" Kaia asked.

"Just . . . just shut up a sec," Alfie said to Kaia. She looked offended but did as he asked. His mind was spinning; he didn't know what to do, what to say. He couldn't believe he'd messed up so badly, but then of course he could believe it, because he messed up everything, all the time. What was wrong with him? "I'm sorry," he said to Keiko. "I—if I tell you who I am, you'll just be in more danger."

"I'm sneaking a prisoner out of custody," she said. "I'm already in danger."

This was true. Alfie closed his eyes. "I wish you weren't," he said. And when Keiko did not respond to this, he went on. "I'm here as an operative for the Resistance. The Pirate Supreme, specifically. As a spy."

Keiko sat down on her bed. "Shit," she said.

Alfie had never heard her cuss before, and it didn't sound right from her. It was like the auditory equivalent of seeing a dog in human clothes. It might have been funny if he didn't feel so awful. "I didn't mean. I mean, I never wanted to put you in any danger. I'm so sorry," he said.

"Well, you did," she said curtly. She stood and dusted off her skirts, which did not have dust on them. "Come on, then." She took Kaia by the arm. "Let's get this over with."

And in the midst of the most uncomfortable silence Alfie had ever experienced, they walked out of Keiko's room and into the palace.

Getting through the servants' wing was easy. Everyone was so busy attending to their own business that they didn't have time to watch Alfie, Keiko, and the stiff and uncomfortable laundry girl as they went. Kaia had snuck in through Keiko's window—a difficult task for one, an impossible task for three. And so the real test would be getting through the palace. Then the palace grounds. Then the palace gate.

Their story was simple: Alfie was escorting the young women on an errand for the nursery to buy new textiles for sheets and pillows. Only the best for the princesses and Crown Prince. This was a believable story, if a little strange that a kitchen boy had been sent on the job. If they were questioned by a guard, it'd make sense that Alfie would do the talking—he was the only boy present and the best liar of the three. It wasn't a perfect plan. But it'd have to do.

They passed the courtyard with only one stumble—Kaia held her head a little too high as she curiously regarded a few senators as they passed. Alfie could understand why—the golden robes they wore were ostentatious even by Imperial standards, so he couldn't imagine how they looked to a Wariuta person. One of them quirked his brow at her, offended at her impertinence, but he didn't stop arguing with his cohort.

"Don't look at people," Alfie hissed under his breath.

"Sorry," Kaia hissed back in a voice that didn't sound very sorry. But she kept her head down after that.

When they passed the atrium, though, Kaia couldn't help but pause, arrested by the sight of the great dragon skeleton assembled there. Keiko made a small noise of remonstration, and they moved along again before anyone noticed that a laundry girl seemed shocked by such a normal part of palace life.

"For gods' sake, keep it moving," Alfie said just as a senator turned the corner in front of them.

At the sound of a foreign tongue being uttered in the Imperial palace, the same senator regarded them suspiciously.

"New girl," Alfie said, his voice cheery. And then, for good measure, he added in an exasperated tone: "Immigrant."

"I see," said the senator. He looked at Kaia disapprovingly. This time, at least, Kaia had the good sense to keep her head properly bowed. "They'll hire just anyone these days, won't they?"

Alfie laughed as he swallowed his disgust. "You know how it is."

He bowed deeply to the senator, and the girls followed suit. The senator went on his way without sparing them another glance.

"We're not going to make it," Keiko whispered. Her voice was shaky, terrified.

"Yes, we are," said Alfie firmly. He wished she had not had to come along—but without another maid, Alfie and Kaia would look extra suspicious. Kitchen boys and maids did not just perambulate about the palace one-on-one, lest they appear to be canoodling on the Emperor's coin. "Just act normal, and we'll be out of here in no time."

This was a lie, of course. They still had the grounds to traverse. But they were at the grand entrance to the palace now, and the grounds were much less busy than the palace itself was.

When they walked through the great golden doors and down the front steps, Alfie felt a grin pulling at his face. They really were going to make it. None of the guards had even blinked at them as they'd gone. Scared straight by the senator, Kaia was doing an excellent job keeping her head down and eyes averted now, and Keiko—well, Keiko looked terrified, but he suspected he could see that only because he knew her so well.

He hoped that someday she might forgive him for all this. He knew she may very well not.

The grounds were empty save for some gardeners tending to the various trees and flowers, their backs to all as they worked. This was easy, this was pie, and they walked quickly but not too quickly through the grounds.

They were nearly to safety when, as if in slow motion, the gates were pulled closed by several guards. Alfie was not the only one confused. There was some murmuring of confusion among the gardeners.

"No one comes in or out!" a guard called. "Emperor's orders!"

The murmuring grew louder. Not everyone in the palace during the day lived in the palace. Something was afoot.

"What's going on?" Alfie asked a gardener.

The man grimaced. "I hear there's a plot to assassinate the

Prince . . . so till that gets sorted, we're all stuck here. Which is fine by me. Food's better here than it is at home." The man gave a loud chortle. "I'm gonna go see about some milk bread."

Alfie tried to laugh along but could not find the energy.

"What do we do?" Keiko whispered.

"I . . . don't know." Alfie looked around desperately but could think of no alternatives. All the entrances would be heavily guarded. And if what the man had said was true, then . . . the Guard was looking for him.

"Stay with Kaia," Alfie told Keiko. "I need to go. To see if there's any other way in or out."

Keiko gave him a look like he was the worst person she had ever met, which, honestly, he probably was. "Fine," she said. "Come back to my quarters when you can. We'll be waiting."

"I promise I will." He gave her hand a squeeze, tried to let the gesture communicate his earnestness. He would not let harm come to Keiko. If that was the only thing he could do before he was strung up by the Guard, then so be it. It would be enough.

To Kaia he said, "Be gentle with her. I will be back for you both as soon as I possibly can. They've locked down the gates."

"Are they looking for me?" Kaia asked.

"No. Or yes. But I think they're also looking for me."

CHAPTER 35

Evelyn

T hey swam down, down, down. Into the gaping abyss of the trenches far below the world they had so recently come to know. In Flora's hand the quartz stone glowed, lighting their way.

It was cold. Not cold like Crandon was cold in winter, not the biting cold of ice, but the deep, encompassing cold of nothingness. Without the illumination of Flora's stone, Evelyn knew, they would be lost forever. Maybe even with the stone.

As they descended, the water around them grew thick with tiny particles that shone white in the light cast by Flora's stone. Flora pointed the quartz over them, once, and illuminated an enormous shark languidly plodding through the water. Evelyn gasped. It was immense and scarred and paid them no mind. Occasionally, blinking lights flashed, but it was impossible to tell in the encompassing darkness whether they were near or far.

"Are we lost?" Evelyn asked. After all they had been through, still she was like an extra saddlebag for Flora to carry. And maybe she would have felt shame if she were not so cold.

"I don't know," Flora said. Her voice was gentle, was always gentle, with Evelyn. "I don't think so."

"I'm so cold," said Evelyn.

"Yes," said Flora. There was nothing else to say.

Flora took her hand, and for a moment, Evelyn's fingers were warm where Flora's lips kissed her. They held each other's hands after that for some ways, even though it did make the going slower. Clearly, Evelyn was not the only one a little afraid.

They swam farther down.

There was no sound anymore. No whale's song that echoed, resonant and sad. Only silence and darkness, cold and craggy rock. There was no silence, Evelyn realized, on land. There was always something: the sound of a leaf falling, a bird's call. Not so down here. Not even the tiny blinking fish of the deep came this far.

And then suddenly:

"Stop."

They had reached the bottom. The floor of the Sea was not like the ground on land—it began and ended in gradient, a spectrum of diatomaceous earth. Something breathed, the force of its breath sending waves over the undulating floor. Something enormous. And there: the yawning maw of a cavern somehow even darker than the darkness that enveloped them.

Flora's face was lit by the glowing stone, and Evelyn found fear there, worry. And she kissed her then, so that perhaps Evelyn could carry some of the worry for her. Flora would carry a burden forever without a thought to ask for help. It was Evelyn's turn to be strong now.

"Please, Dragon," Evelyn called. And her voice was so brave, she could feel Flora's pride in her swelling in her own chest. "Will you lend us your time?"

Silence.

"Perhaps she did not hear—" Flora began.

But before she could finish speaking, there was a great rumble, like stone on stone, like thunder just after a lightning strike. They both flinched as the great head of the dragon emerged from the cavern.

She was gigantic on a scale Evelyn did not have words to describe. Big like the sky was big, like she might have been limitless. She did not end and begin the way a person did; she was more like a cloud, blurred at the edges, ethereal. She glowed blue in the light of the stone, but she could have been purple or white or opalescent, or a color that Evelyn's eyes did not understand, could not categorize.

"Two souls," the dragon whispered. Her voice was soft for something so colossal, as though she were just a girl passing secrets. One great foot emerged from the cavern, and each of her three toes ended in claws as long as trees were tall. She lowered her head so that her eyes—slit-pupiled and silver—met theirs.

"We come to beg a favor," Evelyn said.

"Ah." The dragon's only reply.

"The fate of the Known World depends on it," added Flora.

"Who sent you?" asked the dragon.

"The Pirate Supreme," Florian said.

"They will destroy the Empire of Nipran," said Evelyn. "And end the Emperor's tyranny. He's been killing and lying and hurting for so long now." She thought of Flora the child, scrounging for scraps while so many had so much. While she had so much. Shame washed over her. "It must be done. Not just for us but for the whole world! To save children, and, and, and mermaids, and—"

"To save the Sea," the dragon finished for her.

At this the dragon emerged fully from the cavern. Her body

was long and sinuous, sliding from her hiding place like an eel. Her great scales flashed white as she moved.

"At last," said the dragon.

Flora and Evelyn exchanged a look. So Flora didn't know what that meant, either. Still, though, the dragon swam toward the surface, and the mermaids followed.

"At long last."

• CHAPTER 36 •

Genevieve

S
he sat with her mother on a set of steps that led straight into the sea. There was nothing to do just then except wait, and so they waited together in uneasy silence. It was odd how quickly she had become accustomed to her mother being the Fist. Perhaps it was because it suited her so well. Her mother was a skilled leader, that much was clear from the quiet way she demanded respect. And Genevieve was left to wonder who she might have become if her mother had trusted her enough to tell her who she was, all those years ago, before the Lady Ayer had cast her spell upon her.

The Fist sat with her knees lazily spread, hunched over a steaming cup of something the witch, Xenobia, had made to help with her voice. It smelled odd, more like woodsmoke and copper than something edible. Her mother gazed out at the sea. In the distance, Genevieve could see whitecaps blooming like flowers beneath a brewing storm. The sea was angry, according to the Pirate Supreme. Genevieve didn't know what that meant, exactly, but it didn't sound good.

"Do you think they'll get the dragon's help?" Genevieve asked.

Her mother took a long sip of her drink. "Hmm. I don't know much about magic." Her voice was a little less raspy, though still deep and different from what it had been when she had been Mrs. Vo the innkeeper. "But I've seen enough now not to underestimate it."

"Why didn't you tell me?" It came out more like an accusation than the genuine question she'd intended. "Who you were," she added in a more conciliatory tone.

Her mother put down the now empty cup and looked Genevieve in her eyes. Their eyes were so similar, Genevieve knew, the same shape, the same shade of tawny brown. "You have to understand. Just knowing that I was involved was the same as a death sentence for you. I couldn't risk it."

"Dai knew," Genevieve said. And the resentment she hadn't realized she had bubbled to the surface, prickling her eyes. She looked away.

"That was his parents' choice," her mother said. "One that got him killed."

They sat in silence with this horror for some time. Genevieve had not known what had become of her former best friend, her former betrothed. The anger she'd felt toward him for years seemed hollow and cruel now. He'd been so young. She had grown so much since then, changed so much. And he would forever be the same. She didn't have the strength to ask how it happened, but she suspected she knew. Traitors were usually hanged.

All this death, all this suffering, and she'd helped cause it. Because a rich lady promised Genevieve she was special, that being a part of this cruelty made her better than everyone she'd grown up with. But the truth was she wasn't special. She was normal, gullible. Eager to believe that the Empire was successful because it deserved to be, because it was just, because it was great. Not because of its seeming unending predilection for murder. She'd forgotten so easily, so quickly, who she was, where she came from.

She'd even let the Lady Ayer change her name.

"Is there any coming back?" Genevieve asked. Her voice trembled, straining against the shame that constricted her rapidly beating heart. "From what I've done? From what I've become?"

"I have done things that keep me up at night," her mother said. "I can't sleep for seeing the terrible things I've done, the faces of the people I've killed or had killed. But I keep going because I know what I'm fighting for is right."

"But how do you know?" She felt a little desperate. To know anything for certain would be a salve. It felt as though nothing in the world was exact, and that everything was complicated, and that she would never be smart enough or good enough or wise enough to parse it. She had thought she was right all those years ago, when she had gone along with the Lady Ayer. She'd thought she was fighting for good. But she'd been wrong.

To her annoyance, her mother laughed. Not a chuckle but a big boom of a laugh, like a cannon being fired. Genevieve glared at her.

"I'm sorry, child. I'm not trying to be cruel. It's just that I don't know. I suppose you never can. But I believe people deserve to be free. And I can't prove that, and I don't know what that's going to look like. Mm? But that belief lives in the same part of my heart that loves you and loved your father. And so that's what I choose to fight for. That's who I've chosen to be."

"I don't know who I am anymore."

"You're my daughter." Her mother squeezed her hand, and she was not only the Fist then, she was also Mrs. Vo. She was still her mother. Was it worth it? To have been lied to, to have fought for the wrong side, to have shamed herself—all to be reunited with her mother, the family she thought she had lost? To see that person clearly, finally, for the first time? Was that enough? She didn't know. But it was the truth, at least. And it was nice to know something true. "No matter what you've done."

She smiled at her mother, let her eyes wander over the face that was at once so different—wrinkled and scarred, burnt by the sun, with lips gone slack at the edges, one eye hidden behind a patch whose story Genevieve did not know—and exactly the same. Her mother was a completely different person and exactly the same person at once. And so maybe she could be, too.

"I think . . . I think I'd like you to call me Thistle again." Thistle. The name was so familiar and so strange. Like putting a lost glove back on her hand and finding it fit just the same. A reminder that, even after all the mistakes she had made, she had something to be proud of. Thistle, daughter of the Fist, child of Quark. "I think that'd be right."

The Fist's eye watered, but she did not cry. "As you wish."

They sat in silence for some time, absorbing all that had been said. The golden light of dusk danced across the sea.

"It's funny," the Fist said. "So much Imperial time and money spent to educate you, to sharpen you into the little dagger's edge you are now. And you're going to use it against them." She chuckled. "Irony can be so delicious."

"You reap what you sow," Thistle said.

CHAPTER 37

Commander Callum

Commander Finn Callum was home. Though his estate in Crandon was not as comfortable as he remembered it. Less grand than what he deserved. Still, he felt a kind of relief as he sat in his library, which did not hold as many books as it held weapons. A sword from the era of the 990th Emperor, a naginata his grandfather had once wielded in the days before gunpowder. A dagger from the Cold World, forged in dragon fire in the days when there were still dragons. All mounted on the walls. His servants had brought him some mediocre tea, which sat on the table next to him, going cold.

When they found Tomas Inouye's corpse on the palace grounds, the girl gone, Callum felt only irritation. Keen and biting, a threat to his calm. Windsor was flogged, discharged, family connections be damned. He sent his men into Crandon to find the girl. It wouldn't take long, he was sure. She stuck out from the Imperial gentry like a donkey among horses.

His return had been an overwhelming disappointment. The parade was not nearly festive enough. He had expected sexual entreaty from at least a handful of ladies, only to receive none. The Emperor's reception had not gone at all as planned. The old idiot could barely keep his head up, let alone declare war. It was so exhausting, he reflected, to be the only competent person in his orbit. What he could have accomplished if only he had adequate help!

Still, it was good to be back. In civilization once more, where real people tended to real business, not just hawking their wares in the open air like perpetual vagrants. Crandon smelled of smoke and horses and the sea, and Callum loved it as much as he'd loved anything in his life. Not that there were many points of comparison. He was not prone to affection. He had, however, expected a somewhat warmer reception from the Emperor's court. Even though the old man was senile, demented, weak, he had assumed the nobles would have his back. But alas, they were as weak as the old man who led them.

Senator Tsujima was exactly on time, as xe always was. Xe wore a particularly decadent haori, and it didn't suit xem. It would be more fitting, Callum thought, on a man. A royal one at that. New-moneyed people were like that, though, forever dressing above their station. Impertinent, really. Xe may have earned enough money through buying and selling slaves in the Cold World to earn a place in the Senate, but that didn't make xem noble. Callum didn't like Tsujima, didn't approve of xem, but xe was useful even if Callum didn't know how to treat someone whose genitals were a mystery.

But Tsujima knew everything about everyone at court. Callum motioned for xyr to sit down, and xe did, with a flamboyant little flourish Callum found deeply annoying.

"Commander Callum," Tsujima said silkily. Xe was forever decorous. "Welcome home. I rather thought you'd invite me here to your lovely abode a little sooner. You must be so exhausted from your exertions upon the Red Shore."

"Battle will do that," Callum replied.

"From what I hear, it was less of a battle and more of a massacre," said Tsujima. Xyr voice was conversational, but there was a barb in there. The disposal of resisters was, Callum thought bitterly, the dirty business the military attended to so that the gentry of Nipran could feign ignorance of it. They were a just and polite society, after all. But murder was murder, and murder was required to keep the ladies in their silks and the men in their gold. Callum was the best at commanding all that bloodshed.

"Our men fought gallantly," said Callum. He gave a short, cold smile. Smiling had never suited him. "I do not imagine, however, that you hinted so aggressively for an invitation here just to give me your compliments."

"Alas, no," Tsujima said with a rueful smile. "Deserving of them though I'm sure you are." Was that sarcasm? "No, I'm here to gauge your interest on a matter of the greatest delicacy. One that requires your absolute dedication to secrecy. It's a secret I think you might be amenable to, if you were to hear it."

Callum quirked a brow. He did not trust Tsujima, did not trust anyone who had never served in the Guard.

"The thing is, it's so delicate, in fact, that in order to tell you about it at all, I must divulge a secret of my own, such that I might, ah, encourage your loyalty." Xyr tone was one of false reluctance, but Callum could feel xyr hunger to exert power over him as clearly as he could see xem sitting there, in his chair, in his home, making veiled threats.

"Go on, then."

"I know about your arrangement with Lord Hasegawa." Tsujima tut-tutted. "Naughty stuff. Sending his daughter off to be killed by pirates so that you would have an excuse to start a war. No, I don't think the court or the senators would be pleased to hear that you'd sent one of Crandon's own daughters to her death just so you could secure some explosives. She was one of us, after all. And it didn't even work. I hear she escaped your grip, slippery little thing, never to be seen again."

Callum kept a mask of impassiveness on his face, but inside, his guts were churning. Tsujima was right, of course. This agreement with Lord Hasegawa was the kind of thing that had to happen in darkness. And even if plenty of nobles had participated in such arrangements, or worse, they could never admit to it publicly. Reputation was everything in court. He'd be ruined.

"You have proof of this allegation?" he said calmly.

"Indeed, I do," said Tsujima. Callum's hand made a tight fist in his lap. "A written testimony from Lord Hasegawa himself. A written testimony I was clever enough to secrete away such that it cannot be destroyed except by me or my secret keeper, who will release it should I suddenly and inexplicably perish."

Callum silently cursed Hasegawa. *The little toad, the little traitor.* "Is that so?"

"Oh, yes, yes, yes. Hasegawa always needs money, doesn't he, more than your little arrangement allowed him. And I was generous enough to lend him some coin. A paltry amount, really, but it did the trick. A small price for such valuable information. So. Am I assured your silence?"

Callum took a deep breath. He didn't have a choice, and Tsujima knew it. "Yes."

"You have likely noticed that the Emperor is . . . not the man he once was."

This was a shocking thing to say aloud. Callum regarded the senator coolly. "I would not say such things if I were you."

"Luckily you are not, and unluckily for his majesty, I am not the only one who has noticed nor who is concerned. I imagine you were somewhat disappointed by his inability to recognize the great gestures you made, your clear entreaty for troops to take the Red Shore? Man like you, in his prime. Certainly leading the offensive there would keep you in gold for the rest of your days. If the Emperor had ordered it, that is."

Callum did not reply. His lips set into a tight line of chagrin at having been so transparent, but Tsujima was undaunted and, apparently, clairvoyant.

"There is a plot, you see," said Tsujima. "A Resistance plot to kill the Crown Prince."

At that, Callum's ears pricked. The heir.

Tsujima nodded. "My sense is that there are several factions of the Resistance working together to see it done. And my sense is also that, if we are careful, it could be aided in happening with precious little interference from us."

Callum saw it then, the hazy edges of Tsujima's motivation. He could not help it; he was impressed. Xe was full of surprises.

"With no heir, the Senate will take over once the Emperor dies." A clever plan, if xyr involvement was not spotted. As a senior senator, Tsujima would become incredibly powerful overnight. Xe had so much to gain. "And this is where you come in." Tsujima steepled xyr fingers and regarded Callum, xyr eyes fixed with cold calculation.

"There it is."

"You have long cultivated a glowing reputation for violence," Tsujima said in a tone that belied both disgust and respect, as if xe were conversing with a useful dog, a beast of burden. "And if you were to aid us in this little bit of tidy skulduggery, why, I imagine the rewards would be . . ." Xe searched for the right word. "Ample."

"I'll need specifics."

"Well, the Senate would be in charge of appointing the new general of the army, wouldn't we?" Tsujima paused, letting that sink in.

Callum could feel his mouth watering, and it tasted like blood. To lead the entire Imperial forces. To be top man in command. General Mirimoto was old now, nearly as old as the Emperor, though his mind was still sharp. He'd need to be replaced with someone younger. Someone hungrier.

Callum smiled, a real smile. Finally. A competent ally.

"I'll need you to put that in writing," Callum said. "Before I can commit to anything."

"Naturally, naturally. I'd expect no less. Anything less would be foolish. And you, my good sir, are no fool."

Tsujima stood, and the two bowed to each other.

"Thanks to the Emperor," Tsujima said.

CHAPTER 38

The Pirate Supreme

The Pirate Supreme waited, along with the representatives, Xenobia, the Fist and her daughter, and Rake. That morning they had awoken with Xenobia in their bed. Xenobia was already awake and sure, she said, that it would happen today. That the dragon was close. She could feel it. And so they waited, all of them, on the steps that led into the Sea, watching for any sign of movement. A pod of whales spouting nearby gave everyone a false start.

When the sun began to set, the Supreme turned to Xenobia. "Are you sure?" they asked at a whisper, for probably the hundredth time.

"Yes," Xenobia said.

The ambassador from Tustwe shifted on her feet, impatient and cold in the dwindling sun. The Supreme feared that she would lose interest entirely and leave before the dragon presented herself, but they kept that worry to themself.

And then, Koa's hyena giggled. High and anxious, the animal's nervous laughter was louder even than the waves that crashed against the stone of the Supreme's keep, a piercing *hee-hee-hee* that sent shivers through them. All watched, transfixed, as the animal started to pace, clearly afraid. Koa tried to shush his familiar, but Tupac would not be comforted.

"She's close," said Xenobia. Even she looked afraid; Kwizera could see it in the way she breathed, short and shallow, the way she held herself taut. They took her hand in theirs, and for a moment they were as they had once been, joined by their fear and their anticipation, together in an uncomplicated way. For a moment, they were just Kwizera and Xenobia, there to protect each other from whatever may come.

But then Xenobia's eyes darted away, scanning the horizon.

She need not have looked so far.

With unnerving quiet, the dragon's enormous head surfaced almost directly in front of the waiting crowd.

Maybe because they were in such shock, or perhaps because the dragon was so strange, so otherworldly that no one knew how to respond, not a one of the waiting crowd made a sound. Eyes wide, they watched as the dragon slowly blinked, taking them in. She could have easily opened her maw, swallowed the entire group whole. But instead, she simply looked at them, as if waiting for them to speak. Which, Kwizera realized, she probably was. They had called her, after all.

The Pirate Supreme stepped forward, and with their best semblance of courage, they squared their body to the dragon. *If you want to do great things*, they reminded themself, *you must be bold*. They were close enough to her that if they reached out, maybe they could have touched the scales that glistened silver and white and blue on her snout. But there was something so odd about her—the way she was both very much right there and also indistinct at her boundaries, more cloud than creature—that they wondered if they could touch her at all. When she breathed, the air around them smelled of rain on stone. She was beautiful the way a distant storm was beautiful, and with just her presence she seemed to tell the Supreme how small they were, how finite.

She was not death, but she was a reminder of it.

"I am the Pirate Supreme," they said, and their voice was loud and clear. "I am the one who calls, to beg your help."

"Yes," the dragon said. Her voice was impassive, but they guessed she was likely impatient at redundancy. Likely the mermaids had told her. She did not say more but waited, as if the Supreme were a child. Compared with her, they likely were.

"We have assembled fighters from all over the Known World so that we can free the colonies from the Emperor's grip and save the Sea from his greed." They motioned to the crowd behind them. "We have waited generations for a realistic shot at liberty," they said. "And the time is now. If, that is, you are generous enough to help us."

"The Emperors killed my children," the dragon said. "Hunted them down. Found them out and took each of their lives. My sons and my daughters, my children, my babies, all dead and gone."

None were brave enough to tell her that a skeleton of one of her children was on display in the Emperor's palace. The Supreme wondered if she knew.

"Nipran is rapacious," they said. "Whatever they consume they consume voraciously, no matter the cost, until it is gone. They must be stopped."

"Yes," said the dragon. She looked then to Koa, who startled backward, nearly tripping over his hyena, who had gone as still as everyone else in the dragon's presence. "What do you think, child?"

She asked this in Sky Tongue, and the boy was so surprised

that it took him a moment to answer. "I agree," he said slowly. "That they must be stopped."

"But," the dragon said.

"But . . ." He looked around at all the leaders and representatives cautiously. "Death makes me uneasy."

"The Emperor must be killed. His Empire burned. His soldiers defeated," the Supreme interjected. They liked Koa, felt an affection toward him, but they would not see him ruin their one chance at overthrowing the Emperor. "Will you help us?"

"Help you kill them all?" the dragon asked.

"Yes," the Pirate Supreme said.

"How small you are," said the dragon. "How limited your imagination."

The Supreme did not know what to make of this. They looked to Rake, whose eyes conveyed bewilderment as deep as their own.

"Is that a no?" they asked, unsure what else to say.

"I will bring justice," said the dragon. And before anything else could be said, she emerged entirely from the Sea, her long body rising like smoke. "Sail now, children," she called back to them. "I will meet you on their shore."

The crowd whooped and cheered as she flew away on the wind, more mist than bird. It looked as if she were swimming through the air, her body undulating to propel her away. In her wake, the Sea stilled, as though she knew that finally, a power great enough to save her was on the move.

And the Pirate Supreme grinned.

The battle of Crandon started now.

PART THREE

The Spy

CHAPTER 39

Thistle

How many times had Thistle looked at her mother and sworn she would never be like her? Countless. But now she watched the woman the Resistance called the Fist and marveled.

Maybe one day she could be like her. If she worked hard. If she was lucky.

If she survived.

Aboard the *Leviathan*, the Fist had started teaching target practice to those unfamiliar with guns. Some were too proud—the gruff chieftain from the Cold World bogs refused to let his people attend, but he was unusual. Much of the underground work of the Resistance had not required participants to learn weaponry at all, and they had but the weeks-long voyage to learn before they would be thrust into battle.

The Fist lined up empty glass bottles along the quarterdeck and barked instructions at her students. Thistle watched with her lips quirked in equal parts amusement and concern. Most of those who attended knew nothing, and it showed. When one of the Widows fired directly into the deck, she couldn't help it, she laughed. Not out of cruelty, truly, but incompetence would always be a little bit funny.

"I suppose you can do better, hmm?" her mother called. It was not an entirely friendly tone of voice. The smile fell from Thistle's face. She was loath to disappoint the Fist, but a sliver of her old irritation with her mother found its way beneath her skin. Objectively, what had just happened was funny. But she tried to take the high road.

"Just hope no one got hurt," Thistle replied.

Her mother stuck her with a challenging glare. "Show her, then," she said. "If you're such aces with a pistol."

She handed Thistle a gun that was much larger than the one the Lady Ayer had entrusted her with. It felt heavy and wrong in her grasp. An Iwei thing, she could tell from the barrel. A cursory examination of it told her that the sight on it listed a bit to the left. In her mind, the Lady Ayer's voice reminded her to count the bullets. She pushed the voice away but counted all the same. There were three bullets in the chamber. Three bottles on the quarterdeck.

Thistle aimed, breathed out. Just as the Lady had taught her.

Three bottles exploded into shards.

The assembled class clapped and cheered, and Thistle did an exaggerated Imperial bow for them. She grinned, and to her delight, her mother grinned back.

"At least she taught you well," she said. She thumped Thistle on the back, then resumed teaching.

Aglow, Thistle sat back down to watch along with Koa, who refused to handle a gun. It took a moment before she realized he was grimacing at her.

She knew he didn't like guns, but wasn't it better to be well trained with them at least? And anyway, she just wanted to enjoy herself. But Koa's eyes were too sad to ignore. "What?" Her voice was a bit more testy than she might have hoped.

"It could have been you," Koa said. "On the shore. Shooting us down. Just like those bottles." He made his hand into a gun and mimed shooting. "Bam. Bam. Me. Kaia. Bam. Tupac." His voice quavered with emotion. "That's what you came to our shore for, isn't it?"

Thistle felt as if she'd been slapped. Not undeservedly, but it stung all the same. "I had been taught . . . so many lies. When we left Crandon, the Lady Ayer told me that we were trying to start a war, yes, but with as little bloodshed as possible. It sounded so smart, she always sounded so smart, and I guess I was just stupid and—"

"But you're not stupid." Koa averted his eyes, let his hand find Tupac, whom he rubbed behind one crooked ear. "I know that, you know that. But you would have killed me on the shore. You pointed your gun at me. I see now you wouldn't have missed."

"No," said Thistle. "I would not. I'm sorry."

It was a weak apology. She tried to think of something else to say, but nothing came. Nothing sufficient. Nothing that could speak to the depth of her error, or the profundity of her ignorance. She had needed to learn so much and so quickly and in the worst way possible. She only hoped that maybe someday she would undo even a fraction of the harm she had caused in her short life.

They sat without speaking for some time. The guns sent a visible jolt through Koa's body each time they were fired. Thistle wanted to reach out to comfort him but worried that might be the opposite of what he wanted. Glass exploded on the quarterdeck, another target hit. The class cheered. Koa sat rigid. Finally, Thistle could not take it anymore and put her hand, tentatively, on his. To her surprise and relief, Koa reached his hand up and clasped hers. It was not an absolution, she thought, so much as an acknowledgment that she was there. That he wanted her there.

"I'm grateful for your friendship," Thistle said. "I do not deserve it."

"No," said Koa. "You don't."

Tupac stood and positioned himself between the two so they both could pet him, and Thistle pushed down a laugh. They were so alike. This boy and his beast. Cut from the same piece of cloth. She scratched Tupac under his chin, just below his enormous canine teeth.

"Do you ever worry," Koa asked, "that you have been made into a weapon without the wisdom to know where best to aim?"

Thistle let her hand fall from the animal. If Koa was indeed her friend, she could certainly count on him for bone-crushing candor. She thought of the Lady Ayer, of her mother. Both leaders. Both with specific ideas about whom she should be. Her mother thought she should have stayed safe. The Lady Ayer had thought she should be an operative, just like her, in service to the Empire.

"I do," Thistle said, and it was the truth.

CHAPTER 40

Koa

The voyage to Crandon was difficult, even on the *Leviathan*—the ship that Koa had been told was blessed by the Sea herself. Rocky and uncomfortable, across waves too tall and too violent. The Sea made herself clear: She no longer favored or recognized anyone, not even the Pirate Supreme, and this was disquieting to all, but especially to Koa's old friend. Koa could see that easily, though it wasn't as though the one called the Pirate Supreme made any pretense of hiding it. They paced the ship, and when they weren't yelling orders to their crew, they sat looking either angry or worried, or most often both.

It was likely due to the witch that the small fleet of Resistance ships had not sunk. She was forever murmuring spells, which was unsettling. Now and then she'd prowl the ship for ingredients, randomly accosting people and asking if they had a blade of grass or a compass on them. And so the fleet made its way.

The witch and everyone else who was not part of the Pirate Supreme's crew spent most of their time belowdecks, watching the lanterns swing as the boat was jostled and tossed by the Sea.

Koa was grateful to have mostly conquered his seasickness, but Tupac was unable to find his sea legs, forever scrambling and toppling. It would have been funny if it were not so distressing to the animal. Koa alternated between frustration and guilt. He needed his familiar, and yet could he keep him safe? He did not know. It seemed not. He tried not to think of Chima, of Puka, of all the fallen familiars. He was stepping into danger, and he was taking Tupac along with him.

It was impossible to explain to outsiders the bond between a familiar and a warrior. It was not just friendship. It was something greater, more encompassing than that. They were partners, each other's shadows. He tried his best to comfort Tupac, to cuddle him and help him keep still, but the animal was forever giggling, squirming, pacing.

He wanted to yell at Tupac, *Do you not see how miserable I am, too? Do you not understand all that has been lost?* But it would have done no good, and so he did not. Instead, he did his best to help the witch when she needed it, which was often. He did not understand her magic, but he liked her and her propensity for cursing in various languages.

It was night when Rake called the passengers to the deck. The moon was high in the sky, though shrouded in the fog that Koa had been warned perpetually lay over Crandon. Koa shivered in the damp of it as they sailed beneath the shadow of an enormous statue.

"That's the Emperor," Thistle told him. She had changed her name back to the name she had been called as a child, apparently. Wariuta often changed their names if something fundamental about themselves shifted: their gender, or their sexuality, or in moments of terrible grief or triumph. He wondered what had shifted in Thistle. He hoped it was good. "They say he watches over us."

"But it's just a statue. Stone, no?" It seemed a monumental waste of effort to build a model of someone, when tales of starving within Crandon reached even the Wariuta shore. Surely there were better ways to spend resources?

"Yes," Thistle said. "Just stone." She shook her head. "I found this impressive once. No more."

The Emperor stared down to the Sea. His gaze did nothing to arrest the progress of the attacking fleet.

Koa had never been so cold in his life. He wrapped the poncho a pirate had given him tight around his enormous shoulders. He looked to the city with his eyes narrowed. Buildings seemed to be stacked directly on top of one another. It was nothing like home.

"It's so crowded," he said.

Thistle looked at Crandon, too, and nodded. The street lamps glowed orange, like the last rays of a bleeding sunset. It might have been lovely.

"Where will the people go?" Koa asked. "When the battle starts?"

"There'll be nowhere to go," Thistle said finally. Crandon was dense with human life, Koa could see that immediately. The hum of it all reached out across the water. Escape would be. Difficult. Impossible, maybe, for some. No passenger ship would be able to board the entire populace and set sail in time.

Koa took a shaky breath. "I'll never understand this world," he said. "They brought blood to our shore, and now what, we bring it to theirs? When does that end?"

"When we dock," she said, "keep your ax drawn."

"But I don't want to kill anyone. I just want to find Kaia."

"I know that. But the Imperial Guard won't. And they will shoot you on sight."

"Do you think . . . They wouldn't kill Kaia, would they?"

"We'll find her," Thistle said. But there was reticence in her voice.

Koa looked at her, but she would not meet his eyes. The Colonizers had brought Kaia all the way back to their own land, had bragged to the world about the warrior they had kidnapped; why would they just kill her?

Thistle opened her mouth but was cut short when Rake called out to the crew to ready the cannons.

Distantly, Koa could hear the city bells ringing their warning of impending attack. They had been spotted. Next to him, Tupac quivered with rising anxiety, his giggles going sharp and jagged. Koa laid a hand on his familiar's haunch, felt the familiar bristle of Tupac's fur beneath his fingernails. Whatever happened, they would go through this together. And though that was little comfort, it was better than nothing.

The *Leviathan*, being the biggest and best and most powerful ship in the fleet, was on the vanguard, carving a path of cannon fire destruction through the docks so that other, smaller ships could make for land. Koa's whole body tensed at the sound of the first cannons firing, and he jammed his fingers in his ears as Tupac ran circles around him, his giggles drowned out by the cannons. All around them it smelled of gunpowder, and Koa could not help but think of the men who guarded the docks, and the bodies and families they would leave behind.

He could hear the screams and shouts of alarm and panic, gunfire, and the slaps as the many rowboats hit the water, carrying the Resistance's forces. And all the while, the hyena laughed and laughed and laughed, his fear a terrible song over the cacophony of the unfolding battle. Koa tried to keep his mind from that horrible sunny day on his own shore, watching his own people fall.

"Come on, then," said Thistle. "Let's go kill some Imperials."

And Koa did not say no.

CHAPTER 41

The Fist

She sailed ashore with the pirates, the Resistance from Quark, and her daughter, pride bursting in her chest. All those years ago, she'd never have believed that Thistle would raise arms with her against Nipran. And now they would fight side by side. As mother and daughter should.

All around them were screams and fire, bullets and bodies. She had never been to Crandon before, never once desired to visit the snake pit from whence the Imperials came. And so it was with great pleasure that she scanned the wide streets and the many tall and narrow buildings and saw them ablaze.

How arrogant they were not to expect this. Not to assume that one day the many nations they had subdued would seek revenge. To forever assume the war would never reach their shore.

The dirty work of the Empire had come home.

They would know the death they had spread throughout the Known World at last. At long last.

An Imperial soldier made the fatal decision to point his pistol at Thistle. The Fist roared, aimed her rifle at him, pulled the trigger. He lay dead in their wake, her daughter safe. They had made it this far together. She would do her best to see that Thistle made it through this. Though, as she watched her daughter, she could tell that the Imperial woman had taught her well. Her sense of tactics, her aim. She did not require her mother's instruction.

As they made their way to the palace, she could feel the heat as the gunpowder barrels—the gunpowder that she had, over years of hard-fought negotiation and battle won for their use—exploded through windows and walls, shattering glass and wood. Its purpose finally achieved. The whole sky was black and orange with smoke and flame. It was like the sun rising over a more just world.

She caught Thistle's eye as they cut their way through Crandon. She was illuminated with the light of the fires that raged. They smiled at each other. This was not the girl who used to peel carrots in her kitchen. She was not the woman who had taught her how. Not anymore.

"This has been too easy," Rake yelled. His face was black with grime and smoke, save for a swipe he had made across his brow.

The moment was broken.

The Pirate Supreme grimaced at their first mate. "The shore was poorly guarded," they said. "The palace won't be."

They would know. They'd been there before, scouted the many halls so that they would be prepared for this moment. A benefit of having kept their face a closely guarded secret for so long. The Pirate Supreme was rarely unprepared, a quality the Fist had long hoped to adopt. It was the mark of a good leader, she thought, to be humble in the face of challenge. To be thorough.

Ahead of them, the Cold World tribes cut a path of destruction, their battle cries sharp even through the deafening reports of guns and, distantly, cannons. She saw one of them, the chieftain of the bogs, take an Imperial bullet, his head snap back. He was gone. This only enraged his people more. The woman who fought at his side threw a spear, and the Imperial guard gasped, clasping at the weapon now buried in his belly. As he fell, more of the tribe swarmed the soldier, obscuring him. It would be a slow death, and a painful one.

It would be what he deserved.

The palace rose above the rest of Crandon like the moon, grand and white and forbidding. How strange that something so beautiful could be the locus of so much cruelty. It was an injustice to the stones it was made of.

A volunteer soldier from Tustwe reported to the Pirate Supreme, yelling directly in their ear. The Supreme nodded and yelled back their orders. A small retinue to the front gates, a distraction. But the bulk of the Resistance would attack the stable gate on the south end of the palace grounds. The Guard was thinner there. The Sisterhood of Widows, the tribes of the Cold World, the Fist, and the guerrilla fighters from Quark, Iwei, and the Floating Islands, as well as the soldiers from Tustwe, would attack there, and with luck they would win. This had long been the plan.

The witch had grabbed the string of pearls around her neck and yanked until the thread that held them broke, but the pearls didn't fall. Instead, they hovered, slowly orbiting her open hand, innumerable and glowing in the red light of war.

The Fist made to go with her people from Quark, but before she could, Rake's hand encircled her wrist.

"Be safe," he said, his voice strained.

She could only barely hear him over the chaos Xenobia unleashed. The pearls became projectiles, hurtling toward the enemy, and as they did, they changed—from pearls into tiny flaming suns, each as hot and as cruel as high noon. The Imperial armor was no match for the heat, and they heard screams and confusion and horror echoing down from the ramparts.

Momentarily distracted, the Fist had looked up to bear witness to this feat. But when she turned back to Rake, his eyes were intense on hers. His feelings were clear. She was still organizing her own. The Fist smiled, then leaned in and gave him a kiss on the cheek. She tried to ignore her daughter, who watched with plain disgust. It was so like children to deny their parents romance, and for a moment it was as if there were no battle raging around them. It was as if they were simply mother and daughter again. And the thought made her smile for just a moment before a fresh volley of bullets snapped her focus back on the battle.

They had hoped the dragon would arrive before they got to the palace, but she was not there yet. Which. Was not ideal. But the Fist had trained her people well, had forged them through battle after battle. They knew what they were doing. Now she needed to trust them.

Thistle and the Wariuta boy ran behind her as they neared the south gate. It was with some annoyance that she saw his ax still strapped to his back. She knew the Wariuta were slow to kill, but still. He was a warrior. Her daughter was adept enough to protect the both of them, and his familiar didn't hurt. So. She would have to trust them, too.

She watched—as best she could—and marveled as her daughter moved. Thistle had always been a fierce thing. Fights in the schoolyard, arguments with teachers, a willfulness that the world, her mother included, had been unable to break. She had just wanted to keep her little girl safe, give her a quiet, predictable life. Why had she not seen? That life was never for Thistle, just as it had never been for her.

It was no wonder she ran away when she got the chance. To

Thistle it would have seemed the best and likely only escape. And how much of a relief had it been to her, even through the pain of Thistle's departure, to return to the life that she was meant for?

And how could her daughter have understood the horror of occupation if her mother was so fastidious about keeping her safe? A safe child needed not question the world. But it was clear that Thistle had now. And it seemed she had settled on some good answers.

The Fist's eye caught a soldier, hidden behind a decorative parapet, aiming his rifle at Thistle. She had moved forward without checking her blind spot first. He was too slow in sighting, and the Fist's bullet caught him before he could squeeze the trigger.

She smiled. Thistle still had something to learn. And, if they survived, her mother would teach her.

• CHAPTER 42 •

Commander Callum

A ll around Crandon the bells tolled. There was an attack
upon their shore. But there was nothing Callum could do
about that at the moment. Inside the Imperial Palace, he
tried to cut his way through the many servants who ran around as
they locked doors and cabinets and gathered provisions to bring
to the nobles already cloistered away in the catacombs. It was pan-
demonium, chaos as all the bodies clambered about, so unused to
threat, so terrified of battle. *Everyone dies,* Callum thought. And
yet people were still scared. Madness.

Though the chaos was to his advantage. Even the guards were
frightened, jumpy. Low-ranking men were often like this, Callum
knew, a side effect of their poor breeding. And none questioned
him, a commander in the Imperial Guard, as he moved through
doors that should have been closed to all but especially to someone with a pair of daggers strapped to his leg and a pistol on
his back.

It was almost too easy.

The Emperor would not be hidden away in the catacombs, which were liable to collapse if the ramparts were hit just right. He would instead be hidden in a secret cell within the Imperial Palace. Callum only knew where it was due to his time serving in the Emperor's Guard in his earlier years, a post often given to young men of noble blood hoping to carve a place for themselves in court.

Callum got there with such speed that it startled even him. When the coup happened, he would have to talk to Tsujima about better security. It was only when he got to the passage that led to the cell that he was given any bother.

General Mirimoto was in the antechamber to the cell, rather than leading his men. This was not unusual. One of the perks of high rank was to stay mostly safe from the bloody exertions of battle. He was able to send his commands from safety and comfort this way and concentrate only on strategy. *Someday*, Callum thought, *that will be me.* Mirimoto ordered a couple of his guards off to go see to this or that, leaving him woefully alone. This was a farce.

Mirimoto's wrinkled face regarded Callum coolly. "Ah, good. I need another message run to Commander Imanaka."

Callum couldn't help it; his face contorted into the shape of resentment. Mirimoto's eyebrows pulled up, shocked at his impertinence.

"Now, Soldier!" His voice impatient, as if Callum was someone he could command. Now. With them alone, and Mirimoto unguarded.

The pistol would be too loud. So instead, Callum stepped toward the general until they were so close they could have kissed. With dawning realization that something was terribly, terribly wrong, Mirimoto opened his mouth to call for a guard, but it was too late. Callum clamped a hand over the war hero's mouth and pinned him to his war table, their eyes locked in this strange and intimate moment, Mirimoto's wide, Callum's determined.

Once, the general had been something of an idol to Callum. But then he had ignored the young man again and again, his accomplishments never enough to gain favor in court. And so Callum had shipped off to the colonies, hoping to make a name there. It was only through the blood of so many, riches shipped back to Imperial stores, gold won, and land conquered that Callum had returned. And still nothing. From Mirimoto or the Emperor.

"Can't ignore me now, can you?" Callum hissed. He pulled the key that hung from a chain around the general's neck, the key to the Emperor's cell, pulled hard enough to leave red welts on the old man's skin and hard enough that the thin gold chain snapped. Callum pocketed the key.

General Mirimoto stared at him with bewilderment that simply stoked the flames of Callum's anger.

The dagger cut through Mirimoto's chest with ease. Callum had not fought for years, trained so many men, not to know where and exactly how to push a dagger into a man's heart.

A gasp, a groan, and the general was gone. His body crumpled at Callum's feet, just another carcass. Callum smiled. He stepped over what was once the great general of Nipran, careful not to let his feet track blood, and unlocked the door to the Emperor's cell.

There were no windows, of course, no egress or ingress that could not be guarded. So the room was much dimmer than the rest of the palace, alight with a decadence of ornate paper lanterns. The Emperor lay on a bed, dozing, as his two guards stood beside him.

Callum closed the door behind him, knowing that the room was soundproof. No sounds in, no sounds out.

"Who—" one of the guards started, but Callum was too quick for them. He pulled his pistol, and both men were dead before they could fully unsheathe their swords.

The Emperor stirred in his bed and blearily blinked his eyes open.

"Is it over?" he asked. His voice was so soft, so weak. Callum smiled. He sat down on the bed next to the Emperor, relishing this moment of trespass. To be so close to him, the supposed god, who smelled faintly of the stale urine his perfumed robes could not hide. The old man's face was vacant, his eyes clouded. Callum reached out a hand and brushed the man's face gently with his fingers. His skin was like paper beneath Callum's touch.

"Yes," he whispered, as if to a lover, his voice low. "It's over now."

Then he wrapped his hands around the Emperor's neck and squeezed.

The man thrashed a bit, but not with much force. He was so weak, his spindly fingers trying to pry Callum's hands off his neck to no avail, his legs kicking but finding no purchase. Callum watched, unblinking, not wanting to miss a thing, as the man who had determined so much of his disappointing life writhed beneath him.

Watched with delicious glee as the life faded from the clouded eyes.

"Thanks to the Emperor," he said. And he dropped the body back on its bed, eyes still open, mouth still agape, frozen in its final moments of horror.

Carefully, Callum stepped back through the cell, avoiding the pooled blood of the dead guards, and returned to where General Mirimoto lay dead. The bells were closer now, and he could tell that the Resistance had broken through the gates, much earlier than expected. He'd need to be fast if he was to find the Crown Prince first. He pulled a dagger from the general's hilt, and after only a moment of reluctance, stabbed himself in the side. He knew enough not to pierce anything vital; it was mostly a flesh wound. It would take time to heal, and it'd be uncomfortable, but it was a small price to pay.

He took a deep breath, clutching the wound at his side, letting it bleed over his fingers.

Then he thrust the door to the passageway open and shouted, "The Emperor is dead! General Mirimoto! He . . . killed him!" And he collapsed, theatrically, to the ground.

◆ CHAPTER 43 ◆

Alfie

The palace was mayhem, but Alfie could maneuver through that. His whole childhood had been a sustained flow of mayhem. The problem was that he wasn't sure what to do.

That wasn't exactly true; he knew what he was supposed to do. He was supposed to find the Crown Prince, and he was supposed to either hand him over to the Pirate Supreme's forces or kill the infant himself.

It was just that he wasn't sure he could.

If he didn't, the Pirate Supreme would have Alfie killed. Or Senator Tsujima would order him killed. But if he got caught trying, he'd be killed by the Guard. Most likely, he was not going to live through the night.

In the meantime, he figured, it would be good to be armed. The armory would be stripped. The guards' normal posts, too. The dungeons would be shut down, no one in or out. The only way to get a weapon, he realized, was to pull one off a dead body. It'd hardly be the first thing he'd pulled off a corpse, but it did mean heading directly into the chaos instead of, more sensibly, away from it.

Alfie steadied himself and then ran toward the battle that now raged within the palace itself.

Maybe he'd get shot before he had to make a decision. Maybe that would be some small mercy. Maybe his string of luck in surviving the unsurvivable would come to a predictable end, and no one would remember him, and no one would be disappointed by him, and maybe that was OK. Maybe that was fine, actually.

He ran.

He found what he needed in the atrium. The dragon's skeleton that had once hung from the ceiling was just a pile of gray rubble—equal parts bone and ceiling—on the floor. Beneath the enormous rib cage was a puddle of viscera and limbs that told Alfie the bodies below had been crushed to death by the fall. He would not be strong enough to lift the ruins, but if he could just find one whose weapon was close enough to the edge . . .

He was scrounging about unashamedly when he heard the clack of a pistol cocking. He froze. How had he not heard the approach? He must have lost his sense of what was close or far in the cacophony. Slowly, he put his arms over his head.

"Please—" he started.

"Who are you with?" demanded a voice. "What side do you fight for?" The accent was easy enough to place as Crandon born. But Alfie knew full well that plenty of Crandon natives fought for the Resistance. Without turning to see what the man was wearing, he'd have no way of telling which side he was on.

"I—" Alfie started, hoping he could make a pretense of conversation before having to commit, but the man jabbed him hard with his pistol in the back of his neck.

"Stay where you are!" he barked.

265

"I just want to get out of here," Alfie said. And for once he was telling the truth. "I don't want to fight anyone." Maybe the Alfie who had served on the *Dove* so long ago would have been embarrassed by his tears. But the Alfie who stood in the atrium with the blood of soldiers and the dust of a dragon's bones on his knees and hands was not. Could not be. He simply did not have the energy anymore. "Please."

Outside the atrium, Alfie could hear shouts echoing as those in battle called out to one another. In his rational mind, he knew who the fighters were. Guardsmen, of course, and plenty of them. But pirates, too. People from all over the Known World, all taking one last shot at the Empire before likely being crushed into oblivion, only to be remembered in cruel tavern songs about their flatulent corpses. And he was hit, hard, with the stupidity of it. The pointlessness of all of it. Probably nothing would change. Probably humans were too intractably violent in their nature to ever create any meaningful change. Too greedy, too hungry, too ugly. Fighting for right or for wrong, what did it matter? It all ended the same. Death, death, death, all the way down.

"I just want to live," Alfie said. His voice was quiet but without shame.

"Everyone wants to—" But the man's scoff was cut short.

The report of a rifle. A spray of something hot and wet on Alfie's back. He ducked, but the attacker clearly had had no interest in him; Alfie'd have been too late anyway. By the time Alfie turned all the way around, he was alone again, save for the man who had, until just moments ago, been holding him at gunpoint. There was a gaping hole in his back, still smoking gently from gunpowder. He'd been an Imperial guard after all.

The man looked to be perhaps ten years older than Alfie. Old enough to have a family, if he was inclined to one. He had the red hair of someone with parents or grandparents or great-grandparents buried in Quark. His eyes, open, were the ruddy brown of fields after the rain. How had he come to wear the uniform? Why did he come to die for his Emperor? *Everyone wants to live,* he had been about to say. Alfie was sure of it. And yet he had not, and Alfie had. Alfie wanted so badly for that to mean something, to make sense of the rat's nest of reality that swirled around him, but he could find neither sense nor meaning. The question of who deserved to live or die remained as arbitrary as ever.

Alfie relieved the corpse of its weapon and moved on.

· CHAPTER 44 ·

Koa

Koa hated it.

Hated the cold, hard streets, uneven and untrust-worthy beneath his feet. Hated the smells of smoke and burning metal and the strange chemical scents that coated his tongue. Hated the sounds of people, everywhere, too many people, shouting and yelling and shrieking, crying, hysterical as their lives either fell apart or ended. Hated that, as Tupac ran at his side, the animal felt so far away from him, as if they were running at the same pace but on different shores.

But most of all, he hated that he had anything to do with this destruction. Though he had not once lifted his weapon, he was still a part of this fight, was as guilty as anyone else as soon as the first cannon had fired and he did nothing to stop it.

For Kaia, he told himself.

For Kaia, at what price?

He wondered what Ica would have done.

He saw a child crying frankly, tears running pink streaks down his soot-covered face—his house was burning, and the child watched this calamity with unbridled despair. Koa wanted to run to him, to cradle him in his arms and whisper to him that all would be well, but it wouldn't be, would it? His parents may have died, probably had. He broke away from the group to go collect the child, but Thistle held him back, her fingers tight on his wrist.

"This way," she said firmly. "For Kaia."

When Koa turned to look at the child once more, he was gone.

Their destination was an enormous building that seemed to swallow an entire corner of the city. This was where the Resistance had said Kaia would be. But that was all he knew. It did not look beautiful, as was promised. It looked like the physical embodiment of greed: too big, too tall. Garish in the way that the Colonizer uniforms were garish, glints of gold and lacquer. And as he looked at it, the Colonizers finally started to make sense. They had worshipped at this palace, been told this was the greatest to which they could aspire.

No wonder their souls were broken.

It was the soldiers from Tustwe who made it through the gate first, leading the others. By the time Koa and Thistle walked through, only a spattering of dead bodies remained, and Koa was glad he could not see the blood that spilled in the dark of the night on the grounds. He could smell it, though, and hastened his step, did not look as Tupac helped himself to the carrion.

Thistle's mother was yelling at various people, who took her orders without question. She was a good leader, Koa could tell from the way people seemed to calm under her direction. Ica had been like that. It was easy to follow her orders because she always knew what she was doing. You could trust her with your life. And it seemed these people trusted Thistle's mother with theirs. He wished he felt the same. She yelled something at Thistle, who nodded.

"We go inside with the Sisterhood."

Koa pressed his lips into a thin line. Inside there would be slaughter, indiscriminate. As if reading his mind, Thistle flashed something like a smile—and a bit like a wince.

"Only soldiers now."

Koa took a deep breath. He whistled for Tupac, and they plunged into the building that was all wrong. If he thought it was cold and unnatural outside, nothing had prepared him for what was within—the walls seemed to hold the stale air in, suffocating and cloying, as if he were breathing only screams and bated breath. Thistle led him through strange and narrow passages, the clamor of their footfalls bouncing off the walls disconcertingly. Tupac stopped giggling, but his eyes swiveled everywhere, his head bowed as he ran. He looked as afraid as Koa felt. He should have lent his familiar courage, he knew. He had none to give.

It was hard to tell what sounds were coming from where in that dead building, and so when they turned a corner and ran headlong into two Colonizer soldiers, Koa's shock was double.

They all blinked at one another, but Thistle acted first. A deafening crack, and one of the soldiers fell. The gunpowder was thick in the air, and Koa gagged on it, spit filling his mouth as he tried not to look down at the soldier who lay dead on the floor—there was no question of that: he was definitely dead, and blood pooled around him—and soon it was not spit but bile that rose in his throat, and Koa could not stop staring at the body, the place where the man had once been. There was shouting around him, and activity, but Koa could not pull his eyes away from the death Thistle had made, final and permanent.

When he looked up, he saw Tupac in a fierce tug-of-war with the second soldier. Though that was not exactly what was happening—the soldier's hand was in Tupac's mouth, and Tupac was pulling, pulling, pulling as the man screamed and tried, with his one hand, to get the pistol at his side. If Koa did not act fast, the man would shoot his familiar, that much he could see, and it was as if everything slowed down as Koa pulled the ax from his back and threw it at the soldier just as the man pulled the safety back on his pistol.

There was a thwack as Koa's ax found home in the man's chest.

There was a heart-stopping bang as the pistol fired.

There was a cry of pain.

◆ CHAPTER 45 ◆

Keiko

Keiko needed to get to the catacombs, now. But where were the guards? She wasn't to carry the Crown Prince anywhere without a retinue of guards. The many princesses had, thankfully, been down at dinner when the attack had started, so hopefully they were already in the catacombs. But how had the guards neglected the Crown Prince?

She could hear the gunshots, and they were so close, maybe even in the palace already, and she rocked the baby in her arms as he mewled grumpily. She hoped he could not feel her heart as it drummed in panic.

She had left Kaia in her room, but that was before the attack. She could have been anywhere now and was probably gone. The chaos of the battle would have been more than enough cover. Good riddance. She had enough to worry about without harboring a fugitive, even a beautiful one. All the other nurses were gone. Alfie was, too, and a spy to boot. She hadn't even had a moment to take in this information before her world was torn apart again when the bells rang of invasion on the Imperial shore.

When an explosion went off just outside the nursery window, sending shards of glass and wood and stone flying, Keiko knew she had to move, guards or no. The Crown Prince howled in fear. She tried to hold back the tears that ran down her cheeks, but she couldn't. Gently, she kissed the Crown Prince on his little sweaty brow. If not for herself, then for him. She needed to be brave.

Clutching his highness to her chest, Keiko peeked out the door to the nursery but pulled her head back in quickly as a man came running down the hallway, laughing maniacally, smashing the many vases and kicking over the statues that lined the hallway. She wasn't sure what side he was on and didn't care to find out. He didn't seem interested in anything other than gleeful destruction, and soon the sounds of his voice and the crashes died down and were gone.

The nursery and the catacombs couldn't have been farther apart, which on a normal day made sense. Why keep life so close to death? But that terrible night, it felt like an insurmountable distance. She would have to move quickly and carefully, and so she darted out of the nursery, thankful for the years in the Hasegawa household that had taught her to move in silence.

She pretended then, as she went, that she was back there. That she was simply slipping down the hallways to Evelyn's room, that soon she would be snuggled against Evelyn's warm body, her fingers tangled in the hair Keiko herself had brushed with a thousand strokes before the lights went out. Evelyn was waiting, she told herself. Go, quietly, go.

Keiko scurried past a hallway where she could hear screams and shots, her stomach rolling. There was a part of her that wished she could stop and help, to save whoever's voices were being cut short, but there was a much larger part of her that knew, beyond any doubt, there was nothing she could do. She had one life to save, and if she could do that. Well. Her life would have been worth it.

She felt strangely out of her own body as she ran, as if she were watching herself from above. She had not been, for her entire life, a person of much consequence, and she had been just fine with that. All she wanted was to go about her own business, love whom she loved, and leave the room a little nicer than she had found it. And yet here she was now, ducking invaders and hiding behind doors as she carried the fate of the Empire in her arms. If she hadn't been so terrified, she might have laughed. How had it come to this?

They were about halfway through the palace when she heard her name called by a familiar voice. The pure shock of it stopped her in her tracks. She was suddenly very much back in her body again, her blood pumping, her breath shaky. She turned.

Alfie stood there, a pistol in his hands.

"Keiko!" he said, and he smiled, but she did not wait to hear more. She turned to run.

She had not made it far before she felt his hand on her arm, his grip tight on her skin. She tried to writhe away but could not without risking the Crown Prince, and so she had no choice but to let him catch her.

They regarded each other for a surreal moment, both panting, both ignoring the shots fired and the yelling and the explosions that rocked the palace.

"Well?" Keiko said, her voice alien to her own ears. She felt such a burning and consuming fury at this boy, this boy she had trusted, who was going to ruin everything. She clutched the Crown Prince ever tighter to her chest. "Are you going to kill me, too?"

"No, Keiko, I—" His eyes were sad. Good. She hoped he felt it every day for the rest of his life, hoped it crushed him beneath its weight. "I wanted to—"

But she did not find out what he wanted. There was a cry of delight, and Keiko whipped around to see two people turning the corner.

"The Crown Prince," the woman said.

"Good work, Alfie!" said the other. They were grinning the wide grin of the victorious. "I knew you could do it."

Alfie didn't so much whisper as he breathed: "The Pirate Supreme." His grip fell from Keiko's arm, and she turned to run in the opposite direction, but a wiry red-haired man came from that direction, his pistol pointed.

"I wouldn't," he said coolly.

Keiko gulped down a sob. It was all over. She was surrounded. She was practically crushing the Crown Prince in her arms, but what else could she do? They would have to pull him from her cold, dead hands.

So consumed with the sureness of her own impending death was she that Keiko did not notice when Alfie carefully, subtly moved her behind him, so she was marginally blocked from the Pirate Supreme and a more difficult target for the man with red hair.

The woman quirked a brow at them. "I do not think he's on our side."

"I am," said Alfie, but his voice was unsure. "But. I—I can't let you kill him."

The Pirate Supreme laughed, a big, merry laugh that was so wrong amid the despair and destruction of battle, it made Keiko flinch. "Come on, kid," they said. "That's the Emperor's son! You know what evil he'll bring into the world. He's everything we're fighting against."

"He's a baby," Keiko said. Her voice was so much bigger than she thought it could be, bigger even than the hiccupping sobs of the Crown Prince. He may not have understood exactly what was happening, but he clearly knew to be afraid.

The woman laughed. "Now he is. But it won't be long before he's a tyrant, just like all of them before him."

"Rake," Alfie said, turning to the man with the red hair. "Please. You know this is wrong."

But the man just shook his head sadly. "It's gotta be done. You know that."

"You promised," Alfie said to him. "You promised Flora you would protect me."

"I said I'd do my best," said Rake. "But I can't protect you from yourself. If you're asking me to choose between you and the Resistance"—he cocked his pistol and pointed it at Keiko—"I choose the Resistance."

"Rake—"

"Don't make me choose."

Keiko turned and saw the Pirate Supreme stepping quietly closer to them, their arms outstretched, their hands open, ready to receive the Crown Prince. "Give me the Prince, girl. There's no reason you need be hurt, but I will if I have to."

"OK," Alfie said, and Keiko's heart dropped into her feet. "OK, just . . ." He turned to Keiko then, his face unreadable. "Duck," he whispered.

Keiko looked back at him, puzzled. Alfie met her eyes, and she could see his message in them. She ducked.

Many things happened so quickly that Keiko could hardly track any of them.

Alfie fired his pistol at Rake, catching him in his shoulder. As

Rake fell to the ground, his own pistol fired, and Keiko could feel it more than hear it as it flew past her head and grazed Alfie's arm.

Alfie cried out in pain as the Pirate Supreme advanced, their hands scrabbling at the Crown Prince as Keiko thrashed away from their grip until there was another bang and a cry, and the Pirate Supreme staggered back, blood blossoming from their belly.

Alfie's pistol smoked, and he looked as shocked as everyone else that he had fired again. The woman howled and caught the Pirate Supreme as they fell backward, their face a mask of shock and pain.

"Run!" Alfie cried.

Keiko did not need to be told twice.

CHAPTER 46

Kaia

Kaia abandoned the room where Keiko had left her and ran into the palace, which was shrouded in chaos and cacophony. It was never the Wariuta way to revel in the death of anyone, even an enemy, but Kaia did not care. It was not enough, but it was still a small justice for her people that left Colonizer soldiers' bodies scattered throughout the palace. It would not bring her mother back. She did not care. The more of them that died the better; let them taste blood in their own mouths for once, let them wallow in a fraction of the pain they had left in their wakes.

If she had to kill some, then so be it. She could square herself with that. This was not the time to be the gentle-hearted leader Ica had encouraged her to be, and she knew in her heart that Ica would agree. Death blows were raining down on the Empire. It was more merciful at this point to kill it quickly. Decisively.

She tried to remember the route Alfie had taken them on before to get out, but all the many corridors looked the same, and she had no idea where she was—even the windows offered little help, since the grounds were dark save for the spots where things were aflame. It was near impossible to tell what was what in the unfamiliar landscape and amid all the destruction.

She picked a sword off a fallen soldier and gave it an experimental slice through the air. It wasn't her weapon of choice, but she could wield it. It was lighter than her ax, anyway. She felt a pang of sadness—that she did not have Chima by her side, that she was, in this strange place, only half the warrior she had been before.

And because her familiar was in her thoughts, Kaia did not think anything of the hyena giggle she heard at first. It was her mind, her memory, playing tricks on her in this desperate circumstance.

But when the giggling got louder, Kaia's breath caught.

That was a hyena.

Here.

She ran toward the sound.

If it was possible that other people kept hyenas, Kaia didn't know, didn't have the breadth of mind to consider as she sprinted through the cold halls of the palace, because it was possible, so possible that maybe, maybe, maybe a Wariuta person was here, in this nest of the Colonizers, and if there was, then she was not alone, after all this time, she was not alone, and perhaps maybe, maybe, maybe she was not the sole survivor of her people, and then maybe, maybe, maybe she would survive. They would survive. She would see to that. She could feel tears streaming down her face but paid them no mind. She had something to live for now, something greater than the fall of Nipran, something pure and good and loving and right. She would find her old self, the one who could imagine a future. Maybe.

The giggling was high and loud in her ears. She turned a

corner, and before she could fully understand what she was looking at, a great force knocked her over and pinned her down.

Kaia gasped but then felt the rough kiss of a hyena's tongue across her cheek. The animal pulled back, and Kaia's eyes focused.

"Tupac?"

The animal growled his pleasure at seeing a familiar face. And as he did, the great possibility of what could be set Kaia's heart racing. She could hear the rush of blood in her ears. She shakily got to her feet. She felt herself moving as if she were moving through sand, impossibly slow and unwieldy.

And there he was.

Koa.

She let out a sharp cry, a noise she did not know her body could create. She had never let her heart even entertain the idea that her sweet, good brother had survived the massacre, it was so unlikely, so impossible. But there he was, his big, warm body so out of place in this terrible, cold country. Koa and Tupac, as intact as if the Colonizers had never come. Like a dream of a better life, a better world than the one she lived in. She had never loved him more than in this moment, when he was here and alive.

But he had not seen her. His hands were covered in blood, and he was trying his best to stanch a freely bleeding wound in Genevieve's thigh. The girl. Why was Koa trying to save her? Surely she would fight even now for her beloved Empire. Only Koa would try to save an enemy's life in the heat of battle. It was his foolishness, his soft heart that made her see that this was not a dream. This was real. Koa's softness had always been real. She tried to stifle the relief she felt when she realized that was another thing the Colonizers had not killed.

"Koa." Her voice sounded far away in her ears, an echo from the horizon. "Step back."

Koa's head snapped around, and his face lit up like the sun but only for a moment. His eyes narrowed at the sword in Kaia's hands. "What are you doing?" he asked, but it was clear that he thought he knew exactly what she was doing. He stood and put his body between them.

"Kaia," Genevieve croaked. "I am so . . ."

But Kaia did not want to listen. "You—" she raised her sword.

Koa put his hand on her arm, forced her to meet his eye. And just like that, she was back in Yunka again, her brother's gaze calming her from one of her many rages. The thrumming blood in her ears quieted. "She's on our side," Koa said.

Koa pulled her into a tight hug, his big arms around her. She hugged him back, barely registering the warm slide of blood on his skin. He kissed her forehead.

"You're alive," she murmured again and again. She could feel her tears pooling between them and she did not care, did not care that her nose ran or that they were in the middle of a battle or that Genevieve lay on the floor bleeding to death.

"I'm not the only one. There are more of us," he whispered. "In Puno."

More. She had been so sure she was all that was left of her people. It was as if she had been struck by lightning. She pulled back, her shoulders square again, the Kaia who needed to lead her people emerging from the ashes of the massacre. She could do this. She had to do this. And distantly, she was aware that the thought no longer scared her. It was time.

"Why are you here?" she asked finally.

He gave her a quizzical look, then smiled his big sunrise smile. "To rescue you, obviously. To take you home." He knelt back down next to Genevieve and resumed tying the makeshift bandage he'd been attending to earlier. "I couldn't have gotten here without her."

Genevieve's eyes were going soft around the edges. She was losing a lot of blood, and consciousness was clearly becoming elusive. Her eyes fluttered, and Koa's hands shook as he tried to make sense of the wound and the blood that would not stop pouring. She could let Genevieve bleed to death, let her bear witness to the slow evacuation of life from her own body. But if Genevieve had brought Koa to her . . . then she was not the girl Kaia thought she was.

"Give me that," Kaia barked, and Koa stepped aside. He had done some good, getting the wound well covered. But he had been too gentle to tie the bandage tight enough to actually stop any bleeding. The girl would lose her leg, but she could survive. Together, Koa and Kaia tied the bandage tight, tight enough to wake the girl momentarily, tight enough to exorcise some small fraction of Kaia's hate. She had to be better than that now, for her people. She needed to survive, and she needed to get home. And maybe Genevieve could help her get there. "Done," she said, proud of her handiwork. She'd always been excellent at patching wounds. "That should stop the bleeding."

With a grunt, Koa lifted Genevieve's body. Her face was white, but Kaia could see her chest rising and falling with breath. She was alive.

"Come on," Koa said. "I think I can remember how we came in. Let's go." He started in the opposite direction from which Kaia had come.

Kaia hustled after him, sword at the ready. "Where?" she asked.

"Home," Koa said.

As if it were as simple as that.

Kaia hoped he was right.

CHAPTER 47

Kwizera

Xenobia's arms felt like home. Kwizera looked up into her eyes. She was crying freely, her face a mess of tears and spit and snot. They had never loved her more. They reached up, ran their fingers across her cheek, tried their best to wipe the tears. There was not enough strength left in them to do this. They let their hand fall, tried to focus their mind, to find the words.

"Hold on," Xenobia said.

Kwizera knew they could not.

Distantly, bells rang, different bells now, the bells that marked the death of the Emperor. For a moment, it seemed that the world went still as all of Crandon realized what had happened.

"We won," Kwizera rasped.

"Yes," Xenobia said. "Yes, my love, you did it."

Kwizera smiled past the taste of the blood in their mouth.

"Do something!" Rake yelled, but both Xenobia and Kwizera ignored him. Not even Xenobia was powerful enough to stop death.

"I should . . ." Kwizera tried to find their breath, it was so hard to speak. "I should have never left you."

Xenobia coughed a laugh through her tears. "No," she agreed. "You shouldn't have."

"Do you forgive me?"

"Yes," Xenobia replied, so easily, so fervently that Kwizera knew she was telling the truth. "And look what you've done," she said, her voice steadying. "The Emperor is dead. Nipran will fall."

It was so hard to hold their head steady, and Kwizera felt it loll to the side. Outside the window, the first sliver of sunlight was just bleeding into the blackened horizon. They smiled. The sun would rise on a new world today, a world they had helped make.

"Use my blood," Kwizera said.

But Xenobia shook her head.

"End it—" They coughed, felt blood dribble down their chin. "With both our blood, she will hear." Xenobia caught their face again and kissed them hard on the mouth. She pulled away, and their blood was streaked across her lips. She was so beautiful, and Kwizera wanted to tell her so, but there was a rattling in their chest, and they knew the blood was in their lungs now.

They tried to say *I love you.*

They could not.

• CHAPTER 48 •

Rake

R ake watched in mute horror as the life faded from the
Pirate Supreme's eyes. Death had come, and it had come
for the wrong person.

He fell to his knees. He could see the witch screaming her
grief, but he could not hear it. He could not hear anything except
the ringing in his ears, the high-pitched tone of rage as unceasing
as a toothache.

Xenobia lifted a dagger then from the Supreme's body and held
it aloft. The sounds of the world came rushing back to Rake then—
the battle, the distant explosions, the beating of his own heart.
And the witch. She was chanting words Rake could not follow, in
a language he did not speak, her eyes streaming tears, her nose
flaring with effort. She cut herself then, a clean line across her
wrist. Before Rake could try to stop her from doing more damage
to herself, she plunged both her hands into the Pirate Supreme's
wound. Rake watched, open-mouthed in revulsion.

But as she chanted, Rake started to hear screams rising from outside the palace. He looked out the window and immediately saw why.

A wave, an enormous tower of water, taller even than the statue of the Emperor, loomed over Crandon's coast.

"Xenobia," Rake whispered, fear rendering his voice faint. "You can't—"

"Let it be done," she said. Each word was like a bullet. She slammed her hands onto the ground, smearing the mix of her and the Pirate Supreme's blood upon the palace floor.

The wave fell.

The crash was louder than the firing cannons, bigger than the sky. He watched as the water slammed through buildings and rushed its way up the many cobbled streets, an ever-expanding spread of destruction. Even there, so far from the water, he could smell the brine of the Sea. For the first time in his life, the scent did not bring him comfort.

Rake did not have to see the docks to know they were gone. Did not need to see the small fishermen's houses that lined the water to know that nothing would remain. He would not mourn the Emperor's navy, but this. This was such a wide swath of people, and he could not be sure they all deserved to die. But they were gone. He blinked in shock. They had already won.

"This is the boy's fault. Your little spy," Xenobia hissed. The sound of her voice made the hair on Rake's arms stand on end. He turned slowly to face the witch, found that he could not resist her words. "Find him," she said, and it was a command. A command he could not decline. "Kill him."

And so he ran. To find Alfie. The boy had run, naturally, run for his life. Rake would see that Alfie would not make it. His feet pounded the beat of vengeance on the marble floors of the palace as he ran. The boy. That stupid boy. How stupid Rake had been to trust him.

He did not think of the promise he had made to Florian.

He could not protect the boy from himself.

A trail of drips of blood led him to Alfie, who had made it all the way to the kitchens on the first floor. He'd nearly made it out but had been foiled by his lack of care. Incompetent as ever.

Rake roared. He aimed his pistol at Alfie, but when he pulled the trigger, nothing happened. He was out of bullets. Alfie, eyes wide, tried to run off, but Rake was too fast for him. He was taller, bigger, stronger. He tackled Alfie, and both their bodies fell hard on the stone floor. Rake could hear Alfie's head smack the ground, and he felt no regret. He wrestled the boy down—it was easily done—and pinned him beneath his body.

"Please!" Alfie cried.

Rake punched him, his fist slamming against Alfie's jaw. His temple. His chest and his belly.

Alfie's face was a bloody thing, his breath ragged and wet.

Hadn't Rake taught him better? All those years aboard the *Dove*, had Alfie learned nothing from him? *Keep your head down. Do as you're told. Be safe, please.* Years-old anger burned inside him as he looked at the boy, the boy he couldn't teach, and saw his own failure looking back at him.

No. Alfie deserved this. He had killed the Pirate Supreme, and for whom? An Imperial prince? That kindness had only created more pain, had punished the wrong people, and he would pay, he would pay with his life for his terrible judgment, his stupidity, his—

Rake felt it before he heard anything. A disturbance, a change in the air, like his body was light and his mind was blank. Vaguely, he was aware of Alfie sputtering, his breathing ragged and desperate, but he paid the boy no mind. He stood and followed his feet out of the palace.

They all did. Everyone who was still inside filed out from their hiding places, their hands limp at their sides. The survivors of Crandon. They stepped over the bodies of the fallen, no one even pausing to look down. They all looked up.

The sun cast its light over Crandon, blinding except for the coiling shadow as long as the horizon.

She sang. A song with no melody, but undeniably a song, music that caught in Rake's throat. He could feel it as much as hear it, and it was like loneliness and kinship, loss and love, the emptiness he felt when he looked at the Sea, the possibility the Sea promised. No one spoke. They all listened.

And as the First Dragon flew, her song washed down over them.

To his surprise, Rake knew the words.

Two souls fight
For love, to be
True love's might
To save the Sea.

• CHAPTER 49 •

The First Dragon

I do not come because they asked. I come because it is time. Every epoch, this day comes. When some destructive force becomes too great. When I must remind the humans of who and what they are. Of what they have done. So that the Sea can be restored once more. So that creation can return to this world.

This time is no different than all the other times. Every time I return, they learn. And every thousand years, they forget. My life is long, and always the same. I breathe in, and oceans rise. I breathe out, and empires fall.

I know they call what I do a song, but it is not that, exactly. My song is a song because that is the closest word for what it is, but that is an approximation. They will hear me, and they will hear what I have heard. They will see what I have seen. They will feel what is real. And the balance will be made. This is not justice—the dead will stay dead. There is no eye for an eye that will do true justice.

There is only reckoning. And that is what I will give them.

As I call down to them, I can see and hear and feel each and every one of them.

Still clutching the Crown Prince in her arms, Keiko staggers. She has never raised her hand to another person, never once allowed another to suffer if she could help it. But all the same, she lives here, lives comfortably off the backs of strangers on distant shores whether she thinks of them or not. Now she sees the children forced to dive into dangerous, rocky waters in Iwei, to catch those oysters she likes to eat. She shivers with their cold, she trembles with their fear. But still she stands. She is stronger than she thinks.

The witch, Xenobia, does not stagger, does not fall. She knows who she is and what she has done. There is no part of her engaged in self-deception. Still, tears cut down her face, through the blood of her beloved. She feels the blast of icy water as it hits the shore, feels the last gasps of air of the drowned. She cries out with their shock and their pain, feels the terror of so many lives cut short in an instant. The anger that burns inside her, the flame of rebellion ebbs at long last. There is no need for defiance in this world she helped make.

Rake does fall. He crumples to the ground, crushed beneath the weight of all the corpses he has made. He feels each death as if each were his own. And when that is done, he feels the fear he put in Alfie. Feels the constant shame he instilled, the shame that should have been his own. That he could not protect him or Florian, that he failed them as the only father either of them would ever know. That he could not protect their innocence, or their bodies, or their minds from cruelties too vast and unending for children. That in his singular purpose to redeem himself with the Sea, Rake allowed Alfie to be the collateral damage. He howls his agony.

Kaia—the warrior, the leader—kneels. She does not weep, does not cry. She accepts the pain of Tomas Inouye's death with what humans might call grace. She sees his parents receive the news, watches as his body, cold and still, is revealed to them, feels their hearts break in her breast. If she feels regret, it is not for Tomas but for all the lives she was willing to take this day. She makes her hand into a fist and raises it to me. A salute that I accept.

Safe at home outside the manor xe bought with ill-begotten coin, Senator Tsujima witnesses the many people xe enslaved. I make sure xe sees each and every one of them, every man, woman, and child xe traded and sold, their sadness and their soul weariness. I make xem feel the salt water in their throats when they were tossed overboard to evade antislaving navies. I lay down on xem the pain of watching their children walk away in chains, knowing they will never see them again. My reckoning passes through xyr body like flames, and xyr body cannot bear the magnitude of the suffering xe has caused in the world. Xe asphyxiates on it, xyr breath leaving xem slowly, xyr eyes bulging with pain. I do not mourn xem when xe dies.

Xe is not the only to die under the weight of this reckoning, but xe is the one that pleases me most.

The woman who calls herself the Fist gasps with pain. She has not killed many in her time, but she has ordered the men who did kill. She feels the blight on their souls, feels the taint of blood spilled that haunts their dreams. She sees the faces of the fallen. Feels the loss of their families, their mothers. She fights for freedom, has always known it is a bloody business, that power seeks only to retain power, no matter the cost. And so she can stand this pain, can weather its storm. It is a grave responsibility she is willing to carry for Quark, and for all those who writhed beneath Imperial boots.

Koa weeps. He sees the children of the soldier he killed, his little girl and his baby boy. Sees them as he scoops them up in his arms and covers their face with kisses. He feels the pain they will feel when they are old enough to understand that they will never see their father again. And while I sing, he shares their tragedy. He will never kill again. I hope he will never have the need.

In the Sea, the mermaid called Evelyn writhes in torment, her body racked with Keiko's hurt at being forgotten, with the children in the Cold World's devastation as they watch the forest they called home destroyed for the wood in the trees they called their friends, the same wood Evelyn's own casket was built of. But her love is there to hold her, to soothe her. She will be comforted, even if she is not comfortable.

Flora has already punished herself enough. How many nights has she replayed the murder of that merchant? A crime committed for survival, a crime she has never once forgotten, not even in the moments of her greatest happiness. This is how it should be. Humans never have clean hands. But she has already reckoned with herself and her regret—my song for her only treads a well-beaten path.

Though she cannot stand, Thistle lets her body go slack, lets herself slip from Koa's arms. She does not feel her body hit the ground. The cries of the Wariuta children echo in her ears. She feels the flames of their homes being burnt lick against her skin. She feels the rope of the noose tied around Dai's neck, feels his urine run down his leg, as he realizes he is about to die. She feels the bullet cut through her mother's neck. She retches.

Clutching his hand to his chest, Alfie hiccups a sob. His toes go numb with the biting cold of a winter he survived but those two children he stole bread from did not. He feels the crushing sadness that Flora felt when he stole their gold to spend on

mermaid's blood, the keen slash of disappointment but not surprise. The destruction of her hope. He feels the sharp betrayal
Keiko felt when she found out what he was. But worse, he feels
Rake's betrayal after he pulled the trigger, feels the witch's pain as
her lover crumples to the ground. The pain is crushing, so much so
that he yearns for death, and he does not know if he will survive.
He can, of course, we both know. He has lived with guilt before.

Outside the home paid for with his daughter's life, the Lord
Hasegawa screams in pain. He has never truly suffered, despite
having caused so much suffering, has never had any real consequences for his frivolousness and his malice. It is not my reckoning
that will kill him—but when he passes out, he hits his head hard
on the stone fence that surrounds his good fortune, and it is that
blow that ends his life. His wife, the Lady Hasegawa, weeps into
her kimono as her daughter wept, knowing she was unloved by
her mother. But she survives.

Within the depths of a constabulary jail, Jung Hoon laughs. It
is not happy laughter, but he cannot cry, not anymore. His tears
dried long ago. He does not laugh for the man he killed—the pimp
who beat him, who had to die so that he could possibly be free—he
laughs for the child he once was, the one he walked away from and
never thought of again.

All across Crandon, the humans that comprise Nipran weep
and scream, they collapse and they lose consciousness. Those who
walked by the homeless and the destitute without even a moment's
fleeting sympathy. Those who shooed the starving orphans from
their storefronts so they would not disrupt business. Those who
traded in goods they knew caused destitution and war in nations
far enough away that they simply did not care.

There are deaths, of course, many in the Senate and the constabulary. Those who viciously bolstered Imperial supremacy,

those who knew, on some level, that their place on the top of the world was precarious and had to be jealously and violently protected. Those who knew that their greed wreaked human and natural destruction but did not cease. Those who understood that the price of their great nation was paid for in the blood of shamans, witches, and priestesses, their wisdom snatched from life and memory in the name of a false god, a small man, already unthinkably rich. They leave behind this world they tainted, and though some will be mourned, none will ultimately be missed.

I do not spare the children of Crandon. If they do not know, if they do not see, then they will live to see all this suffering done again. But I am gentle with them. I show them the children not unlike themselves, made into refugees by Imperial troops. I show them the myriad injustices committed in their names. Some of them weep. Some of them fall. But they will all live to remember this day, to speak of it to their children, and to their children's children. Generations later, the children will forget, but I cannot stop that.

Only Finn Callum glares up at me, curious but unmoved. Every epoch there are those like him. Broken, somehow. Unable to hear me, unable to be reckoned with. It is exactly this deficiency that allows him to kill without bother. To seek power and fortune through the blood of others. His time will be short, but the shadows cast by his victims are long. There is no salvation for someone like him.

Like I said. This is not justice.

I sing and I sing as I circle over Crandon. I am responsible for their remorse, and it is my duty to bear witness to them. I hear their cries. I feel their pain, immense and sharp. Their reckoning fills me, my belly swells with it. In one hundred years, I will lay a new clutch of eggs, and once again, my children will fly through this world. Once again, they will be hunted down and killed. I always hope this time will be better for them. The words to my song are always the same. Each time two souls fall in love. Each time their love sets the world in motion to seek redemption. Each time the powerless topple the powerful. It is always the same, has always been the same.

The Sea is forever destined to forget. And I am forever destined to remember.

The remembering is my labor, and I shoulder it alone.

Perhaps if I were stronger, if I could stand to do this more often.

Perhaps then the pain would not be so great.

I will never know.

◆ CHAPTER 50 ◆

Xenobia

After the song, the First Dragon landed on the Imperial Palace, her claws crushing the ancient stone in their grasp. All watched as the legacy of the Emperors crumbled down, nothing left except rubble, and the bodies within.

Xenobia knew that now the people of Crandon and the Resistance alike would find and bury the dead. That Kwizera's body was somewhere within those stones. But she could not bear to see them battered and gone, not again. Her hands were still sticky with their blood.

So she walked to the Sea.

Across Crandon were the sounds of turmoil, of grief. People still wailed their horror and their regret, their pain and their sorrow. Xenobia paid them no mind. She knew what she needed to do.

The Sea was calm now, though pieces of what used to be Crandon's coast washed gently against the new shore. Xenobia watched a bloated body come in with the tide. A woman in a tattered yukata, her face submerged. Xenobia moved on.

The water was cold around Xenobia's feet, though it smelled more of oil and smoke and destruction than the Sea. She scanned the horizon. The great tidal wave had decimated the statue of the Emperor. All that remained were his feet, standing bodiless, reigning over nothing. She could not smile, but she did feel as glad as was possible.

She looked down at her hands. They were red, her skin stiffening as the blood dried.

She walked into the Sea.

The mermaid that would be born of Kwizera's blood would not be Kwizera. But they would hold the memory of them, of their service to the Sea. Of their love and their bravery. Of their great deed in ending the Empire of Nipran.

If the mermaid would find her, she did not know.

If the mermaid would remember her, she could not ask.

If the Sea would resurrect her as one of her daughters, she doubted.

But it was a small price to pay, to know that some part of Kwizera would live on. That they would be rejoined with the Sea they loved so much. Her power for their memory. Her life to breathe life back into theirs.

Without them, there was nothing left. No purpose.

The water swirled around her neck as she walked farther into the Sea, and just before her head was submerged, she thought of Kwizera's wide smile, the smell of their hair.

When the Sea swallowed her, she smiled.

CHAPTER 51

Koa

I t felt at first as if there was no moving forward. That they all would simply perish where they stood or lay or knelt. But slowly, there was the quiet hum of activity across what was left of the palace grounds. Melancholy movement. Koa had picked up enough of the Colonizers' tongue to understand some. Whispers of how to find the bodies and where they could be buried. No one spoke of what had just happened because no one needed to.

He watched as a Colonizer girl approached Kaia, and was a little surprised that they seemed to know each other. She was carrying a baby, who was sleeping soundly. Koa felt a pang of affection for the baby's soft little face, his complete separation from what had just happened. He deserved his sleep. He was innocent.

The girl did not speak Sky Tongue, and Kaia did not speak the Colonizers' language, but they stood together in silence and in solidarity. Kaia ran a gentle thumb down the baby's cheek. The girl smiled at his sister, and Koa smiled, too. Maybe life would go on. Maybe one day Kaia would fall in love. Maybe that had already started.

Thistle's mother cradled her in her arms, Thistle openly weeping. Koa stepped away. It was not his place. He scratched Tupac behind the ear. The animal was bewildered but calm. Koa knelt next to him, trying to grapple with the feeling that nothing made sense and everything made sense simultaneously. He wondered if Ica could see him now, in this moment when he missed her so deeply.

He looked up only when he heard the terrible commotion. A man yelling, shouting, screaming at everyone. It was a man he recognized.

Commander Callum.

Koa stood. He had dropped his ax long ago, but he was still big, bigger than Commander. And he would not let him hurt anyone else.

"Lies!" Commander shouted. "Weakness!"

People gasped and turned away from him, horrified by his lack of respect in this holy moment in time. His desecration of the sacred event they had all shared. He defiled the peace that had washed over Crandon.

When Commander saw Kaia, he picked up a fallen sword, pointed it at her.

"You!" he yelled, and his voice was like a malediction. A curse. "You will let this savage take the Prince?" the man shouted at the crowd of people who scurried away from him.

Koa knew that Kaia did not understand this, but she didn't need to. She stepped between the Colonizer girl holding the baby and the man who was now screaming at her. Koa tried to move in front of her, but she pushed him back with her short arm. And Koa knew better than to disregard his sister.

She readied her sword.

Commander's eyes were wild as he charged at Kaia. With a great swing of his sword, he aimed a slash that would split her head in two. But Kaia's blade met his with a mighty clash, her strength a match he did not expect. He stumbled back in shock.

"You will kill no more of the Wariuta," she said. Her voice was not angry so much as certain. Firm. It was like a command. It was like Ica's voice. "Not today. Not ever."

They circled each other like hyenas, and Tupac giggled with anxiety that Koa shared. Kaia was a fearsome warrior. But the sword was not her weapon of choice; it was the weapon of Colonizers. And he also knew that it was easier to kill if you had no conscience. Commander clearly did not.

Koa blinked, and in that momentary distraction, he missed Kaia make her first move, a feint to the man's left, and once again their blades met, the clash of metal echoing over the now silent crowd. People watched, their mouths open, but no one spoke as Kaia and Commander fought. Commander kicked Kaia's stomach, and she stumbled back, winded. He tried to take advantage of this, tried to drive his sword directly through her belly, but she moved out of the way at the last possible moment, their bodies practically entwined. It was like a dance, except without joy.

Koa didn't want to watch, but he also couldn't look away.

He winced at the sound of the swords as they slid against each other, the shriek of steel on steel. But it was when Commander's sword slashed Kaia's sword-bearing arm that Commander cried out in triumph and Koa cried out in dismay. It was involuntary, a cry of fear ripped from his chest. There were gasps as Kaia's sword clattered onto the stones.

With a malicious grin wide across his face, Commander lunged with his sword once again, but this time when Kaia moved out of the way, she grabbed him around his neck and hurled him to the ground.

Commander's body slammed down, and the impact of it jolted the sword from his hand. It skittered away from him, and he made to crawl for it, but Kaia was too fast for him. She tackled him, and their bodies became a blur of punches and biting and growls and grunts, until, to Koa's infinite relief, Kaia wrapped herself around Commander from behind, her legs holding his body down, her arm around his neck in a tight stranglehold. A move their mother had taught her.

She squeezed.

Commander thrashed and writhed in her grasp, his hands seeking purchase but finding none. Kaia was too strong for him. She gripped him tight as the fight slowly drained from him. First his legs, then his arms. His mouth gawping like a fish's.

When she stood, the man who had killed their mother, who had killed their people, was gone. His eyes still open, frozen in his final moments of fury and fear and agony. No one stepped forward to press them shut.

CHAPTER 52

Thistle

The *Leviathan* still sailed. Improbably. Impossibly.

Her many sails still intact. Her mermaid figurehead still beautiful, hair forever flowing in a windy moment captured so long ago. She rocked gently in the sea, her anchor still holding fast. Rake, Thistle, her mother, and the few pirates who remained of the Pirate Supreme's crew had paddled out to her to see what remained.

Though seaweed and a few dead fish were strewn across her deck, she was entirely whole. Rake surveyed the scene with open-mouthed wonder. He seemed unable to find the words he needed to command the men.

"Clean up the decks," the Fist said. Not unkindly, but the men still followed her orders without question. "And check below for water damage."

Thistle found that somehow it was easier to keep her balance on her crutches and new wooden leg on the ship than on the shore. Maybe it was the cradling of the sea. Maybe it was simply that here she need not balance on uneven cobblestones. Whatever it was, she felt oddly at ease here on this pirate ship she had spent so long seeking to destroy.

Overwhelmed by the magic of the *Leviathan*'s survival, Rake staggered to a barrel that was tied to the deck and sat down. He ran trembling fingers through his bright-red hair.

"What do we do now?" Rake asked the Fist.

Thistle's mother put her hand on his shoulder, gave it a little squeeze. "We bring the Wariuta home. Koa has said that they are willing to take in the Crown Prince and the princesses, raise them among their own. At least there those girls will have a chance at a good life."

Thistle smiled. Koa would be a great carer for them. It was what he wanted, after all. To care for the children. And Kaia, Thistle knew, would be the leader the Wariuta needed to come back from the devastation. The princesses' nurse, Keiko, would be joining them, which would hopefully make the transition some-what less abrupt.

"And then what?" Rake asked.

"Then . . . we hunt down every vial of mermaid's blood in the Known World." The Fist looked out over the Sea, her eyes thought-ful. "And we return it to where it belongs. The Pirate Supreme may be gone, but that doesn't mean we need abandon their cause. We will do what's right."

Rake stood then, and he was the steady, sure man Thistle had first met not so long ago. He wasn't smiling, exactly, but it was as if there were a smile caught in his eyes as he looked straight at Thistle's mother.

"The Pirate Supreme isn't gone," he said. "She's right here."

The Fist raised a brow. "If anyone would take up their mantle, I'd think it would be you, Rake. The crew already answers to you. You were their first mate."

But Rake shook his head. "I can't. Not after . . ." He took a deep breath. "I can't be trusted with that much authority. But you. You could lead us. If you're willing."

The Fist pressed her lips into a thin line. "Hmm. We'll ask the crew to take a vote. I won't take a throne I haven't earned."

Rake smiled this time in earnest. "Fair enough."

"And you?" Thistle's mother asked her. "Will you serve aboard this pirate ship?" She smiled warmly at her daughter. "Your life is your own. It's for you to decide."

Thistle thought of Koa and the Wariuta. Of Quark. Of Crandon, still fraught with devastation and trauma. "Can I think about it?"

"Of course." Her mother took her hand and brushed a gentle kiss across Thistle's knuckles. "You have all the time in the world now."

The girls who had been princesses all peered over the side of the *Leviathan* as the Red Shore came into view. They cooed and whooped with excitement, making the hyena calls Kaia had taught them. Koa had helped them choose new names for themselves, and Rake had taught them to tie knots in his spare time. They seemed to have come alive on the voyage, happy and content to be allowed to decide things for themselves, to let their hands get dirty, to be as loud as they pleased. For his part, Tupac seemed content to receive whatever snuggles the princesses were willing to sit still long enough for.

The first rowboat carried Kaia and the vast majority of the girls. Kaia gave Thistle a perfunctory goodbye wave, which Thistle was glad to receive. It was more regard than she expected.

"Are you coming?" Koa asked. He had one foot in the second

rowboat that would carry him, Tupac, and a handful more girls, the other foot still on the deck.

Thistle swallowed hard. She had been considering this moment for the whole voyage, changing her mind daily, hourly, about what was the right thing to do. Now that it was here, she felt sure but sorrowful. She shook her head.

"I'm sorry, Koa," she said. She brushed a tear from her cheek. "I don't belong in Yunka. I'm . . . I'm going to stay with my mother. I'm going to help make sure this never happens again."

Thistle wasn't sure what she was expecting, but Koa bounding across the deck to wrap her in a hug so tight it whisked her off her feet was not it. She laughed through her tears as he squeezed her in a warm embrace.

"I'll miss you," he said. He was not crying as Thistle was, but he looked wistful. "You know, pirates used to stop on our land all the time—always had the best stories. It's a tradition you should continue."

Thistle smiled. "I wouldn't want Tupac to miss me too much."

"Don't be a stranger." He gave her one last smile, then boarded the rowboat with the girls and disappeared over the edge of the *Leviathan* as they were lowered down.

Thistle watched as they made their steady progress to the shore. She watched until all the girls were safely on land. They waved back at the *Leviathan*, and then, following Kaia, they took off at a run toward Puno.

The Pirate Supreme came and stood next to Thistle. She put her arm around her daughter.

"Are you ready?" her mother asked. Behind them, Rake was barking orders to the men, to lift the sails, to batten things down.

Thistle grinned. "Let's go make something of this world."

The Sea

The blood of so many of her lost daughters returned in a flood, and now the Sea can do nothing except birth them anew, one by one, until she is restored. Only not entirely. So much is still gone. So much is new. So much is still in flux.

She can hear her mermaids, but she cannot speak to them, not yet. She wants to offer them words of love, of comfort, but finds that she cannot yet command her voice. She has too much healing to do. So instead, she watches and listens to them. Some rejoice. Some mourn. Two entirely new mermaids, Kwizera and Xenobia, find each other, find home at last, at last, at last. Someday the Sea will join them in their happiness. But not today.

This will happen again, she knows.

There is nothing she can do to stop it, she knows.

But the First Dragon is back in her cavern, nestled into the scar tissue of the Sea's own formation. The dragon alone knows her mother this intimately, understands that the architecture of where she lives is the scar tissue of the Sea's becoming. The echoes of volcanoes that changed the shape of the world are carved into the Sea, forming valleys that are deeper than mountains on the land are tall. And that is where the Sea must focus her attention now, on her dimmest, most secret corners.

It hurts, *says the Sea.*

It always does, *says the First Dragon.*

I will never recover, *the Sea laments.*

You always do, *the First Dragon replies.*

Far from what some called the Known World, the reverberations of her great trauma hit the shores in rogue waves, too large and deadly to be understood on a human scale. They will never know what caused this disruption to their lives, never understand the many forces that fit together to create their sudden tragedies. Some will call it the work of gods. Others will call it fate. The result is the same. Death, destruction, loss that they did not earn but suffer anyway. Perhaps one day a world will exist in which no one is punished for the crimes of others. More likely not.

But there, in a kelp forest: a baby otter is born, completely unaware of all the turmoil that preceded it. Her mother licks the fluids of her own body off her child. They are unbothered by circumstance. The Sea watches them with interest.

She does not know if the baby otter will survive. Many do not. But she hopes it will.

・ EPILOGUE ・

Alfie

FIFTEEN YEARS LATER

Jung Hoon dumped a steaming pot of thick white noodles into the bubbling fish broth Alfie had spent all morning preparing. The lunch rush would start soon, and Alfie's food cart had gained a large and loyal clientele of fishermen and merchants. Now and again, when the *Leviathan* made port in Crandon, Rake would come visit. He was a softer man now, and Alfie was glad for that. They hugged whenever he left.

It was more than Alfie could have ever dreamed to ask for.

Alfie sliced scallions by rote as he watched the people of Crandon walk by. Most days were the same. Alfie would wake up before the sun, head to the fish market, and get what he needed from the same people who'd come later for his signature noodle soup. He'd gut the fish and boil down their bones along with the various aromatics he'd collected in the marketplace as he called hello and how are you to the other early risers. Eventually Jung Hoon would join him, and the day would start in earnest.

It was a good life. Quiet and gentle.

It was the life Alfie had always wanted. Almost.

"Here they come," Jung Hoon said as the line started forming. "I'll just take my break now."

It was the same joke every day.

"You leave and you're fired," Alfie responded, his script unchanging.

"Oh, you don't mean that. You'd miss me too much."

Alfie shook his head. "I'd miss you like I miss a pebble in my shoe."

Jung Hoon chuckled and started dishing out soup.

Alfie made cheery small talk with his customers, doled out their chopsticks and their napkins. But the smile drifted as he heard the beating of a single drum and yelling. He craned his neck and saw a small procession of men with their fists in the air.

"THE SONG WAS A LIE," they chanted. "THE MERMAIDS MUST DIE!"

Alfie closed his eyes. Callum's Army, they called themselves, but they were more like a cult. Now and then they hosted these processions, and usually people turned away from them in disgust. The people of Crandon had, for the most part, accepted the dragon's song and struggled to reshape society accordingly. There was no more Empire, only free nations that traded with one another as they pleased, each responsible for their own laws and their own customs. There was also no longer any kind of certainty, of consensus; conflict bloomed—though at least now each nation fought for their own rights and interests as opposed to the Empire's. And there were still some Imperial holdouts, and Finn Callum had become their martyr.

And lately it seemed like there were more of them.

Jung Hoon followed Alfie's gaze to the procession as they passed. "Just ignore them, boss," he said. "There's no fixing stupid."

"MIGHT IS RIGHT!" they chanted. Some of the onlookers hissed their disapproval at them. One customer threw a bowl at them, and it shattered on the ground at the feet of the procession, splashing Alfie's painstakingly cooked broth onto the cobblestones. A brief tussle ensued, and Alfie had to dash forward to pull the shoving match apart. One of the protesters spat at Alfie before moving on, and he was grateful that that was the worst of it.

Alfie watched with relief as the procession turned the corner, still shouting, still beating their drum. He wished he could brush them off as easily as Jung Hoon did.

When the lunch rush was over, Jung Hoon took the dishrag from Alfie's hand and pushed him out from behind the cart. "Go on," he said. "You need a break. And I'm sick of looking at you."

"You sure? It's a lot."

"You can pay me extra."

Alfie laughed.

He took off his apron and walked, as he often did, down to the docks. The afternoon sun was just warm enough to cut through the fog, but the sky was gray. Alfie liked it that way, liked the chill of the air, the scent of the Sea. He walked to the end of a fishing dock, sat, and took off his shoes. The damp wood of the dock was cold beneath him. The tide was in, the water high, and so his feet just skimmed the surface of the Sea. It was too cold, really, to put his feet in the water, but he did anyway. He always did, no matter the weather.

A disturbance in the water ahead of him told him he'd made the right choice coming down that day. His luck wasn't always so good. The visits were becoming more and more sporadic as time went on. But today. Today was lucky. Something like solace washed

310

over him, and he felt his shoulders loosen, his jaw unclench. He grinned.

A familiar face surfaced, wearing an easy smile. Her voice was less like a voice these days and more like the echo of waves trapped in a seashell. And though Alfie had filled out, his stomach boasting a comfortable roundness, his eyes just starting to wrinkle at their corners, the mermaid looked exactly the same as she had more than fifteen years ago when she stepped off the *Leviathan* and into the Sea. Somewhere not too far, Alfie knew, was another, and the knowledge she was close by was a great comfort. He wanted their happiness.

But Alfie was here to see the missing piece in his life.

"Hello, brother," Flora said.

The Mermaid, the Witch, and the Sea

THE EXCITING PREQUEL TO
THE SIREN, THE SONG, AND THE SPY

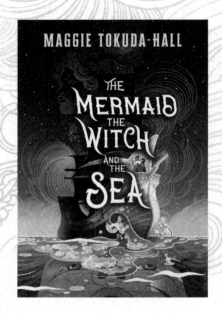

The pirate Florian, born Flora, has always done whatever it takes to survive—including sailing under false flag on the *Dove* as a marauder, thief, and worse. Lady Evelyn Hasegawa, a highborn Imperial daughter, is on board as well—accompanied by her own casket. But Evelyn's one-way voyage to an arranged marriage in the Floating Islands is interrupted when the captain and crew members show their true colors and enslave their wealthy passengers. Both Florian and Evelyn have lived their lives by the rules, and whims, of others. But when they fall in love, they decide to take fate into their own hands—no matter the cost.